PRAISE FOR THE NOVELS OF JOHN LANTIGUA

HEAT LIGHTNING

"Vivid . . . a masterful detective story."
—*Chicago Tribune*

"A great who-done-it with political insight."
—*Los Angeles Times*

"A very clever plot and a well-drawn hero. Ought to give the Edgar Awards people something to think about."—John Katzenbach

BURN SEASON

"A superior job all around."
—*New York Times Book Review*

"A darkly gripping read."—*Publishers Weekly*

"A fresh, clever cast in a taut and authentic tropical thriller."—Carl Hiaasen

TWISTER

"The author's observations . . . are as crisp and clear as anything you hear."—*New York Times Book Review*

"The characters are extremely well-drawn, and the feeling of place is just about perfect."
—*Daily News*

"I recommend *Twister* with one reservation: not to be read when the winds outside are gusting."
—*Washington Post*

Player's Vendetta

A Little Havana Mystery

John Lantigua

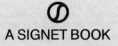

A SIGNET BOOK

SIGNET
Published by New American Library, a division of
Penguin Putnam Inc., 375 Hudson Street,
New York, New York 10014, U.S.A.
Penguin Books Ltd, 27 Wrights Lane,
London W8 5TZ, England
Penguin Books Australia Ltd, Ringwood,
Victoria, Australia
Penguin Books Canada Ltd, 10 Alcorn Avenue,
Toronto, Ontario, Canada M4V 3B2
Penguin Books (N.Z.) Ltd, 182–190 Wairau Road,
Auckland 10, New Zealand

Penguin Books Ltd, Registered Offices:
Harmondsworth, Middlesex, England

First published by Signet, an imprint of New American Library,
a division of Penguin Putnam Inc.

First Printing, August 1999
10 9 8 7 6 5 4 3 2 1

To Douglas, Edwina, and Ana, with love.

ACKNOWLEDGMENTS

The author wishes to acknowledge the invaluable assistance of the following people: Elly Chovel, Billy Taylor, Lino Piedra, Monsignor Octavio Cisneros, Monsignor Bryan Walsh, Lieutenant Bill Schwartz of the Miami Police Department, Orlando Aloma, Cathy Leff, Linda Robinson, Marice Cohen Band, Steve Satterwhite, Alberto Fundora, Holley Bishop, Bernardo Benes, Rosario Moreno, Fabiola Santiago, and the late Alicia Parla. Thanks to my agents Kim Witherspoon, Gideon Weil, and Josh Greenhut of Witherspoon Associates; to my editor, Joe Pittman, for his acumen, and also to Whitney Baker. Paul Goepfert was, again, a trusted friend. Michelle Urry was an inspiration throughout. Elise O'Shaughnessy served as my muse. And I owe the people of Kermit, Texas, from last time.

Cuban children smuggled into U.S.

WASHINGTON—The United States government revealed today that thousands of Cuban children have been smuggled into the U.S. since the Castro regime took power Jan. 1, 1959.

With the help of the Catholic Church and foreign diplomats, those children, from infants to adolescents, have traveled to Miami with false travel visas. Many of them are now in orphanges and foster homes in some 50 cities in 35 states around the country.

The smuggling scheme had been kept secret for the past three years as the flow of children continued, but a crackdown by Cuban authorities in the wake of the recent Cuban missile crisis has stemmed the exodus.

"We don't know when or if their parents will ever be allowed to follow them," said a State Department spokesman. "Those parents are obviously opposed to the regime and we worry for their safety."

The children have flown to Miami one at a time or in small groups, without adult accompaniment. Because of that they have come to be known in the Cuban community as Los Niños Pedro Pan, or the Peter Pan Kids.

Chapter 1

Willie Cuesta swung gently in the hammock and looked up at a mango that hung heavy on the bough. It was a sweetheart—swollen, golden yellow with just a blush of red on the underside. About the size of a softball, it would be good for at least four frozen mango daiquiris. Inside the house he had stashed away a case of five-star Haitian rum, partial payment for recovering a sailboat shanghaied from the Miami River. He had a bucket of ice and an industrial strength blender too. All he needed to do was nudge that mango and he would have paradise in a glass.

He eyed the mango but he didn't move. From inside the house the CD player spouted a song by a Colombian crooner about thwarted desire.

> My mind is on fire
> From always thinking of you

Willie would have to delay that daiquiri at least another ten minutes. It was not quite six o'clock and he was waiting for a potential client who might still show. He had his rules, even though this had been a busy day already.

First had come a referral from the Miami police on a pair of runaway teenagers from the Midwest. He had spent the morning slogging from one end of South Beach to the other, flashing faxed school photos to lifeguards and bartenders, with promises of shared rewards.

Then came a call from a lawyer in Panama. "A boy from a good family" caught at the airport with condoms full of cocaine in his stomach. It couldn't be true.

Willie visited a Customs agent he knew who had viewed the X rays.

"The kid's stomach looks like a surprise party just before the guest of honor arrives," the cop said. "Lots of balloons and no lights."

Willie called the lawyer back, told him there was nothing he could do, and billed him for only half a day.

Finally, there had come a phone call from one Ellie Hernandez, a lady who sounded hesitant, nervous, and wouldn't discuss what was distressing her. She would come to his office after work and would get there before six. Willie had provided her with directions. His place of business was right on Southwest Eighth Street, also known as Calle Ocho, the main drag of Little Havana. You found it in a narrow doorway right next to a Cuban coffee joint, across from a Cuban bakery, and just down the street from a Cuban Santeria priest's waiting room. The priest exhibited fortune-telling seashells and human skulls in the front window and a Mastercard sticker on the door.

Willie's place always smelled of espresso because of the coffee bar next door. The mango tree, surrounded by hibiscus, areca palms, and scarlet bougainvillea, grew in the backyard and the hammock hung under that. He had tacked a note to the door letting Ellie Hernandez know he was waiting for her around back. Meanwhile he swung, studied the fat mango above him, felt the air swell with rain, and listened to the crooner.

> Don't make me wait, *mi amor.*
> Or I'll go up in flames.

Willie was six feet tall and thin, so that the sides of the hammock curled over him like a cocoon. At the moment he was dressed in cream-colored linen pants and a long green shirt imprinted with large crimson palm trees. His skin was olive, gone a golden brown because of the Miami sun. The eyes were also brown, but flecked with green, eyes still attractive behind a skeptical squint.

"What are you so suspicious about?" his now former

wife had asked him when they'd first met. "It's the sun," Willie had answered, even though it was night.

In childhood his nose had been straight, but by the end of high school it had developed a break. A schoolmate who had called him a racial epithet had "developed" it. That was in the pioneer days when Cubans were still a small minority in Miami. In return, Willie had endowed the schoolmate with a nose that looked like an obstacle course. This and other such incidents in his early years had left Willie with that suspicious squint.

The only other mark on him was a scar above his left eye, a memento from his days in the Intelligence Unit of the Miami Police Department. A stray bullet had grazed him in the midst of gunplay with some Colombian gangsters. The scar was a faint gash with a tail on it and over the years ladies had told him it looked like a small shooting star. If any of them had wished on that star for something permanent with him, it unfortunately hadn't happened. Since his divorce years before, Willie had lived alone.

He watched the dying afternoon light turn golden on the mango above. And then he realized someone was watching him. A smallish woman in a flower-print suit stood near the gate, staring. He emerged from inside his hammock, feeling like a tropical Bela Lugosi.

"Can I help you?"

"Mr. Cuesta?"

"That's right."

"I'm Ellie Hernandez. I hope I'm on time."

Willie let her in and shook hands. Standing next to her, he realized she was very small, no more than five one. Her features were small and fine as well. Her eyes were brown, her skin fair, her hair auburn, with maybe a little help. She was probably in her late thirties. Under the suit she wore a white blouse and a tiny gold cross hung at her neck. A small black purse was clenched in her small fist.

She didn't let go of his hand right away, a bit dazzled by him. Willie led her to a canvas chair under the tree.

"Can I offer you a mango daiquiri?"

"No, thank you." She shook her head nervously, like a hummingbird.

Willie sat. He would have to wait. In the background, the crooner was still longing as well.

"How can I help you?"

"I need you to find someone for me."

"Who's that?"

"My fiancé."

Willie's squint deepened. Looking for runaway spouses, or in this case a reluctant groom, was not his favorite sport. You could find them easily enough. It was getting them back that was difficult. Ellie Hernandez could apparently read his thoughts. Umbrage and intelligence flashed in her eyes.

"It isn't what you think. Roberto didn't run away to avoid marrying me."

"I wouldn't think so," he said and that brought her chin up again. "Roberto who?"

"Roberto Player."

She opened the small purse, removed a color snapshot, and handed it to him. It showed her and a man, about forty, standing on a beach in bathing suits, their backs turned to aquamarine waves, a palm tree nearby.

Even at first glance they appeared oddly mismatched. The man was much bigger than she was, maybe six three, dark, hairy chested, and husky. The expressions they wore were totally different as well. She was smiling eagerly, while he was solemn, his eyes full of wariness, vulnerability. It was a look you might expect to find in a troubled teenager, not a grown man. Willie didn't say that.

"He looks like a serious fellow."

"He is and he's a good fellow too."

"When was the last time you saw him?"

"Ten days ago. We spent the night at his condo in Coral Gables . . . and we had a fight."

"Over what or . . . ?"

He let the question trail off, but again she was ahead of him.

She shook her head. "It wasn't a who. It was a what. We were both born in Cuba and he had decided to go back there."

"To stay?"

"No, only for a few days."

Willie shrugged. "Lots of people go back these days to visit family. They have to sneak over through Mexico or the Bahamas, but they come back alive. It's not anything to worry about."

"That's just it," Ellie Hernandez went on. "He has no family there. He's an only child and his parents were killed in Cuba more than thirty-five years ago. They smuggled him here just months before they died. He was one of the children they called the Peter Pan kids."

Willie's eyebrows went up. "Really?"

"Yes."

It had been years since Willie had heard mention of the Peter Pan kids. In the early sixties, when it was almost impossible to get out of Cuba, some citizens who opposed the government there had managed to smuggle out their kids through a secret pipeline. With the help of foreign diplomats and forged documents, they put them on planes to the United States where the kids lived in orphanages and foster homes for years until their parents were finally allowed to leave Cuba. They were called the Peter Pan kids because they had taken to the air without adults. The story was one of the legends of the Cuban exile.

"But you say Roberto's parents didn't follow him to the U.S., that they died before they could."

"They didn't just die. They were found murdered in their home."

"Murdered by who?"

She shook her head. "We don't know that for sure and that's what this is all about. His parents were in the hotel and entertainment business in Havana. They controlled one of the most successful casinos. They were well known. But six months after he came here, he suddenly stopped hearing from them. He was six years old and he lived in an orphanage up in Michigan with a bunch of other Cuban boys who were constantly communicating with their folks. The nuns who ran the orphanage wrote to his old house, but got no answer. Someone got in touch with the Cuban government and they were told that

Roberto's mother and father had been killed by thieves. Their friends here didn't believe that. They said Bobby's parents had been murdered by the government because they were part of the anti-Castro underground."

Willie's eyebrows danced again. The underground was another legend beloved in Cuban Miami. It had been almost entirely wiped out back in the sixties, some members killed, others imprisoned, and a few eventually able to escape. In his teens Willie had played pool at a local billiard hall with a dark, rail-thin man named Marcos who told tales of midnight sabotage missions and escaping through Havana roof to roof.

"So they were in the underground."

"That's right. Although it isn't clear what they did or exactly how they died. Anyway, after the orphanage, Bobby was moved into foster homes. Other Peter Pan kids went through the same thing, but eventually their parents were allowed to come from Cuba and reclaim them. He had no one left to be reunited with. I don't know if you can imagine how hard that was on him."

Willie nodded in commiseration. "Very hard, I would think. Who raised him eventually?"

"Some old friends of his parents took him in for a while and then he was adopted by the family of another Peter Pan boy who had lived at the orphanage with him. The head of that family is Sam Suarez, a banker here in Miami. Maybe you've heard of him."

Willie nodded. "Yes, I've heard the name. South Florida Federal Bank. A big wheel."

"That's right. Bobby's smart and did well at school. He won scholarships, went to law school, and works as counsel for Sam's bank now. But he never stopped wondering about his parents. What had happened to them? How had they died? It has haunted him for years."

Willie glanced back at the photo. That was the look in the eyes all right. Someone haunted.

"So that's why he went to Cuba?"

"Yes. We planned to get married this year. But he said he couldn't do that until he resolved all those questions. He couldn't settle down and start his own family until he found out what had happened to his parents. Where they were buried and how they had died. Of course, he didn't tell the Cuban government that. He said he was a Cuban who simply wanted to see where he was born and he was allowed in. He didn't tell anyone here besides me where he was going."

That didn't surprise Willie. Trips to Cuba weren't talked about much in some sectors of Miami exile society. On the one hand, people said it was treason to go to the island and deposit even one dollar in Castro's economy. On the other hand, these very same people went on the sly to visit relatives they loved and couldn't see any other way. The Cuban government was aware of the weakness exiled Cubans had for their families. It didn't stamp American passports, so nobody would ever know who went. Willie's old history teachers had once taught him about what was called the "open-door policy" of American immigration. In Miami they had what was called the "back-door policy." Don't ask, don't tell. Bring back cigars. Not too many, but a few.

"And? Did Roberto make it back?"

She nodded, irritated now. "Oh, yes. He came back three days ago. He didn't even bother to come to visit me. Instead he phoned and said he wouldn't be able to see me for while. Just like that, out of nowhere."

"Why?"

"Because he had something much more important to do. In Cuba he had uncovered something, or at least he said he had."

"And what was that?"

"That his parents were definitely dead, but the people who had killed them are not in Cuba. They are right here, in Miami, and he's going to find them and make them pay."

Willie frowned. "Why did he think that? Who are these people?"

"I don't know for sure. But like I said, his father ran one of the biggest gambling houses in Havana, Casino Cuba. Roberto said his father was an honest businessman himself, but he had American business associates who weren't."

"The American Mafia," Willie said. "They ran that industry in Cuba back then."

Willie had seen the old films and his father had told him about the high life in Havana in the days of the casinos. It had been a kind of Caribbean Monte Carlo, crowded with men in white linen suits and beautiful women in daring evening gowns amid the royal palms. All of it designed by members of America's own Cosa Nostra and their Cuban partners.

"So he's looking for certain Mafiosos who he thinks killed his parents. Is that it?"

"That's the only thing I can think of."

"He's going to go after Mafia guys. And he's a bank attorney?"

"Yes."

Willie winced. "Does he own a gun?"

She nodded. "But I've never seen him hold it and I'm sure he doesn't know how to use it. Now you understand why I'm so worried."

There was pain in her face as if she were watching her guy being gunned down right in front of her.

"Did he tell you anything about where he was going to find these people?"

She shook her head. "Oh, no. He wouldn't tell me anything. Not who he spoke to or where he went in Cuba. Nothing. He said he didn't want me involved because he didn't want me to get hurt. Of course, as soon as he tells me that, I start worrying myself to death. But that doesn't seem to bother him. Me, the person who loves him more than anyone, who has been trying to give him the family he never had. . . ."

Her voice started to crack then. She didn't cry, but she stopped talking and looked off into the areca palms as she composed herself.

Willie watched her. Ellie Hernandez said she wanted to give Roberto Player the family he'd never had. But she was near forty and if she didn't have kids already, her time was almost up. Her chance was slipping away, although she didn't seem the sort who would come out and say so. She was a tough, smart little woman and Willie liked her.

He touched her hands, which were still clutching the small purse. "Don't worry. I'll try to help you find him. What did he do once he got back to Miami? Where might he be?"

Her head gave that hummingbird shake again. "I don't know. He stopped going to work, which is another problem. Sam Suarez is very angry about it. Bobby's going to lose his job. Mike Suarez—that's Sam's son and Bobby's best friend since the days at the orphanage—is trying to calm his father down. But it isn't doing any good."

"And I take it Bobby isn't showing up at home, at this condo in Coral Gables."

"No. He went there the first night he was back from Cuba. He left the suitcase and some clothes. I have a key and I let myself in. He hasn't come home or called. He has never done this before, hiding from me."

Willie squeezed her hand. Even if Roberto Player's story was true, it seemed likely that the people responsible for his parents' deaths might be dead now too, or at least very old. The whole thing certainly sounded a bit crazy, but then Cubans tended to be crazy about family and old scores.

Willie got phone numbers for Player's old pal, Mike Suarez, and his boss, Sam Suarez. He got the address of Player's condo in Coral Gables and Ellie also gave him the key so he could go have a look around.

Finally, she reached into her small black purse, withdrew her small fist, and opened it. In her palm lay an old red poker chip, which had been cut in half with either scissors or a knife, so that its edge was irregular. It had originally been stamped with the words "Casino Cuba," Willie figured. Now it said "Cas Cu." It looked like a jagged, red half-moon.

"What's that?"

"Carlos, Roberto's father, gave it to him when he put him on the plane to Miami all those years ago. Carlos kept the other half. He said when they saw each other again the chip would be whole and the family would be whole too. Roberto showed it to me a long time ago and I found it on his dresser when I went to his condo two nights ago. I don't know why he had it out."

Willie took it from her, studied it, and asked her if he could hold on to it. She said he could.

They discussed his fee, came to terms, and she wrote him a check that amounted to a one-day advance. Then he showed her out and said he would be in touch. He watched her get into her car and drive away.

Willie returned to the backyard rubbing the chip between his fingers, the way you might rub something for good luck. The CD had come around again and the crooner apparently had found luck.

No, *querida*, don't leave me now
This love fever won't break till morning

Willie was still standing under the mango tree when he heard a rustling above him. He looked up, stuck out his hand, and caught the fat one just before it hit the ground.

Chapter 2

It was a little after dark when Willie strolled out his front door and headed for Roberto Player's place. He reached the parking lot around the corner and climbed into his car—an old red LeBaron convertible with a black top and white pinstriping, received as payment for his handling of a Nicaraguan divorce case. He started the car, flipped on the radio, tuned into a brassy Willie Colon medley, and breezed west through Little Havana.

Willie had grown up in this neighborhood. His family had immigrated before the revolution and he later looked on as it grew crowded with tens of thousands of his Cuban compatriots escaping the island. Those Cubans arrived with not a stick of furniture and only a few threads of clothing, but they imported their island way of life. They had wrapped it in an obsessive nostalgia and preserved it in Little Havana. Roberto Player was certainly not the only Cuban hung up on his past.

More than thirty years later, Little Havana still looked nothing like its namesake. Where the old capital was famous for its baroque Spanish colonial architecture, Calle Ocho was a long commercial strip marked by minimalls, with the occasional palm tree and tin tables where dominos were played. That strip was heavy on health clinics for its aging population, but still featured the tryst motels where younger Cubans and other lovers met to carry on their *amores*. Many Central American refugees had moved in over the years, but the streets were still saturated with what they called *cubania*—Cubanness. Corners of it smelled of Cuban coffee and sounded of mile-a-minute guttural Spanish and conga rim shots. For a man like Willie, who had come of age there, the whole neighborhood was charged by the looks in the eyes of Cuban women, sometimes amused, other times haughty, and still other times nakedly interested.

Now it was eight o'clock and the streets were bustling. People were still out foraging for food in the brightly lighted supermarkets and the cluttered bodegas. Or they were heading for the old, familiar restaurants, some of them resettled from Havana decades before. Willie cruised past a music store with speakers out front and heard a chorus of trumpets and the rattle of a tymbal, and he danced a little salsa in his seat. He eyed a woman in a red dress that was tight around the hips and he couldn't help but notice the lovely rocking of her walk in rhythm with the music.

A few blocks east, Willie's mother owned a small botanica where she sold a combination of herbs, potions, and religious imagery. Just blocks south, Willie's brother, Tommy, ran a nightclub called Caliente—Hot—and it was the hottest club in the city. Willie helped his brother by overseeing security there and he was planning to go to the club later in the evening.

But now he left behind the conga music and the beckoning rhythm of hips and turned south into Coral Gables. As time had passed, the Cubans who had done well had moved on to tonier neighborhoods, especially the Gables. Within a block after you crossed the line you knew you were out of Little Havana. You began to pass the tall, tinted-glass office buildings, the art galleries, and then the homes with manicured grounds that were each worth almost as much as a whole block in the barrio.

Three months before, Willie had handled a case for a man who ran a fancy restaurant in the Gables. A customer had welched on a very large tab for a private party. The story on the street was he had taken off for Pago Pago or Bali. Willie had found him closer to home, hiding out on a houseboat up in Lauderdale, and he had impounded the guy's car as payment.

Now Willie turned where Ellie had told him to and pulled up to the condominium complex where Roberto

Player lived. It was a Spanish colonial place called the Monastery, three stories high, with white stucco walls, barrel tile roof, graceful, black wrought-iron balconies, and an old *campanario*—a bell tower. Royal palms rose majestically all around it, and the rest of the grounds were beautifully landscaped in tropical greenery. If this had ever really been a monastery, Willie thought, then the monks had lived very well indeed.

Willie passed it, parked down the street, and then walked back. At the base of the bell tower a glass lobby had been constructed and Willie could see a uniformed guard seated at a desk. He didn't want to speak with him right then, so he walked around the block to a wrought-iron gate at the rear.

The ring Ellie had handed him held only one key and it didn't fit. So he looked around, took from his wallet a small thin strip of metal he had peeled off a vacuum-packed can of Cafe Bustelo, and easily jimmied the gate. He closed it silently and then headed up stairs lined with blue-and-white Spanish tile in a clover pattern.

On the second floor he found the thick wooden door, affixed with black metal studs, of apartment 2G. The lights were off behind the window, but he tried the wrought-iron knocker just in case. He waited, got no answer. He let himself in with the key and flipped the wall switch.

Roberto Player wasn't there. Willie could tell that right away. What *was* there made Willie stop and stare. Player might have waited a long time to actually travel to Cuba, but he had apparently spent years and years bringing Cuba to him, piece by piece. The old Cuba of his parents' day, that is. He had created in his apartment what appeared to be a small, crowded, private museum or shrine to that era.

Willie began to walk around and touch the furniture. Beautiful old mahogany rockers with woven cane backs, like those he had seen in photos of his grandparents' house in Havana. He examined other finely carved pieces from the Spanish colonial era, including a couch in one corner and a love seat near the balcony, both covered in colorful fabric imprinted with a pattern of banana leaves. A china closet was filled with platters, all hand-painted with scenes of sugarcane being harvested by men with machetes. Overhead hung a vintage, wooden-slatted ceiling fan that had to be sixty years old.

Cigar boxes and humidors sat on surfaces all around the room. Whether they were filled with genuine Havanas Willie didn't know, but the apartment was infused with the sweet, pungent aroma of tobacco. Where there weren't humidors he saw tasteful old vases full of birds of paradise and other tropical flowers. Potted palms stood in large glazed pots.

The walls were covered with framed landscapes of Cuba, all lushly green. Mountainsides, rivers, tropical valleys. A corner was decorated with old black-and-white photographs of the streets and buildings of Havana. One photograph caught Willie's eye. It depicted the inside of a casino, its gambling floor crowded with people, and a bandstand in the background where black jazz musicians in white jackets played. Some couples danced. Everybody was having a good time, not yet worrying about what was to come.

Everywhere Willie looked in that room he saw a relic of a Cuba forty years removed; vintage rum bottles, drink coasters from the nightclubs of legend—the Tropicana, the Caribe, the Sans-souci—an old record player with a stack of 78 rpm records by the world-class Cuban singers and cabaret stars—Beny More, Rita Montaner, and others. Willie could almost hear the music, and because the place had been closed up for days, he could feel the Havana humidity and heat.

He drifted around inspecting it all. What Ellie had said about Roberto Player, growing up without his parents to guide him, had echoed in Willie. His own parents had come ashore in the United States without speaking the language or knowing the turf. Willie and his brother, Tommy, had been left largely on their own to learn the ropes. A lot of the time they might well have been orphans on the loose in the city. They had stumbled into dangerous areas. Their innocence had probably saved them. Back then being a wide-eyed stupid kid who spoke

broken English could get you walloped but not killed.
There had been scrapes, but no serious injuries or serious
arrests.

And they had learned the city and learned to be Americans. In the end, they were hybrids, both Cuban and
American. Many of the older generation never wanted to
be anything but Cuban and never gave up hopes of some
day going back. To them, the Cuba of old was like Atlantis. A place full of magic that had sunk, but might still
re-surface. If you belonged to the younger generation,
you had to establish how much of each world you belonged to, Atlantis and Miami. Your tastes, your lifestyle,
how you loved, your soul. If you were smart you found
yourself with the best of each. Roberto Player had taken a
route that seemed extreme—an attorney for an American
bank at work, and a radically nostalgic Cuban at home. It
was as if he led a double life.

Willie went into the bedroom and found more of the
same. In particular, on the night table next to the bed
was propped a photo, an old black-and-white, five-by-
seven. It pictured a well-dressed couple, in their early
thirties it appeared, and a boy about five. They posed in
front of a two-story house with a balcony and sun shutters. A palm tree stood next to them and you just knew
this was Havana.

It wasn't easy to see the older, brooding Roberto Player
in that boy. The kid was smiling, his eyes shining, not like
the solemn man of forty Willie had seen in Ellie's beach
photo. But Willie knew it was Roberto and his parents.

The Players were an extremely handsome, elegant couple, with a romantic air about them. Roberto's mother,
wearing a dark dress with white rose print and a white
rose in her hair, had been a very attractive woman, small,
slim, and fine featured—a lot like Ellie Hernandez. Roberto resembled her very little. Where Willie did see a
ringing resemblance was in Roberto's father, a tall, robust
man with a pencil-thin moustache, decked out in a gleaming white suit. He carried the same wary look in his eyes
that Roberto had now. The couple had not been killed for
some time after the photo had been taken, but Mr. Player,

unlike the people in the photo of the casino, had already been worried.

Willie put the photo down and began to look in and under things. He opened drawers and searched beneath cushions. In a shirt pocket in a laundry basket he found a slip of paper with writing on it. It said "Aurora—305-555-2117." Aurora might be the name of a shop, but it was more likely that of a woman. Willie tucked the paper away in his shirt pocket.

He kept searching. On the top shelf of the bedroom closet he found what appeared to be an old diary and next to it a folder for legal briefs. Some very old letters, written on onionskin paper, were tucked into aged airmail envelopes. They were addressed to "Master Roberto Player" at the St. Joseph's Orphanage in Michigan and postmarked Havana 1960 and 1961. The letters were written in a feminine hand, almost certainly by his mother in the months before she died.

Willie suddenly caught a whiff of perfume. It was strong and for a moment he thought it came from the letters, even after thirty-five years. Then he sensed someone behind him. He whirled and found a lady, a very provocative Latin lady, standing in the doorway of the bedroom. Willie froze and she did the same. Willie's eyes dropped to the chrome-plated gun in her hand and then went back to her face. He raised his hands and gave her his biggest, sunniest Miami smile.

"Buenas noches," he said.

Chapter 3

She didn't return the smile, so they stood and stared at each other a bit.

The lady was certainly a sight. In fact, she was a show. Latin, extremely tall, close to six feet, she wore high heels that jacked her off the ground several inches more. She was middle-aged and rail thin except for a very ripe chest. Her tight, short, low-cut green dress showed off her decolletage and also displayed legs that were as long and slim as palm trees. Draped over her shoulders was a boa that matched the dress. Her dark, lustrous eyes were heavily made up, her lashes long, and she wore brown gloss on her pouty lips. From her ears dangled rhinestone earrings the size of small chandeliers. Her black hair was pulled back in a bun and behind her ear she'd stuck a red hibiscus that was a bit wilted. In her hand she held that small, chrome pistol, which wasn't wilted at all.

Willie lifted his hands even higher. Her lashes fluttered at him nervously.

"Who are you and what are you doing here in Roberto's apartment?" she asked in a heavy accent.

"My name is Willie Cuesta and I'm looking around."

"Roberto knows you are here?"

"Not exactly."

That worried her and her hand tightened on the gun. "You broke into here?"

"No. I have the key." Willie reached delicately into his shirt pocket with two fingers, plucked out the key and held it up. She frowned at him suspiciously.

"Where did you get that?"

"From Ellie Hernandez, a friend of Roberto's. She

hadn't seen him in a few days and she was worried. I'm a detective."

Willie dipped into his pocket again and brought out his laminated credential. He held it up and she stared at it. That made her a bit less suspicious. The angle of the gun changed so that it was pointed vaguely at his knees.

"Do you know Ellie?" Willie asked.

The woman nodded, her rhinestones swaying. "Yes, we know her. We know her ever since she and Bobby they start to go out together."

"We?"

"My husband Rico and me. My name is Olga Tuzzi. My husband is Rico Tuzzi. We know Bobby since he is a baby. We know Bobby's mother and father in the old days in Cuba."

She jiggled the gun in the direction of the photo on the night table.

"In the casino business?"

"Yes. Rico he worked for Cozy Costanza," she said proudly.

"Really?"

Cosimo "Cozy" Costanza was a legendary Miami mafioso, a historical personage. He had been big in Cuba and had moved to Miami after the revolution. He was very old now.

"So your husband worked for Cozy."

"We still work for Cozy. We run the gambling boat for him. It's called the *Treasure Coast,* at the Port of Miami. All legal, all very legitimate."

Willie nodded. He had seen the ads for offshore gambling. He glanced at the photo on the night table and back at her.

"Your husband must have known Bobby's parents pretty well back then?"

She tapped her exposed breast bone with a finger. "Me, I knew them too."

"How?"

"I was a dancer in the show at the hotel, a featured dancer. I was very popular."

She put her free hand on her hip and tilted her head

back as if she had been introduced on stage. For a moment she was back in Havana, an artifact from the past, just like everything else around her. In her time, Olga Tuzzi must have been a bombshell. She was still fairly explosive.

"Those must have been special days," Willie said, trying to soften her mood even more.

Her eyes narrowed as if she were staring through him and into the past. Olga Tuzzi had a greater taste for nostalgia than for violence. That was clear. She seemed to forget she held a gun in her hand. "You are too young, so you don't know," she said. "It was beautiful then. We had fifty people in the show. Musicians, singers, dancers. The club, the casino, they were very classy. The people all dressed so expensive, so elegant. Everyone had a good time. When I danced they came to watch me. And after, they invite me to the gambling tables. They give me money for the roulette. If I lose, I lose. If I win, I keep it and I buy beautiful clothes, shoes, perfume. And the men, Cubans, Americans, and everyone else, they would fall in love with me."

She smiled lazily, mischievously, warmed by her own memories.

"I'm sure they did," Willie said.

Willie had heard such tales before. He had once interviewed a whole chorus line of women in a Cuban cabaret show on the beach. One of the dancers was involved with a South American army officer who was smuggling stolen luxury cars from Miami to Medellin. Willie had spent all night in a dressing room surrounded by G-strings and plumes. He had heard all about what guys were willing to do for Cuban chorus girls. It had taken hours before one of the dancers had finally fessed up and told him where to find the guy.

But Mrs. Tuzzi was lost in her reverie. She was staring at the photo on the night table. "Carlos Player, he was the best boss and most wonderful man I ever know," she said.

"Is that right?"

"Yes. I come from the sugarcane fields, from nothing. But still he made me the star of the show and he pay me good. He sits at the bar with me and listens to me when I have problems. He tells everybody to treat me nice. Maria, she was good to me too. That's why I always remember their baby, Roberto. I want to adopt him when he was a little boy and all alone, but the government here it don't let me."

"Why?"

She glanced at him suspiciously, as if he had suddenly become too nosy. Olga Tuzzi might have made a great mother, but on the surface she didn't look like prime material for the role, not to an adoption agency. Ladies who had worn pasties and mirrored underwear on stage probably drew extra scrutiny. Being married to an organized crime figure wouldn't be a plus either.

"Eventually you married one of your admirers from your days in Cuba," Willie said. "Mr. Tuzzi."

Olga Tuzzi's expression went solemn and the warm memories evaporated.

"Yes."

"That name doesn't sound very Cuban."

She shook her head. "My husband he is an American. That's how he could bring me here with him. We were married in Havana just before we left. That was the only way I could come here."

She looked unhappy about that situation even now, more than three decades later. Maybe she had reason. If Rico Tuzzi was one of the partners Ellie Hernandez had talked about, he was a mafioso. Maybe he had something to do with the deaths of Roberto Player's parents. Maybe he wasn't a nice man to be married to either.

"Did you leave before Bobby Player's parents were killed or after?" Willie asked.

"We leave the next day, after they found the bodies at their house."

That made Willie's eyebrows arch in interest, but she didn't notice. She shook her head so that her rhinestone earrings swung again and she pressed her puckered lips together in dismay.

"It was terrible what they did to them," she said.

"What do you mean?"

"Maria, they tortured her."

Willie frowned. "How?"

"They took off her clothes and they burned her with cigars on her body." Her free hand drifted to her breasts. "And maybe they did more to her before they shoot her. We don't know."

"And Carlos, Bobby's father?"

"Carlos they just shoot. In the head. It was terrible. Another day or two and they would be alive."

"What do you mean?"

"The people who killed them, they did it just before Carlos and Maria are going to escape. Carlos said soon they would take all the money they had, sneak out of Cuba, and come here. They would start a new hotel with a show. I would be the star. But then someone kills them and takes all the money too."

Willie's eyebrows danced a bit. "Someone stole money from them?"

She nodded once. "That's right. All of it."

"How much are we talking about?"

"The whole bank for the casino and all the profits they make for that last year. Carlos he was scared to put it in banks because the government took over the banks. Rico said it was half a million dollars."

Willie whistled. "A half million dollars. That's a lot of money, especially back then. So who do you think killed them and took it?"

She looked at him and scowled. "Who? The government down there, that's who."

"Because they were in the underground?"

She became wary again. "I can't talk about that. But Rico said the government killed them. He knows."

"How did Rico know?"

She shook her head once. "I told you, I don't talk about that. Rico he never talks about it, not even to me." She appeared offended by that after all those years, as if she'd been kept in the dark for her own good, the way a child might be. Willie could tell she had questions that had never been answered and they nettled her.

"Well, Roberto Player doesn't think the Castro government killed them," Willie said. "He went to Cuba and someone there told him it was people here who murdered his parents."

Her pouty lips formed a perfect "O" in surprise and her eyelashes swung open in shock as if they were on hinges. "That's *loco.*"

"Maybe, but Roberto doesn't seem to think so. In fact, Ellie thinks he's going after some guys his father was in business with down there. I wonder if he's going after your husband."

It took her moments to put it all together, but then her face stormed over in anger.

"We know Bobby since he's a baby. Rico he don't do anything to hurt him or hurt Carlos and Maria Player."

Willie watched her. She was married to a gangster, but a gangster with some principles. Or at least she hoped so.

"How about some of Rico's associates, other people in his organization who were in business in Cuba? People like Cozy Costanza. Could he have been involved?"

She was shaking her head, but there were doubts deep in those large, moist, dark brown eyes. They were doubts that scared her.

"I should speak to Rico," Willie said. "Where can I find him?"

She liked that idea even less. The gun that had fallen to her side came up and she shook it at him as if she were wagging a finger.

"You leave Rico alone. You don't want to make him mad. You tell him something like that, maybe he kills you."

She backed away from him toward the bedroom door, as if he was crazy, contagious, or at least very bad luck.

"When you find Bobby, you tell him to call me. You tell him his Aunt Olga is angry with him because he don't call her. And that I'm very worried about him too."

She shoved the pistol back in her bag, and pulled her tight dress down on her hips. She looked Willie up and down appraisingly, as if she hadn't had a chance to do it before. It was clear she approved of what she saw. She was a piece of work, Mrs. Tuzzi.

"Nice to meet you," she said demurely.

Willie bowed. *"Encantado, señora."*

She turned then and tottered out on her spike heels.

Chapter 4

Willie watched her go. Then he finished his search quickly before anybody else showed up and pointed a gun at him. He found nothing of consequence. Most important, he didn't find the gun that Roberto Player owned. Roberto was probably carrying it, which wasn't good.

Willie took the photo of Player and his parents from the frame, stuck it in the legal file with the letters and the diary and headed out. On a table behind the door he noticed for the first time an answering machine. Its message light was blinking so he pushed the button and listened.

The first two messages were from Ellie Hernandez, both recorded earlier that day. They were the same. "Bobby are you there? Please pick up if you are. Please, please call me."

Then another, very different voice came on, a man's voice.

"You there, Bobby? Kick in if you're there. It's me, Barnacle. I've got the cargo from Cuba sittin' here, amigo, and you nowhere in sight to pick it up. Ya understand? I can't sit here much longer. These waters ain't friendly, you get my drift?"

The voice was gruff, non-Hispanic, American, wired, maybe altered by drugs. Not at all the kind of voice you would expect to call an attorney for a bank. It waited for an answer and didn't get one.

"You there or what, Bobby? You better get over here to Matheson Hammock Marina, amigo. If you ain't here before midnight with the money, I'm gonna take this cargo of yours I have on board and haul it back to the island. Ya hear me, Bobby?"

Barnacle sounded like an old conch from the Keys.

Boat owners in the Keys had been smuggling goods and
people to and from Cuba since long before Castro came
on the scene.

"Or maybe I'll save myself the fuckin'trouble and just
topple it into the ocean," the voice said. "Let the sharks
eat it. You won't like that, will you? The 'cargo' won't
like it either, amigo, but I'll do it. Right down to Davey
Jones's locker. You get my drift? So bring the three thousand. My boat's the *Wayward Wind*. I'm tied up at the
back pier."

Then he hung up. The message, according to the machine, had been delivered less than an hour earlier.

Twenty minutes later, Willie was driving on a two-lane
road under a dark canopy of banyan trees, approaching
the shore of Florida Bay. Matheson Hammock was a park
and marina about six or seven miles south of the city. The
air there was full of the smell of jasmine hedge, the sea,
and heat.

On the radio, an old bolero was playing:

> My love is shipwrecked
> In the dark sea of my life

Air plants and Spanish moss hung in tangles from
branches and power lines and reminded Willie of the last
time he had visited the marina at Matheson. Years ago,
when he was a cop, he had gone there to identify a young
woman found floating in the bay. She was a New York girl
who had worked as a runner for a counterfeiting ring,
smuggling bogus U.S. bills into the country from the Cay-
mans. Willie had been looking for her, but he wouldn't
have to look any more. Somebody had hunted her down
before him. She lay bobbing face up, eyes open, about five
hundred yards from shore, her very long hair floating
about her, looking a lot like that tangled moss he saw now.

The houses on either side of the road gave out and
Willie picked out the entrance for the park. The gate was
open, even though the sign said the grounds closed at sunset. He followed the narrow road, crowded on either side

by tall vegetation. He passed through a stretch of mangroves, his headlights sweeping across them so that they looked like nests of snakes tied in knots.

He came out into a clearing and saw the marina off to the right, a small forest of masts. Most of those boats were owned by weekend sailors who didn't drive out here during the week and especially not at night. The place was abandoned, the marina office closed and dark. He followed the road to the parking lot, where he saw only one car, a black Mercedes. He got out, touched the hood, and felt it was warm.

He walked by it, down the main pier, toward the last berths. The smell of the sea was stronger now. A breeze made the riggings clank against the aluminum masts. As he approached the end of the pier he spotted a lone boat and heard voices, an argument in urgent Spanish. He couldn't understand at first and then he heard a man's voice clearly, in English:

"Listen to me, Bobby. This is smuggling and it's illegal. Don't get mixed up with these people. They're gangsters. You'll get hurt."

Another man answered. "I'm going to do what I have to do, Mike."

"You mean kill somebody?"

"If I have to."

Willie was close enough to see them clearly, two men silhouetted on the pier, maybe ten feet from the boat. The larger one was Roberto Player. Willie recognized him from the photo Ellie Hernandez had given him. Mike Suarez had to be the other, smaller and wiry. Willie had gotten close enough that Suarez looked up and noticed him.

"Who are you?"

"A night sailor."

"Well, why don't you go sail someplace else."

"Because I'm looking for Mr. Player here."

He walked up to them and Player scowled at Willie and his loud palm tree shirt.

"Who are you?"

Willie introduced himself. "Ellie Hernandez sent me to look for you. She's worried."

"You tell Ellie to stay out of this. It's dangerous for her."

"That means it's probably dangerous for you too, amigo."

Suarez shook a finger at Player. "That's what I'm tryin' to tell him."

Bobby Player looked from one of them to the other, just barely in control of himself. "It wasn't your parents who were killed. It wasn't your mother who was burned and tortured by animals. It wasn't the killers of your parents who got away free. So you can't tell me what to feel or do, can you?"

He was staring at Willie now, but Willie didn't answer. He had learned as a cop not to try to talk people out of their tragedies. It only made them more distraught and emotional. Miami was full of folks with revolutions, coups, and assassinations in their pasts, people with all kinds of phantoms. When it was your parents who had been killed, your own blood, it had to be hard. Willie would have felt the same, but he didn't have a chance to say that to Player.

Another man stepped off the boat, bare chested, with shoulder-length hair and a full beard. A handgun protruded from the waistband of his sweat pants.

"The tide's goin' out and I'm goin' out with it, Bobby. I need my money or I head back to sea with these people. You get my drift?"

This had to be Barnacle, the smuggler. He came up to them, tattoos all over him like some kind of sideshow pirate, except for the gun. That wasn't just for show. It looked real.

Roberto Player dug into a pants pocket, pulled out a wad of money and put it in the pirate's hand. Barnacle wet his thumb and started to count it.

Suarez grabbed Player by the arm. "Bobby what are you doing?"

Player pulled away from him. "I'm doing what I have to do. These people will help me find who I'm looking for."

"Who? The people who killed your parents? They're in

Cuba. These people are lying to you, just using you to smuggle them into the country. You're in over your head. I'm not letting you do this."

Suarez moved toward the boat captain who was still leafing through the bills. Player reached out with a beefy arm and pushed him back. The smaller man went at him now and they grappled.

Suddenly, Barnacle stepped forward, pulled the pistol from his waistband and smacked Suarez across the side of the head so that Willie heard metal meet bone. Suarez went down on all fours and rolled over holding his head.

Willie had longer arms than Barnacle and was quicker too. In a moment he had the freak's tattooed arm in a lock, twisted it, heard him screech, and saw the gun drop to the dock. Willie kicked it into the water. You didn't let geeks from the Keys come to Miami and act tough.

Willie reached to pull his own .38 from a back holster, but he stopped. While the scuffling had gone on, two people had gotten off the boat, a man and woman, also known as "the cargo." They stood just feet away now, each carrying a small suitcase, the kind that thousands of refugees from Cuba had traveled with over the decades. In his free hand, the man also gripped a handgun. It was pointed right at Willie's gut.

An uneasy silence followed. Barnacle took advantage of it to jump back aboard the *Wayward Wind*. Suddenly, the engines of the boat roared to life. The smell of brine filled Willie's nostrils. Barnacle jumped down from the bridge, untied from the dock, and sprang back up to the wheel.

"Ahoy, Bobby. Anytime, mate." And with a roar and a churning white wake, he raced away into the night. The wave he caused made the riggings of the other boats clank louder.

Willie knelt next to Suarez, who was still holding his head. Roberto Player looked down at them.

"Let me do what I have to do, Mike. I want some peace in my life."

Willie glanced up at him. "So you're going to go hunt-

ing old mafiosos?" Willie asked. "You think that's going
to bring you peace?"

Player scowled. "What's it to you?"

"I don't think Cozy Costanza or any other made man is
going to let a bank attorney shoot him, no matter what
you were told in 'Kooba' and who you brought to help
you."

"This is none of your business."

"It isn't mine, but it is Ellie's."

Willie stood up to discuss that point, but then "the
cargo" stepped closer. The guy and the gun were deadly
still and Willie knew right away not to challenge him the
way he had the smuggler. He'd be dead quick.

Willie could make out the other man's face now and he
didn't like what he saw. It was angular with sharp cheekbones and sunken cheeks and was extremely pale. The
kind of wraithlike face sculpted by a very rough life. The
hair was cut short and bristly gray; the eyes were dark,
cold, and emotionless, glinting like the black gun in his
hand. The look said, "Give me reason, I'll waste you
without a second thought, *hermano*." On his gun hand,
between thumb and forefinger, was tattooed a small star,
the kind worn by gang members or guys who'd been in
stir. Willie had dealt with this kind of individual before.
Cuban jails had a reputation as extremely nasty places
and turned out some very bad boys, cold-blooded killers.
Quite a few had made it north to Miami. This particular
specimen had a small jagged scar under his left eye that
made him appear even more lethal than usual. He looked
to be about sixty, old enough to have been in Havana
when the Mafia was hanging out there. Old enough to tell
Roberto Player who had murdered his parents. Or to lie
about it for that matter.

Willie looked from him to the woman standing just behind him. She, on the other hand, was not old enough to
have lived those days. About thirty or thirty-five, she
stood an inch or two taller than her traveling companion.
Her skin was café au lait, her hair long and dark. Her eyes
appeared large, but maybe that was the effect of fear.

From what he could see, she was very beautiful. They made a strange couple, Willie thought.

But now Roberto Player put himself back in Willie's face, a gun wrapped awkwardly in his hand. "You mind your own business. We won't shoot Mike, but we'll shoot you if you try to stop us. Now get out of the way."

Willie didn't jump to it. On the case only a matter of hours, he'd already found the man he was hunting for, but was about to lose him again. Not only lose him, but have him disappear in the company of a guy who looked like very bad business indeed. Willie got a good look at that scarred, gaunt face, fixing it in his memory. What this ghost was really doing in Miami, God only knew. The other man glared back, as if deciding whether Willie was worth shooting. Apparently, he wasn't. Without changing expression, the man stepped around the fallen Suarez and led the other two away. They hurried down the pier and moments later Willie heard the engine of the Mercedes crank up. It drove away into the darkness.

Suarez was struggling to get to his feet and Willie gave him a hand. Blood trickled down the other man's face and Willie handed him a handkerchief.

"What's going on here?"

Suarez shook his head. "He's trying to wreck his life. That's what's going on."

"So it seems, but why did he bring you along?"

"He arrived at the bank offices tonight to get that cash, I was working late and I forced myself into his car and wouldn't get out. He had to bring me."

"So who are those people and what were they doing on the boat with that crackhead?"

Suarez started to speak, then stopped. He suddenly realized he didn't know Willie from the wolfman, or Adam for that matter.

"You want me to guess, *hermano?*" Willie asked. "Okay. I will. She's Cuban and he's smuggling her in. He traveled to Cuba, came across a beautiful, stormy island girl. She gave him a hot time and now he's bringing her in as contraband. He had to drag her nasty old uncle along as part of the deal. He's dumping Ellie Hernandez because she's a plain Jane and he's concocting some story about his dead parents as an excuse to put distance between them."

Suarez shook his head as he daubed at the blood. "He isn't making it up. He believes that whoever killed his parents is here. This woman or the old guy or both of them told him that. Bobby's convinced he's going to get revenge, but all he's really going to do is get himself hurt."

"You mean by going after mafiosos?"

Suarez shrugged. "Maybe. His father worked with those guys in the casino business in the old days."

"Did Player give you any idea where he was taking these two who came in?"

"No."

They were walking back to the parking lot. Willie's LeBaron stood by itself. They got in it and drove back toward the city. On the way, Willie milked Suarez for information about the years he had been pals with Player. Suarez had turned fourteen just after he arrived at the orphanage in Michigan, while Bobby had been a little boy of six.

"Most of us were already in our teens. Our families sneaked us out because they were afraid we might get drafted into Castro's army or sent to some commune or to the Soviet Union to study. Those were the rumors. We snuck out with doctored documents that you got through an underground pipeline. Once we got here, we lived in a large tent city out near the Everglades. When they sent us, our parents thought it would only be for a short time and that things would return to normal soon in Cuba. But later, when Castro didn't fall, we got sent off first to the orphanage and then to foster homes. It got hard. Bobby, he was the baby in the bunch. Our fathers did business together back in Cuba. My father was a banker and he handled the accounts for the hotel and casino Bobby's parents ran. I just started taking care of Bobby."

"It looks like you're still taking care of him. Or at least trying to."

"Well, it looks like he needs it. Don't you think?"

Willie didn't think forty-year-old men should be taken care of. Roberto Player obviously didn't think so either. He was packing a gun to help him now.

"You said your father was the banker for the casino. Does that mean he held money for the mafiosos too?"

"That's right. It was all perfectly legal back then in Cuba, the casino and all. In fact, Cozy Costanza still keeps accounts in our bank here today. IRAs. The works. He's been very loyal."

"Yes, mafiosos are known for their loyalty," Willie said.

The sarcasm got lost because they were just pulling back into the city. Willie offered to take Mike Suarez to a hospital emergency room to have his wound tended. The bleeding had stopped, but his hair was matted with blood.

"I'll be all right and I don't want them asking me questions about how this happened. Just drop me at my car outside the bank if you can."

Willie complied. At the bank, Suarez thanked him.

"If you find Bobby again, let me know," Suarez said.

"I will, if you do the same."

"It's a deal."

Willie handed Mike his business card and then waited for him to find his car and drive off. Then he headed for his brother's club. He was already running late.

Chapter 5

It was turning eleven o'clock when Willie pulled up outside the club and found a long line of people waiting to get in.

Old folks around town always recalled the glory days of the Tropicana, the Montmartre, and the other great glitzy nightclubs of Cuban history. These days in Miami, the place to go, the nightclub that carried on that honored tradition, was his brother Tommy's club, Caliente.

Waiting in line stood the young *haute monde* of Latin Miami. The women were bare shouldered, bejewelled, and beautiful; the men, slicked back, buttoned down, and shined up. Every time the door opened, music hot and brassy spilled into the street and made the bare shoulders shimmy and the temperatures rise.

Willie handed his car keys to the chief valet, Esteban, pulled on a cream linen sport coat over his palm tree shirt, cut the line, and went inside. There he found Billy Blanco, the big-bellied, black Cuban who ran the door. Billy flashed him a smile as bright as the flashlight he used to check IDs. Willie shook his hand.

"How we doin', brother?"

"We're cookin', Willie. We're fine."

Willie ducked through a black curtain into the main room. Caliente was constructed like an amphitheatre, a Roman circus, with concentric circles of tables three levels high. The lights were turned low, but candles on the tables illuminated the faces, if you were interested in who else was in attendance, which most people were. At the far end, a wedge cut out of those circles provided a space for the bandstand. Right now the house band was swinging through an old mambo.

Only about two thirds of the tables full so far, but the crowd outside would pack the place. And this was a weeknight. On weekends they turned them away in droves.

The waiters, all in short white jackets, worked from bars on the first and third levels, scaling the aisles quickly and nimbly with their trays held above their heads as if they were circus jugglers. The maître d', another Cuban named Joe Mesa, wore a tux and ushered the newly arrived patrons to tables, like a ringmaster.

Some couples had already taken to the dance floor, working out to the music. Willie's attention was grabbed by a tall, raven-haired woman in a lacy black dress laying down intricate steps. Her long, thin legs moved like a colt's. Her hips rocked in understated, but clockwork rhythm to the percussion.

As her partner turned her, her hair flew around her head and her coal black eyes locked on Willie for one brief, but complex moment. In it he saw the sudden discovery that she was being watched, sultry defensiveness, a glimmer of interest, and then demure retreat. She pulled back to her partner and they fell into a tight-lock, perfectly rhythmic step that had them pressed against each other, cheek to cheek and toe to toe and everywhere in between, as if they had melded into one body in sinuous, sensual movement. When they talked about why God had made women, Willie thought, to dance like that was certainly near the top. *Sí, señor!*

Willie closed his eyes for a moment. When he opened them again he found his brother, Tommy, laughing at him from across the dance floor. Willie dodged between the dancers and made for him.

Tommy Cuesta was most of what Willie wasn't. Where Willie was tall and slim, Tommy had always been short and broad shouldered. Willie had inherited his mother's swarthy complexion, Tommy was light-skinned like their late father and prey to the sun. Maybe that was why he ran nightclubs and stayed up all night, hardly ever seeing the light of day.

Tommy, older by one year, had lived a twenty-year all-nighter. He had developed first a liquor problem, then a drastic drug habit, but had beaten both. Now he stayed straight, a family man with two kids, and the perfect professional host. He was possessed of a smile as broad as the white keys on a piano, an infallible sense of who was who, a mastery of service and ambiance, and a quick eye for trouble. There didn't seem to be any now, as he shook hands with Willie and glanced at the tall lady who was shimmying with her partner.

"Does she look like a security risk to you, Willie?"

Willie shrugged. "Not for the club maybe, but for somebody."

Willie was the chief of security at Caliente. Several bouncers worked for Tommy: Big Billy Blanco and a couple of other Goliaths, who handled the occasional drunks and roughnecks. Willie, when he was on the premises, filled the role of intelligence officer, keeping an eye out for customers running scams. Most often they were drug dealers, people who clocked an amazing number of trips to the bathroom in short periods of time. In those cases, Willie loitered outside the bathrooms and pulled the dealers aside discreetly when they emerged. In the case of men he recommended a urologist, for women, a gynecologist. In both cases, he advised they leave the club right then to go consult the doctor and not come back. If they didn't, he would call a specialist he knew in police narcotics. The patrons in question always complied.

Willie also kept a constant look out for ladies of the night who tried to work the club. These he would ask to dance. While doing a merengue he would recommend that they retreat to someplace where they could be alone. Once outside he would hail a cab, put the lady in it, close the door, tell the cabbie to drop her off at the next club up the line, and wish her luck. Sometimes the girls got pissed, but at other moments they expressed regret that Willie wasn't really going with them. In general, no hard feelings resulted, no public hassles. That was how Tommy

wanted it. It wasn't a case of being a killjoy, just weeding
out people who were trying to turn pleasure into business.

Now Willie sat with Tommy at the owner's white-
clothed table on the ground floor near the stage. From
there he could scan the whole scene, not just the possible
scammers, and enjoy the eternal game that made the
place run. The appraisals at a distance, the come-ons, the
coy responses, the first dances that maybe turned into
closer, hotter dances before the night was over.

Married couples came as well, part of their regular
mating ritual. Because dancing was about that in the end.
Drinks to wash away the day. A man watching the woman
dance, her shoulders shimmying, her eyes smiling confi-
dently or staring mysteriously into a middle distance. The
way she let him lay his hand on her hip and feel it move,
the woman's fingers on the back of his neck—seemingly
incidental, but always calculated—her breast against his,
her breath on his cheek. All of it while they repeated those
steps they had stored in their memories when they were
kids, before they knew what it was all about. Steps that
came in the blood, invented by some wise Cuban woman
long ago, Willie was sure, to make a man want. To make
the muscles warm and make him start to sweat, so that all
thought dissolved into his sense of touch, into his skin,
and his mind was all desire, until he couldn't take anymore and he took her out of there by the hand and dragged
her straight home to the dance of dances.

Willie watched it all and sipped the lime daiquiri the
waiter knew to bring him, as the place filled up.

"What's new?" he asked Tommy.

His brother shrugged as he drank a Perrier. "A new
club opening up out on the edge of the Everglades."

"Too far out. People won't go that far."

Tommy nodded. "Yeah, usually that would be true. But
they cut a deal with the Indians out there, the Miccosukees. They've got a gambling permit."

The Miccosukee tribe had the only license for onshore
gambling in the county. Now that Tommy mentioned it,
Willie had heard on the news about their working a deal with
some Cubans. Tommy sipped his Perrier and grimaced.

"They say their place will be as posh as Havana in the old days." He shrugged. "We'll see how they do."

"You always survive the competition," Willie said. "You'll survive this."

"A lot of money behind this. Sam Suarez, the banker, and some other people."

Willie pulled an about-face. "You don't say. I was just with his kid."

"How?"

So Willie recounted for Tommy the case of Roberto Player and the scene that had played itself out on the bay.

"Fun and games you have for a living," Tommy said.

"It keeps me in daiquiris."

"Who do you think those two tourists from Cuba were?"

"I don't know. I'd like to. The guy looked like an old hood here on business. Who might know about this type of tourist?"

Tommy mulled that a few moments and shrugged. "You can always try Cassandra. If she doesn't know, maybe she'll tell you who does."

Both of them glanced up in the direction of a table on the second tier, around the middle of the house. Willie spotted the woman Tommy was talking about, grabbed his drink, and got up.

"I'll be back in a while."

He crossed the dance floor and then climbed to the second level, to a table kept permanently reserved for Cassandra Vasquez, Cuban Miami's best known talk-radio personality. Sitting right off the aisle, Cassandra made it easy for her sources to sit down for a quick chat, to drop her a bit of gossip between sips of her champagne, to complain about a politician, local or national, to add their two cents to the latest sensation or scandal.

Cassandra would absorb this information, sauce it up even more, and use it on her daily afternoon call-in show, *Café con Cassandra—Coffee with Cassandra*. Every afternoon a large percentage of the Cuban community tuned in to listen to the latest.

Radio represented the native drum of the Cuban community. It carried all the crucial messages, especially to the older generation of Cubanos. It made heroes and fingered blood enemies. It could call the tribe to battle. Little old ladies could be routed from their rocking chairs and turned into rowdy, even violent demonstrators with a few well-chosen words. In his police days Willie had been forced to deal with those demos and had been gang attacked by grandmothers with rocks in their hangbags more than once.

Politicians and civic leaders made sure to stay on Cassandra's good side. They fed her information about what was coming down in Miami, or between Miami and Cuba. Cassandra was clever enough not to reveal state secrets. On her show she dropped hints about shady goings on, without giving details that would kill the goose that laid the golden eggs.

Tonight it was business as usual for her. She was entertaining a couple of low-level neighborhood "sources," but as Willie approached she beamed a big smile at him.

"Willie Cuesta, *como está?*" She shot him a saucy, lascivious wink.

One look at Cassandra and you knew right away why she had put her talents into radio and not television. She was a very large woman, tall, broad in the beam, the bust and hips as well. Round, pillowlike cheeks dominated her pale face. On the right one sat a large mole.

On the other hand, her hair was a magnificent, amazingly thick, black mane. Her coffee-brown eyes exuded intelligence, nasty humor, guile, and high-spirited lust. Her girth tapered down to a pair of surprisingly shapely, lovely legs. She always dressed tastefully. At the moment she wore a wine-colored dress, draped in a beautiful mantilla. She had seduced not just a legion of listeners, but many wealthy and powerful men, at least that was the gossip.

Willie proffered his hand. "Will you give me a dance, Cassandra?"

Her lustful eyes lit up with delight. She turned to her guests.

"You'll have to excuse me. Willie is one of the best dancers in the city and also one of the sexiest men around. He loves to dance with me. I can't say no."

She held her large hand up daintily and Willie led her down to the dance floor. They fell into a salsa step to an Oscar D'León number, Cassandra extremely light on her feet for someone her size. Like many hefty Latin women she could engage her hips in an effortless rocking motion that kept time perfect. She pressed her large breasts up against him, her face just inches away from his, smiling suggestively. He put her through a turn and she came back close to him again.

"You are still wonderful on your feet, Willie. It is a pleasure."

"Igualmente, Cassandra."

"You must be good off your feet as well, although I guess I'll never know."

Willie's squint narrowed in embarrassment and Cassandra laughed.

"Now let's be honest, Willie, you don't really want to dance. You want to know something, isn't that right? Don't lie to me." She pinched the skin at the back of his neck playfully.

"I want both, Cassandra." Willie sent her into a more complex turn, switching hands, spinning her by the hip, and hugging her back close.

She laughed good-naturedly. "So what do you want to know?"

"I need to know a Cuban who's had good connections with the Mafia over the years, the Italian Mafia, especially someone who knew them during the old days in Cuba."

"Why do you need to know that?"

Willie shrugged. "I'm just curious."

He felt her fingers at the back of his neck again. She pinched him just hard enough to make him wince. "Don't lie to me."

"Okay. I have a reason for asking. A case I'm on."

"You know I don't give information away for nothing, Willie."

She assumed her lascivious leer again, but that wasn't the exchange Willie was interested in.

"I have something to offer, Cassandra. Some information of my own."

Cassandra's gaze narrowed. "And what is that?"

"It's about two people who got smuggled into Miami just tonight."

"Who are these people?"

"I don't know their names, but they were smuggled in on a pleasure craft by a captain from Key West. They arrived in Florida Bay just a little while ago."

Cassandra's keen intelligence focused on him. "You don't say. Your average Cuban who comes here doesn't get that kind of service."

"One is a young woman, but the other is a man with all the marks of an old gangster, a Cuban gangster."

Willie swung her into a turn again, stopped her halfway around, brought her back, and spun her the other way. They closed back together belly to belly.

"I think this guy I saw might have something to do with the Mafia," Willie said. "With the old mobsters who managed the casinos back in Cuba in the old days. If I can find somebody who knew them, that might help me."

"Tell me more about this man," Cassandra said.

Willie described the suspect he'd seen on the dock—his age, his look, the tattoo on his hand.

Cassandra nodded. "There were gangsters in Havana before Castro took over, not just American Mafia but Cuban gangsters. Many of them lived in Old Havana and other barrios near the port. Generally they were smugglers and they gambled. They'd run the old lottery, the *bolita,* or dice games. But some of them also were involved in gunplay. Sometimes they were even recruited by political groups who wanted to go after their enemies, scare them or even kill them. I don't know what happened to those gangsters later after Castro came to power. My family didn't move in those circles."

"Could a person like that have had anything to do with the Italian mobsters down there?"

Cassandra shrugged in rhythm again. "It seems unlikely, but I don't know. The Mafia had very upscale oper-ations in Cuba and these other guys gambled in alleyways. But they were both in the same business, so it's possible they knew each other."

Willie twirled her again and when she came back, she pressed extra hard against him with her large breasts. He held her tight and they moved in lockstep. She looked into his eyes.

"It's interesting that you are asking me this, Willie. Lately certain rumors have circulated about those old Italians."

Willie frowned. "What rumors?"

She got a canny look. "First you tell me why you want inside information about them. These people who sailed in tonight, why do you care?"

"Just some private business. Nothing that could have importance to an influential person like you, Cassandra."

"Private business interests me more than any other, Willie. You know that."

They sized each other up as they danced. Willie won-dered if Cassandra had really heard any rumor at all about the Italians. That was her way of angling for information, dropping a hook into the water with no real bait on it. If he thought he could trust her, he might take a chance and fill her in about the Roberto Player case. But given Player's position at his bank, Ellie Hernandez had insisted every-thing be kept on the q.t. Cassandra survived by swapping information and if she would swap with Willie, she would swap with other sources. She stuck so many irons in the fire around town, Willie didn't know who she might talk to or how he might get burned. So, for the moment, he kept his details to himself.

She pulled her head away and kept her lusty eyes on his as the music wound down.

"Okay," she said finally, "I won't tell you about the Italians and you won't confide in me about your case. But I'll nose around and if you hear more that you can tell me, you'll tell me."

"Agreed."

The music ended then and he escorted her back to her

seat and her other sources. She smiled wickedly at him
again.

"Now you can go find some company for your bed
tonight, *mi amor.*"

He tried to deny any such plan of action, but she
shooed him away. Her eyes flashed across the dance floor
to the third level. "The one with the skinny legs you were
looking at, she wants you. She's been staring at your nice
ass all night."

She laughed her big horselaugh then and Willie headed
back to his table. As he crossed the dance floor, his eyes
drifted to the third level and found the lady of the lacy
black dress and the colt's legs watching him. Cassandra,
she was right about everything.

Chapter 6

It was just after noon the next day and Willie was barreling over the bridge that crossed the bay to the Port of Miami. From the very top of the span he could gaze down Miami Beach. Bands of turquoise and aquamarine water worked their way over the sand and then the coral reefs and out to the dark blue sea. As always, it was beautiful.

Willie hummed an old bolero:

> The sea knows well what it is to lose a love.

Yes, indeed.

He came off the bridge and stopped at the tollbooth leading to the docks. The uniformed man on duty, a guy with washed-out blue eyes and a large sunburned nose, told him the gambling boat *Treasure Coast* was docked at Pier Seven.

"Lucky Seven," the man said.

"I hope so," Willie said.

Willie found the parking lot and then the dock and then the boat. An aging pleasure craft about a hundred feet long, its name was stenciled on the stern with dice painted on either side of that. As Willie walked up, a Latin man carrying cleaning equipment was coming down the gangway. Willie asked for Rico Tuzzi and was told he was on board.

Willie strode up the gangway stairs, through a red-curtained doorway and into the main gaming salon of the boat. The *Treasure Coast* was one of the older gambling boats around. It resembled a casino on land, but crammed into a much smaller space. In fact it looked and smelled like a larger casino that had fallen into the sea and shrunk.

Near the entrance were two long rows of slot machines with rust around the edges, the effect of the salt air. On the starboard side stood several quarter-moon blackjack tables. A half dozen long craps-tables with the high bumpers were crammed forward. The center of the gaming room was reserved for three roulette wheels and their green betting grids.

At either end of the room were service bars to keep the gamblers well lubricated and betting. An arrow pointed to a restaurant the next deck up. Dice, playing cards, and martini glasses were painted on the bulkheads all around. In general, the place smelled just a little dank and was just a little seedy.

Willie nosed around some. He peered into an open closet and saw deepsea fishing tackle and nautical charts. The closet next to it was stacked with bright orange life preservers on the bottom and racks of gambling chips on top, which were locked behind a metal grill. Willie wondered which one the gamblers would reach for first if the boat started to go down.

He was turning away from the closet just as a man walked down the stairs from the restaurant level carrying a cardboard box. The guy was short, barrel-chested, built like a fire plug, probably around seventy, with a cigarette stuck in the corner of his mouth. His head bore absolutely no hair, his skull as smooth as shaved dice. His eyes were small, dark, and close together, like snake eyes. He wore a white shirt with a design of playing cards on it and dark green polyester slacks, so that he resembled a walking green-felt poker table. From the sour look on his face, his luck had run bad for a long time.

He noticed Willie now and stopped at the bottom of the stairs. "If you're here to gamble, we don't open until the nighttime and then only outside the three-mile limit," he said with an accent out of the borough of Brooklyn.

"I'm not here to gamble, Mr. Tuzzi. You are Mr. Tuzzi, aren't you?"

Tuzzi stared at him as if Willie had just pulled a card

from his sleeve. Like his wife, he was quite a specimen. He looked as if he'd been preserved in olive oil for a few decades.

"That's me. What about it?"

"My name's Willie Cuesta. I'm a private detective and I'd like to ask you a few questions."

The old mafioso shuffled to the nearest blackjack table and put the box down.

"You the one broke into Bobby Player's apartment last night? The wife told me about you."

"I didn't break in. I was given the key by a friend of his. We're trying to find him."

"Well, I don't know what your game is, and I don't know where he is. It's my wife keeps in touch with him, not me."

He began taking packs of playing cards out of the box, feeding them into dealers' boots.

Willie drifted over. "Nice place you have here."

Tuzzi gave him a withering glance. "Don't kid me."

"I wasn't kidding."

"This is nothing. It's a rowboat, but it pays the bills." He crammed another pack of cards into a boot.

"Well, I guess it doesn't compare to the set up you had in Cuba way back," Willie said. "I understand you worked in the casino business there."

The old man snorted, fiddling with the boot. He didn't want to talk to Willie very much, but, like his wife, found mention of the old days too much of a temptation. "In Cuba, what we ran was something totally different," he said. "The government that was there before, they wanted professionals who knew the business. They invited certain of us to go in there and run it for them on a big scale. Real casinos, floor shows, musicians, the works. You could fit this whole boat just in the baccarat room there. We ran a class operation."

Willie nodded. Tuzzi was making it sound as if he'd been a big player back then. A Meyer Lansky, a Bugsy Siegel, or at least a Cozy Costanza. He could probably be classified as more of a bagman, but Willie wasn't about to call his bluff. The old were entitled to a bit of exaggeration.

"That's what I've heard, that it was like Las Vegas."

Tuzzi shook his head. "Better. Vegas was built in a goddamn desert. We lived in Havana, a gorgeous city, cobblestone streets, beautiful buildings, palm trees, a waterfront. The customers we had were class. They dressed to the nines, not in fuckin' shorts the way they do in Vegas. We drew people who didn't mind droppin' some real money. They could afford it. We ran everything legit. We paid the government for a license, went into business with the hotel keepers, and split the profits."

"You split with hotel keepers like Carlos and Maria Player."

The mention of the Players forced Tuzzi to pause just a moment. "Right again."

"Then your luck turned."

Tuzzi lifted his snake eyes to look at Willie. "Then everybody's luck turned."

"Carlos and Maria Player, their luck turned even worse than yours. They ended up dead."

"Yeah."

"Who killed them?"

"Who killed them? The same people who closed up the casinos and raked up all the chips. The new government, the communists, that's who. Where were you, on the moon?"

"I was only a baby then."

"Yeah, well, the government killed them, no matter how old you were."

"That's not what Bobby thinks."

Tuzzi's scowl deepened. He looked as if Willie had just laid a wager he hadn't expected. He didn't like it.

"Then he's wrong."

Willie upped the ante. "He thinks maybe some of your people killed them."

Tuzzi's voice went hard and cold. "Bobby shouldn't say that. That's a dangerous thing ta say."

"Why would Bobby think that?"

"How am I supposedta know?"

"I'll tell you. He went to Cuba and somebody told him the people who killed his parents live right here in Miami. He even smuggled two buddies back with him, snuck them in to help him find who did it."

Tuzzi rammed a deck into the boot. "Oh, yeah? Who's that?"

"A young woman and a guy about sixty. Real thin, deep cheeks, a scar under one eye. Looks like a bad guy, a Cuban bad guy."

Tuzzi's hands continued to function, but you knew his mind had drifted far away, no longer on that boat. Thoughts, memories, worries rattled around behind the old mobster's eyes like roulette balls looking where to settle. Willie watched him.

"Sound familiar, Mr. Tuzzi?"

Tuzzi didn't look at him. "No, it don't. Why should it? He sounds like some kinda loser."

"Maybe he is. But Roberto Player believes this guy can tell him who killed his parents. And maybe they'll be coming to see you."

Tuzzi fixed on Willie again, now with his toughest tough-guy stare. "Why would they come to see me? What are you sayin'?"

Willie shrugged. "I'm not accusing you of what happened to Carlos and Maria Player, but that's maybe what Bobby believes. You did beat it out of Cuba the day after they bought it."

Tuzzi's teeth showed. "I got out because I was smart. There's a time to fold 'em and go far away. That's what we did."

"And Carlos Player wasn't smart? He didn't fold 'em soon enough?"

"That's right and he's dead."

There wasn't even a hint of regret in his voice. The deaths of Player and his wife resulted from a bad bet, bad odds, that was all. It certainly didn't sound as if Tuzzi held the Players in the same esteem his wife had. Willie remembered how Olga Tuzzi had waxed on about Carlos Player. "The best boss and most wonderful man I ever knew." Olga had quit Cuba with Tuzzi only after Player was dead. Willie wondered if what he was hearing now from Tuzzi was old jealousy.

"What kind of guy was Carlos Player?" Willie asked. "From what I hear he had a lot of friends."

The old bagman shrugged. "He didn't have enough friends. He's dead and he's been dead a long time."

Well, that answered that. Tuzzi hefted the box and shuffled toward the next table. Another old bolero was echoing in Willie's memory.

The hour will arrive that can't be delayed
When the old debts just have to be paid

He trailed Tuzzi. "Who do you think those people with Bobby Player could be?"

Tuzzi put down the box hard. "I told ya I don't know. Maybe you should hunt up somebody else to ask questions."

Willie shrugged. "Maybe you're right. Maybe Cozy Costanza will answer them. Maybe he has the skinny on what happened to Bobby Player's parents too."

Tuzzi grunted. "Cozy's an old man, eighty years old. He don't recognize people or remember things anymore. Even when he was young and could remember, he couldn't remember. Ya understand?"

"Yes, I think I do."

"Good."

Willie recalled that Costanza had forgotten many things before congressional investigating committees and grand juries over the last decades.

"It's just that your wife told me there was money that went missing when the Players were killed."

Tuzzi slammed another deck in. "What about it?"

"I understand it was a large amount of money, a fortune at the time, and it belonged to your partners. I figured you'd be interested in what happened to it."

"My wife talks too much."

"Didn't you and Cozy Costanza ever wonder what happened to it? And how the people who killed them knew it was there?"

Tuzzi looked up and laid on Willie his nastiest "you don't know nothin' " gaze. "Let me advise you of somethin', amigo. The communists in Cuba worked a system. They kept tabs on everybody and everything. All the time. They had spies in the casino, in the neighborhood where the Players lived, everywhere. The Players were an easy mark."

"There were spies in the casino?"

"That's right. The communists closed the casinos when they first took over, but they let them open again for a while because it put too many people out of work. That's what they said. But I think they really did it because casinos were a good place to put spies and find what people with money were doin'. One of them spies lives right here in Miami now." He gestured vaguely in the direction of the city. "By the name of Del Rey, Victor Del Rey. He worked as a pit boss in the casino and at the same time he was spyin' for the government, keepin' an eye on the Players. Later he turned against Castro supposedly and showed up here. But some people say he never changed sides. He's still a spy. Go talk to him."

"Where can I find him?"

"Last I heard he was workin' as a projectionist in some theater in Little Havana that shows old Spanish movies."

"The Mirage?"

"That's it. Go grill him about what happened to Carlos Player. Maybe he knows."

Tuzzi turned back to his dealer's boot. Willie squinted at the suddenly helpful gangster. He wondered if the mafioso wasn't sending him on some wild goose chase. He wondered if Tuzzi and his bosses hadn't simply whacked the Players for all the profits from the casino and then skipped Cuba the next day.

"Why would he be spying on the Players?" Willie asked now.

Tuzzi scowled at him. "Whaddya mean, why?"

"Was it because they belonged to the underground?"

Tuzzi fixed on Willie and pronounced the next words very precisely, in a voice as dry as the sandpaper he might use to fix a pair of dice.

"They were mixed up in more than that. And they were tied in with people you'll never know about. Stuff you'll never find out. Never. Ya got it?"

Willie's brow clouded over. "What do you mean?"

"Like I said, you ain't gonna get nowhere, so don't ask."

Tuzzi busied himself again with the boot, his cards tucked close to his vest now.

"I'd like to say hello to your wife," Willie said.

"I betcha would, but she's not here."

He put down the boot and led Willie toward the head of the gangway. Willie pulled out a business card and laid it on a table there. Tuzzi sneered at it, as if it was a card that had put him over twenty-one and busted him.

"If you hear from Bobby Player, I'd appreciate a call," Willie said.

Tuzzi didn't answer. Willie wasn't going to hold his breath waiting for further word from the bagman. It turned out he didn't have to.

As they stood there, a car wheeled into the lot, a big lumbering old Chevy at least twenty-five years old, green and rusted, with a ragged old white convertible top. The front doors creaked open and two guys got out. They both had long straggly gray hair, Panama hats, and wraparound shades. They wore vintage leisure suits, one blue in color, the other red. Given the car, the clothes, and the need for haircuts, they looked like they'd been cruising around a few decades searching for someplace to gamble.

Willie looked more closely and realized what appeared to be very old drooping skin on their faces was really rubber masks. He also realized these gentlemen hadn't arrived to play roulette. Each one lifted a machine gun, braced it on his respective door, and then tried to sink the boat by shooting it full of holes.

The barrage sent Willie diving behind the low bulwark. The bottom of it had an extra-thick brace bolted to where it met the deck and he ducked his head behind that. The shots ripped through the thinner metal above him, sounding like a jackhammer in overdrive.

Tuzzi lay on his belly on the other side of the gangway.

He held a chrome-plated pistol, just like his wife's. Maybe Mafia couples exchanged them on significant anniversaries. Tuzzi was trying to angle it around a post, pulling off shots without being able to see whom he was shooting at.

The rounds from below blew out a casino window, raining glass down on them, and ripped into the slot machines, sounding like a payoff. The firing stopped for seconds, apparently as the gunmen changed clips, and commenced again. It made a racket. One round hit the overhang above Willie, ricocheted, breaking a caged deck light, and landed next him. It was flattened and rolled like a slug for one of the slot machines. Willie groped for his back holster and pulled out his .38. He expected to hear the shooters come plodding up the plank, which meant he and Tuzzi with their little pistols would have to shoot it out with two goons wielding rattle guns. Very bad odds.

But then suddenly the barrage stopped. Willie heard two doors slam and gravel being kicked up. Tuzzi struggled to his feet and fired a wild shot at the retreating car, which carried no license plate and had enough holes in it that he could never tell if he'd hit it or not. It slid out of the lot and rumbled toward downtown as if it were disappearing back into the past.

Willie holstered his gun, inspected the shattered window and the Swiss cheese bulwark. Tuzzi was craning over the side. All the bullets had hit above the water line, so the boat wouldn't sink, but it looked bad. Willie's heart was pounding.

"What the hell was that?"

Tuzzi was still gripping the little chrome pistol. He sneered back at Willie as if he were nothing but pure bad luck.

"Get outta here."

Willie's ears were ringing and he didn't hear the words, but he could read Tuzzi's lips. He had been raised to respect his elders and not to goad people with guns. He did as he was asked.

Chapter 7

Willie walked down the gangway and climbed into his car. He prodded his ears until the ringing went away. He also thought about heading over to South Beach, picking up his search for the two teenagers from Iowa, and forgetting about Roberto Player. The teens might spray him with some beer, but not with bullets. The father of one was a rich doctor, not little Ellie Hernandez. It was easy money.

He thought that but he didn't move. He kept an eye on the gangway of the boat, but Tuzzi didn't disembark. The mafioso was probably phoning Cozy Costanza. Willie decided he wanted to confer with the capo as well and now would be a good time.

He waited a while longer, but when Costanza didn't show, Willie turned on the car, crossed the bridge again, and pulled into a gas station on Biscayne Boulevard. A useable directory actually hung at the pay phone. He checked, but of course Cozy wasn't mentioned in it. Crime bosses tended not to be listed.

Instead Willie placed a quick call to a friend of his, former Detective Sergeant Clarence Ross, retired from Miami PD and Willie's mentor when he worked with the Intelligence Unit. Ross had dogged the Mafia in the old days and kept up on them. The old man picked up.

"Haylo."

"Old man?"

There followed the briefest of pauses, the moment it took Ross to recognize his voice. "What are you doin' up so early?" he asked in his flagrant cracker accent. "I thought you people danced all night and slept all day."

"Unlike you, I'm working, and I have a question for you. Where does Cozy Costanza live?"

"In a place called the Coral Arms Condominiums on Collins Avenue around Forty-fifth. He's been aging there for years. Why, what's cookin' with ol' Cozy?"

"I'll drop by later and tell you."

"Sure thing."

Willie hung up then and headed for the beach, traversing the bay on the Julia Tuttle Causeway. The bay almost always reflected a darker blue than the sea. Who knew why? Today it absorbed some of the color of the clouds, a gorgeous, placid gray blue, all the four miles across the causeway.

Willie had never made the acquaintance of Cozy Costanza, but he had researched him in books about the mob. Cosimo Costanza had developed a reputation as a gentleman gangster who had hobnobbed with legends like Meyer Lansky and Santo Trafficante in Cuba and now lived in semiretirement in Miami Beach. In his "family," he delegated day-to-day business to his lieutenants, but those underlings consulted him on any major decisions and supposedly awarded him one tenth of all profits from loansharking, gambling, prostitution, etc., as a kind of tribute. Just like an old Italian prince.

The other Cosa Nostra role he filled was that of a national consigliere. Crime families across the country tapped him to settle disputes between them. A few years back, when a family from Philadelphia tried to muscle its way into the Miami area, Costanza had chaired the Cosa Nostra panel that had designated Miami as "open territory" not belonging to any one family. He acted as a kind of Supreme Court judge of the Mafia. In other words, Costanza was a big cheese, a major player, a godfather.

Willie pulled up to the Coral Arms Condominiums, which rose about ten stories on the ocean side of Collins. He parked in a public lot next to it and cruised in.

The condo architects had designed the lobby as a species of grotto. It was constructed of make-believe coral, actually molded out of cement, with waterfalls and vines cascading down on either side. Propped in the middle of that stood something resembling a Greek column. Who knew why? Hanging from the ceiling was a series of small, but not at all tasteful chandeliers, which if they were ever to fall would turn anyone standing under them to sushi. Willie figured these were supposed to be rain clouds passing over the grotto, somebody's idea of a nature scene.

The guard behind the desk also qualified as a work of nature, a large olive-skinned fellow with curly black hair, a crimson uniform with green piping, and a gold name plate that said Salvatore.

"Can I help you?" he asked in an Italian accent. As he spoke he stood up and there was no mistaking the gun tucked beneath the tunic of the uniform. This had to constitute the entry-level position these days for the Cosa Nostra, guarding the capos in their old age by apprenticing as doormen in their buildings.

"Yes. I'm here to see Mr. Cosimo Costanza."

Salvatore glowered at Willie the way he might have examined one of the cheaper, lousier brands of American pizza.

"Who is calling for him?"

"You can say former Miami Police Detective Cuesta is here to speak to him."

A moment before, Willie had been no more than a questionable Hispanic foolish enough to ask for an audience with Cozy. Now Willie had sunk even further in the evolutionary scale—a former policeman.

"Mr. Costanza he's sleeping."

"It would be good if you woke him up."

Salvatore slipped out from behind his desk and planted himself between Willie and the sliding door.

"And maybe I don't wake him up."

Willie held up his hands. "Take it easy. I'm here to do Mr. Costanza a favor. I'm here to warn him about some people who might want to hurt him."

The doorman's hand drifted to his waist. "Nobody's gonna hurt Mr. Costanza."

Salvatore appeared about as smart as an osso bucco, but he was loyal.

"Well, if you can just tell Mr. Costanza I called." Willie reached delicately into his pocket for a business card and laid it on the desk. Salvatore was about as impressed with it as Tuzzi had been.

"Arrivaderci," Willie said.

He drifted back out to the parking lot and passed through it to the boardwalk in the rear. He shaded his eyes and gazed out over the sand to the beautiful aquamarine surf. He lingered on a topless woman in a red tanga lying on her stomach, her back, legs, and tush the color of mahogany. Her head rested on her folded hands and she smiled at him with teeth that were extremely white in her bronzed face. Willie smiled back with his own white teeth.

He walked to the gate that led to the back entrance of the Coral Arms. He arrived there just as two old ladies emerged carrying a red-and-white striped beach umbrella and wearing straw hats, sunglasses, and white cream striping their noses. He smiled at them too with his white teeth, held the door for them so it wouldn't close behind them, and sneaked in.

The large lobby continued the eclectic design begun in the foyer. Fake doric columns, murals of the Coliseum, and such picked up the Roman theme, but here the scenes were painted on an aquamarine background with fish swimming around, which placed the empire under water. Another large grotto in one corner made noise, a genuine torrent. It was a style Willie thought of as *damp classical*.

From the back of the lobby Willie could observe Salvatore standing guard on the other side of the sliding door, absolutely impassable. Willie found the mailboxes off the lobby and next to them a list of tenants, which told him Costanza lived in Penthouse C. For Cozy.

The main elevator opened too close to Salvatore, so Willie found the freight elevator and rode it up to the top floor. He got out and passed through a fire door into a hallway of red plush carpeting and more underwater Parthenons papered on the walls. He found Penthouse C, listened for a moment to the opera music sounding faintly from inside, and rang the bell.

Moments later it opened. Filling the doorway was an extremely large young man, much larger than Salvatore. His blond hair was long and curly and he was very tanned. He wore a turquoise T-shirt contoured to a sculpted chest and swollen biceps; the handle of a pistol protruded from his flowered, drawstring pants, and he was carrying a duster. Willie figured he was the maid.

"I'd like to see Mr. Costanza," Willie said.

The maid frowned. "How did you get up here?"

"The elevator."

The frown deepened. "You just try to get in here downstairs?"

Apparently Salvatore had called. Willie tried the same smile that had worked on the topless woman and the old ladies. "Listen I just want a word with Mr. Costanza. I want to do him a favor."

"Mr. Costanza don't need no favors. Not from you."

"There's some people who might be coming around to do him some harm."

The maid didn't seem surprised. Tuzzi had obviously called as well. "Ain't nothin gonna happen to him."

Willie heard voices beyond the door. "Maybe I could have a word with him anyway." He started to step forward but the maid placed a big beefy hand on his chest.

Then another man appeared in the doorway. It was not Cozy Costanza, whom Willie had seen in old photos, but a tall, thin, older man who didn't appear at all Italian. A cowlick stuck up from his graying, wheat-colored hair. His skin was very red from the sun and he was smiling. He wore golf clothes—bright red pants, a blue pullover, and white shoes. All in all, he looked like an American flag with hair.

The maid shoved Willie to one side and turned back. "Go ahead, sir. Just a little trouble with someone don't belong here."

The other man glanced at Willie once more and then left.

The maid kept his hand on Willie's chest. Beyond him in a room carpeted in white shag stood an old man dressed in white pants and a black silk shirt and espadrilles. His hair was very thin on top, his cheekbones high and pronounced, his nose large and bent, and his eyes dark, almost black. Stooped and liver-spotted, he had one hand shoved in his pocket. Nothing moved except for his eyelids, like a lizard.

It was Cozy Costanza, Mafia legend. One of the king-pins of old Cuba.

"Mr. Costanza. I'd like a word with you. It's about Carlos and Maria Player. Casino Cuba. The old days in Havana."

The old man's expression hardly changed. His brow furrowed only a bit. He kept his eyes on Willie about ten seconds, only his lizard lids moving. Then he shook his head minimally, turned, and shuffled slowly out of sight.

The maid pushed Willie back, stepped out into the hall-way, and pulled the door closed behind him. "You better go now and don't come back. We don't like people sneakin' up here. Next time you'll get hurt."

"Any idea who just shot up Mr. Costanza's gambling boat over at the port?"

The maid frowned. "No gambling boat was shot up."

"I was there. My ears are still ringing."

"Must be your imagination or too many *mojitos, her-mano.* Now get out of here."

Willie smoothed his shirt where the maid's damp hand had been pressed and thanked him for his hospitality. He took the regular elevator down just as the Meals on Wheels cart was showing up. Willie wondered if Cozy was a subscriber and if the maid had to make sure it wasn't poisoned before he ate it. Who knew?

On the ground floor, he walked out through the lobby where Salvatore was grimacing into the phone, appar-ently being chewed out from upstairs for his lack of vigi-lance. Willie didn't wait to say good-bye.

He made it to his car in the lot and was just about to get in when a voice sounded from behind him.

"Excuse me," it said.

Willie turned quickly and found himself looking at the lean man in the golf clothes whom he had bumped into coming out of Cozy's penthouse. The man held up his hands to show they were empty and flashed a seven-inch smile.

"Easy there. I'm not part of this rumble."

Willie looked him over. He had to be about six two, with square, narrow shoulders and a long, craggy, red face. His most outstanding feature was his eyes, which were as blue as two shards of sky over the Great Plains. In his red, white, and blue clothes he appeared much as Uncle Sam would have looked after finishing eighteen holes. He gave the impression of being old and boyish at the same time.

"What can I do for you?" Willie asked.

The other man was still smiling. "I got a sense there was some trouble back there. I wanted to make sure everything was all right."

"Who are you?"

"My name is James Clancy." He held out a very long arm and a hand that turned out to be hard and smooth.

Willie introduced himself. "I take it you're a friend of Cozy Costanza's."

The tall man shrugged. "Let's say I'm an old acquaintance."

"How old?"

"Oh, very old indeed."

"The early sixties? That old?"

Clancy nodded. "Yes, as a matter of fact, that's when I met him."

"Did you know Cozy in Cuba?"

"Right again."

Willie studied the other man. "What were you doing in a place like Cuba?"

"I was posted at the American embassy in Havana. I was a junior cultural attaché. I arranged for exchanges, Cuban students, artists, and entertainers to come to the States, and vice versa."

"Sounds like a sweet job."

He nodded enthusiastically. "For a farm boy from the Midwest who had studied some Spanish at university and gotten himself into the foreign service—it was like nothing I'd ever known. A paradise." His tone was elegiac, but suddenly an expression of mock seriousness came over him. "But it wasn't easy, Mr. Cuesta. It was tough work. I had to be out in the nightclubs, casinos, and music halls every night until the wee hours doing my diplomatic duty, increasing international understanding."

Willie squinted. "Especially with Cuban chorus girls."

"Yes, I had a special policy for chorus girls. My alliance with them was strategic."

"I'm sure it was."

The other man chuckled. You could tell it was a little joke he had told many a time. "Are you still with the government?" Willie asked.

"Oh, no. I left the foreign service after my time in Cuba, went into business, and then retired down here."

Willie glanced up toward the penthouse he had just left. "Did you arrange for Cozy Costanza to go to Cuba all those years ago as an example of American culture? Is that how you know him?"

"Not exactly. But I did arrange for some Cuban entertainers Mr. Costanza employed to visit this country. And you have to remember that Mr. Costanza was doing nothing wrong in Cuba. Gambling was perfectly legal there. He was a respected businessman. We fell back into contact after I moved here. Mr. Costanza is an interesting fellow."

"If you like gangsters."

Clancy shrugged, not losing his grin. Willie knew that embassy types had to keep tabs on what was happening wherever they were. Sometimes they had contacts from the wrong side of the tracks. It was part of the game.

Willie leaned against the car.

"In your time down there did you ever do your diplomatic duty at Casino Cuba?"

Clancy nodded. "Oh, you bet I did. It was one of the best joints in town. Beautiful gambling facilities. Gorgeous women."

"Did you know Mr. Tuzzi and Mr. Costanza's Cuban partners, Carlos and Maria Player?"

"Of course. Carlos Player was an extremely elegant man and his wife was lovely and charming."

"You know they were killed."

"Oh yes. That was right in the middle of the season, that last season."

"Nineteen Sixty-one."

"Yes, just before we broke diplomatic relations with Cuba and all of us in the embassy had to leave."

"It must have ruined the season."

Given that natural sunniness, Clancy must have weathered sarcasm before. He accommodated it now without blinking or grimacing.

"I understand they were killed because they worked in the anti-Castro underground," Willie said.

That caused Clancy's smile to crimp around the edges. "I've heard that myself, but I wouldn't know anything about that. Another section in the embassy handled those matters. My field was culture, not politics. They trusted me to make policy on chorus girls, but not much else," he said with a shrug.

"And in your rounds of the clubs and casinos, you didn't pick up any intelligence about who might have killed them?"

He shook his head. "It's like I said. Just days later we were all expelled. There was no time to ask any questions."

"Well, their son doesn't think the Cuban government killed them. He thinks whoever killed his parents is right here in Miami. In fact, he thinks it might have been your friend Cozy Costanza and his associates. A large amount of money the Players had stashed away went missing and the next day Cozy and his people exported themselves out of Cuba."

The smile disappeared totally. Clancy seemed like a young boy crushed by an accusation against a hero. "I'm sure that's not true," he said. "Oh, I know what people say about Cozy and his partners. In fact that was part of the draw down in Cuba. Come play where the Mafia plays. Colorful characters. Some criminality in their pasts. But that was all for show. They were always efficient businessmen and cordial hosts. Bloodshed was not part of their economic plan, not in Cuba at least."

"Did Costanza tell you that a gambling boat he owns over at the port just got shot up?"

Clancy frowned. "No. He took a phone call while I was there, but he mentioned nothing about a shooting. Was anyone hurt?"

"No, just a slot machine or two."

Clancy shrugged. "Sounds like a disgruntled roulette loser taking his revenge, most probably. Every business has its hazards." He glanced at his watch. "I better be going now. My tee time is coming up." Maybe, but maybe he wanted to get clear of Cozy Costanza before another disgruntled gambler showed up. He put out his hand.

"I hope we see each other again, Mr. Cuesta. *Ha sido un placer.*"

Willie watched Clancy shamble toward his car, his cowlick waving in the sea breeze. Then he climbed into his LeBaron and headed for the house of Clarence Ross.

Chapter 8

Willie took the bridge back across the bay, cruised north on Biscayne Boulevard, and pulled into a neighborhood called Miami Shores. It was one of the older residential areas around, full of modest, mostly tasteful one-story houses, old palms, fruit trees grown tall, croton and hibiscus hedges, screened-in porches to protect against skeeters, and garages or carports to guard against the blistering sun. Right then it smelled of newly mown grass, humidity, and heat. Air-conditioners were on in a lot of houses—so that the whole neighborhood hummed with them.

He pulled into the driveway of a beige stucco house that featured a red tile roof and a ragged croton hedge. He parked behind an old blue Volkswagen beetle. Next to it was a Chevy pickup almost as old, with a boat hitch and a seventeen-foot center-console Seacraft sitting on it. This meant Ross was definitely home. If he wasn't out on the water fishing, he was home. Those were his two habitats these days.

Willie cut through the garage, crowded with junk, fishing tackle, shrimp nets, sawdust, and part of a bookcase. He opened the door that led into a rundown but authentic 1950s kitchen, complete with a linoleum tile floor and classic Formica counters and table, all in yellow. In a pan on the stove were some instant grits, which in color almost matched the yellow Formica, and might have been from that morning or possibly the morning before. Next to it sat an ancient percolator that made the whole kitchen smell of chicory coffee.

"Hey, old man!"

There was no answer.

"Viejo!"

"Yes, neighbor."

The voice came from the Florida room at the back of the house. Willie found Ross almost totally horizontal in his fake-leather BarcaLounger, a bottle of Corona in hand, watching what appeared to be a college basketball game on the television. A burly, barrel-chested man with an ample waistline, he was still wearing his fishing garb, a white captain's cap with a gold anchor above the bill, aging white guayabera, tan khakis, and laceless sneakers. He hadn't shaved in at least a couple of days and his face bristled with a white stubble matching his cap and shirt.

Directly behind him on the wall hung a bunch of framed commendations from his days on the police force, including two Officer of the Year awards and several citations for valor. There were also photographs, one of the old Miami police station on 12th Avenue, which was later torn down, and a few shots of old colleagues, most of whom were dead. In one of them, Ross was posed with Muriel, his wife, who had died of cancer about a year before. It had been at her insistence that the commendations had been hung and Ross had allowed them to stay after her death, more out of inertia than anything else. It was clear he never dusted them.

Ross peered at Willie from under snow-white brows. "I don't think I've ever seen you standing this early in the day."

"Somebody has to fight crime while you go out and fish and putter in the garage with your band saw."

Ross shrugged. "I promised the widow of an old patrol sergeant that I would make her shelves. She makes very good cornbread and absolutely lovely ham hocks, although you wouldn't know that those are."

He sipped his beer and kicked the cooler next to his chair. Ever since Muriel died it had been as if he was camped out in the place. Willie grabbed a beer, sat down, and together they watched a player run out a shot into the gap.

Willie had met Ross years ago, after he was transferred out of patrol into the Intelligence Unit. Clarence Ross was a sergeant in that unit and a living legend in the Miami police department. Born in a small town near the Georgia border, he had served in the navy in World War II, first in the Panama Canal Zone, then in the Pacific. After the Armistice, he'd knocked around the country some, eventually gravitating back south to Florida and finally further south to Miami, the way a pebble settles in the toe of a sock.

He had taken a liking to water in the navy and he spent a couple of years crewing on pleasure boats sailing for the Caribbean. He took on other odd jobs before finally, surprisingly and providentially, applying to the police department. His time in the service, and nothing else, got him the job.

Despite his travels, Ross had been considered strictly backwoods. He spoke with the thickest of reb accents and had a blue-eyed, square, corn-fed face, as blank as the wall of a barn. His style of working was deliberate, ponderous, cud-chewing, folksy. He came back again and again to the same questions, as if he were slow-witted. He stared at people a lot and might have been watching okra grow instead of trying to catch bad guys. His colleagues on the beat considered him a hick and even a liability at first. Behind his back they called him "the boll weevil."

What Ross did over the next ten years was convince them, superior officers one after another and criminals too many to number, that he was absolutely the smartest hick they'd ever run into. Ninety-eight percent of cases your grandmother could solve, but Ross, with those slow-witted, obvious questions, broke the tough cases, the complex ones. Behind that small-town cracker facade he had an instinct about evil, they said, although Ross denied that.

"It's that certain people loved to lie to me back then," he once explained to Willie. "It must have been my farmboy face. But certain criminals, who thought they were clever, would travel miles over bad roads just to tell me the damnedest lies. 'I didn't kill so and so with an ax, officer.' And I'd say, 'Son, I didn't even know he was dead. Let's talk it over.' I was lucky, Willie, a lucky boll weevil." And then he'd smiled slyly.

Willie knew it was more than luck. But whatever it was, it led Ross to apply for the Intelligence Unit just before things started to get real interesting in Miami. That was at the beginning of the sixties when the city was filling up with Cubans planning attacks to get back their island, which meant they were looking to buy weapons, bombs, whatever. These were folks the city wanted to keep an eye on. Ross, who had picked up some Spanish in Panama and in the Caribbean, was the man for the job.

Eventually, some of them started shooting each other and blowing each other up. Even later there were the Colombian gentlemen who wanted to do "international business" in drugs in Miami, with attendant money launderers. By that time, Willie had joined Intelligence. He and Ross and their colleagues eventually had to keep their eyes on Nicaraguans, Salvadorans, Haitians, Israelis, Palestinians, potential Muslim terrorists of various nationalities, the Russian mob, the Cosa Nostra, activists on one side or another of nukes, abortions, sea turtles. You name it. If any group had secret designs that could destabilize Miami, the Intelligence Unit wanted to know about it. Ross was the best, the eminence gris. You couldn't tell who was who without a scorecard and Ross was the smartest of scorekeepers. As one Cuban detective had told Willie: "He's a redneck. But attached to that neck is a quick mind and a long memory."

Ross's neck was still red, as was his fleshy face. But when retirement was facing him, he had wanted a protégé. He had picked Willie, the youngest Latin in the unit—and, according to him, the smartest.

"You people are taking over this town, so why should I tell what I know to some out-in-the-cold white boy?"

Ross taught Willie a lot. It was through Ross that Willie developed not only dependable FBI sources, but even contacts with foreign intelligence services and from time to time the CIA. Willie knew the Miami Latin community pretty well already, but it was Ross who tutored him on the non-Cuban establishment, both criminal and not, and allowed him eventually to operate everywhere, from the club scene on the beach to the foreign consulates and the offices of the big old law firms downtown to the private islands and gated communities where some of the very old and very new money was.

They became unlikely allies and had stayed that way even after Ross retired and Willie left the force. One had a lot to do with the other. Willie had a reputation as a lone wolf, an independent operator who worked on his own schedule and chafed at any interference on the part of his superiors. It was a work style he had picked up from Ross. He had little tolerance for bureaucracy and did nothing to ingratiate himself with those of higher rank. As long as Ross had been in the office, Willie had enjoyed his patronage. But the moment the old man was gone, the brass began to crowd him. Relations went from bad to worse until Willie took a walk. "You were good enough to be commander of Intelligence if you hadn't been so ornery," Ross told him.

"Why weren't you ever commander of Intelligence?"

"Because I was ornery, too. But I couldn't help it. I was born that way. You just learned it from me."

Willie looked at Ross now. Between them—the old and the young, the redneck and the Latin—Willie figured they had more knowledge of who was who in Miami than any other two human beings around.

"How was the fishing today?" Willie asked, sipping his beer.

"So, so. Yellowtail, but only a couple worth keeping. How 'bout you? How's the fishin'?"

"I've got a particular fish I'm trying to catch but he's still on the loose."

Willie filled him in on the Roberto Player case. Unlike Cassandra, Ross could be trusted with everything, names and all. Ross listened intently. He grew especially intrigued when Willie told him of the shootout at the *Treasure Coast* gambling boat.

"I don't know what I woulda done without you Cuban folks here in Miami. You made my police career much more interestin' than it deserved to be. Even now you keep amazin' me."

"I'm glad we amuse you."

"It would be nice to help this Hernandez lady. She sounds like a nice woman."

"Yes, it would be. You have any idea who this dude with the tattoo and the scar might be? Did you ever deal with the old Cuban gangs?"

Ross shrugged. "I don't know much about the old gangster class in Cuba. I never worked there, I just fished down there—and not for crooks. Of course, we got some with the boat lift in eighty when Castro emptied out all the jails, but that was mostly younger types."

Ross was talking about the boat lift from Mariel when Castro opened that port and over a hundred thousand Cubans came racing to the Florida shores. Of course, he also opened the doors to the jail cells and a contingent of the new refugees turned out to be not such pleasant folks. Some were cold-blooded killers and many of those who weren't soon learned the skill in Miami. Within a couple of years, a number of those freedom-seeking psychopaths had lost that freedom and were back in jail.

"There are so many bad guys from one place or another hidin' out around here these days," Ross was saying, "I don't have any notion where you'd look for this specific fella."

"Well, I wanted to ask Cozy Costanza but he didn't feel like speaking to me. Let's just say this Cuban gangster had something to do with the American mobsters who worked in Cuba in the old days."

"Okay."

"And let's say he really is helping Roberto Player find who killed his parents. Cozy Costanza and his people might have the answer to that. In fact, they might *be* the answer to that."

Ross shrugged. "Well, the syndicate did do business that way. It didn't have much in common with the Red Cross. We know that, don't we?"

"You were already working in Intelligence by then, weren't you?"

"Yes, I was."

"And you were keeping an eye on Mafia people?"

"Oh yeah, especially back then. We didn't want them

to think that since they had been kicked out of Cuba they could come across the Florida Straits and set up business here. Meyer Lansky had already run a big operation years before just north of here. We didn't want him or anyone else to think they would be welcomed back from Cuba with open arms."

"So you went and talked to them?"

"Yes, I paid neighborly visits on people like Cozy Costanza."

"And?"

"And Cozy promised me he wasn't thinking of doing any business in our neck of the woods. In fact, he figured he'd be goin' back to Cuba before too long."

"I guess he had that wrong."

"You might say that. But back then people figured Castro couldn't last. In fact, people like Cozy supposedly were donating money to help get rid of him."

"Really?"

"That's what people were saying."

"To the anti-Castro underground?"

"To anybody who wanted to get rid of the guy with the beard."

"I'm told that Player's parents were part of the underground."

"Well, then they were on the same side as Cozy."

"So you wouldn't think he would have them killed."

Ross chuckled. "Tell that to all the Mafia guys who got cement shoes as presents from their own family members. Those snakes change their skin. They do whatever suits 'em at the moment. Which is why I'd be careful if I were you."

"Right."

Willie drained his beer and got up. "I'll give your regards to Cozy Costanza if I ever get to talk to him."

Ross lifted his beer in a toast. "You do that. And tell 'im I sure do miss seein 'im, ya hear."

Chapter 9

Willie pulled the LeBaron into the parking space around the corner from his office, grabbed the manila envelope he had lifted from Roberto Player's condo the night before, and walked to the Cuban bakery across the street. The few times in his life he had been shot at had always left him hungry. Today was no different. He ordered three *empanadas,* two of meat, one of *frutas,* and a *café con leche* and sat at a table in the window.

He removed the photo of the Players, the letters, and the diary and spread them on the table. He thought about how many people in Miami had hidden away small stacks of documents like these, the only proof of a previous life in a country they'd had to leave, usually in a hurry and traveling light. Lots of people, Willie thought, and not just from Cuba. Working in patrol, Willie had found these stacks of papers in the houses of people killed or detained, often tucked into old, battered suitcases or crammed into the backs of drawers. The people had stowed them away in the same way Roberto Player did, like old identities that no longer were usable. Willie had once answered a call at a house where an old man had died and discovered in his stack not just photos and letters, but a driver's manual for a 1952 Chevy and a map of Havana. Willie had told his mother.

"In his head the old man was driving around Havana in that car still," she said with her profound knowledge of exile eccentricities. "He wants to know how to fix it if the fantasy ever breaks down."

The letters from a mother to her son alone in the States

wouldn't be so whimsical. He removed the rubber band that bound them. How many had been written in total he didn't know, but the stack contained about twenty. All in flimsy, onionskin airmail envelopes, they were addressed and written in royal-blue fountain pen. The ink had faded over the years from age and apparently from having been handled frequently. Roberto Player had wanted to remember his mother's voice. They were all brief, written in Spanish to be read to a six year old, but an intelligent six year old.

The first letter began:

To our little man who we love so very, very much.

You have only been gone less than a week, but already we miss you terribly. We hope everything is going as well as possible there in Miami.

Here nothing has changed, but your father still feels this situation can not go on much longer. People will not accept what is happening here and then our lives will return to normal. You will come back to your empty room very soon. We will go swimming at Varadero and you'll have all you want of the rum ice cream, no matter what I said in the past. You will fill this awful silence your father and I have in our home and our hearts.

We hope you understand this was the only thing we could do and that we love you more than ever. We expect you are behaving like the brave little man you are. We understand you are living in a camp outside the city. Your father says to be careful of the alligators. He is just joking, but I am not. Please take care of yourself.

It was signed, "Your mother and father who will never stop loving you."

Willie folded it away and browsed a few others, stopping at one written a few months later. This one was addressed to the St. Joseph Orphanage in Michigan. In the middle of it you could hear Bobby's mother's hopes fading for any quick change in the situation.

Your father is still working, although fewer people are filling the casino and the government now takes most of the money. We are lonely for our old customers, but not as lonely as we are for you. We don't know how long this can continue.

But that is not something that you should worry about. If matters do not work out here, we will travel to be with you in the United States. We are already making plans. Partners of your father have promised they will help us. It will not be too long before this is decided.

I miss you so much I sometimes think I will die of it. But I know I won't. I know we will be together again, my little man. Please, don't forget us.

Willie finished it and folded it away as well. He figured the "partners" Maria Player had referred to were the mafiosos in the casino business. Apparently they hadn't helped. In fact, maybe they had killed Carlos and Maria.

The third and final letter Willie read was apparently the very last the beautiful Maria Player had written. Postmarked in the first days of 1961, it must have been mailed shortly before the Players were murdered. It was the most worn of the letters, ragged, with finger marks on it. It was apparently written in response to a letter received from young Roberto. Its tone was more anxious.

Please, son, don't despair. Yes, what your friends at the orphanage tell you is true. It is impossible to get permission to leave here now. But they are not right when they tell you that there is no hope. Your friends and you are living far from Cuba and you don't know.

Trust in God and we will be together again soon. We are doing all we can to be with you. Please pray for us. We have never needed your prayers the way we do now.

I dream of you every night. As always, we never stop thinking of you and loving you. Your father reminds you to be mindful of alligators, even up there in

the cold—be careful of who your friends are—and he
sends you all his love.

Willie read it again. He wondered if the "hope" Maria
Player was speaking of concerned the underground and if
the prayers she asked for were for God's help in their clandestine work. Roberto Player had clearly never stopped
wondering that as well.

Willie stashed the letters back in the legal folder and
then opened the diary. He saw now that what he held was
a series of short diaries written on different types of paper, all bound together in the same leather cover. Given
the handwriting and the lined, schoolboy paper in the earliest pages, it was clear Roberto Player had started keeping this record right around the time his parents had died.

Willie flipped through it. The entries, not just the ones
made when he was a child, were strangely inarticulate for
a man with as much education as Roberto Player. They
were all written in Spanish, from beginning to end, as if
he could only speak about his parents in the language of
his earliest years, when they were together. The first, in
faded pencil, started with a lament. It was not addressed
to himself, but to his parents. Maybe before he knew they
were dead, but maybe not.

I don't understand what is happening. I want to go
home. I want to see you.

It was strange, but many of the entries over the years
started with those same words. "I don't understand." Others began: "I need to know who you were . . ." Everyone's curiosity was piqued by who their parents had been
before they were parents, but for Bobby Player it was an
obsession. In other entries, he tortured himself a different
way. "If only I had stayed . . . ," or "If I hadn't let you
send me here . . ." The idea was that they wouldn't have
died. Of course, probably he would have perished as well.

The handwriting was always difficult to read beyond
those first few words, scrawled in the midst of an emotional outburst. The same memories and the same strug-

gle to comprehend emerged year after year, through childhood, adolescence, and into adulthood. He was stuck.

And then Willie reached the entries that began, "I need to bury the past . . ." and "I need to forget it all . . ." and "Please, God, let me forget . . ." Roberto Player was trying to shed his ghosts, but he couldn't. The diary did not contain a story of growing up, but the tale of a man who, at least in one dark corner of himself, was still that Peter Pan kid who had disembarked alone from a plane in Miami decades before. Reading it you understood what had driven him to Cuba and to the course he was on. Reading it also made Willie worry that this was a child going after gangsters.

On the very last page, a short note was scribbled.

Finally, I have an answer to the lies. Finally, I know what to do.

It was written the very day he had returned from Cuba. It contained no more, nothing about the beautiful young Cuban woman or the man with the scar and the tattoo.

Willie put the diary away and sipped his *café con leche*. The man who had read those letters and written those diary entries was in rough shape. He was possessed. But if it were Willie's parents who had been murdered, he knew he would do the same thing. He would hunt down the killers if he could.

Willie looked at the old photo of Roberto Player and his parents. Then he glanced at the phone number of that rich doctor out in Iowa who wanted him to find two pimple-faced boys. Willie figured a few more hours of gawking after super models over on South Beach wouldn't hurt those kids. He drained his coffee and then went after the only lead he had in the Player case.

Chapter 10

The Mirage Theater was a small, old-fashioned movie house just off Flagler, with a marquee outlined in light bulbs. It was wedged between a fruit stand on one side, featuring plump orange papayas just then, and a religious articles shop on the other, featuring statues of the Virgin, as always.

Willie had passed the theater all his life and had stopped noticing it. But from the looks of the place, lots of people had stopped noting or patronizing it. Many of the marquee's bulbs were busted and the few letters left on it didn't form any kind of film title. Willie figured it was just neglect. But if you believed the projectionist really was a spy, then maybe the letters were some kind of code.

Willie parked across the street and got out. Notices in the outside display cases advertised a drama and a comedy, both of them from the fifties. They had dug up a vintage poster for the drama. Painted in lurid colors, it featured a bare-shouldered, raven-haired woman with rouged cheeks, wrapped in the arms of a man wearing a white suit, his eyes full of fire. In the background rose the skyline of Havana, the old Havana. "Mirage" was definitely the right name for the theater. Its business was supplying visions of a vanished world, if only for an hour or two.

Willie found the box office just inside the door, in a dark, dusty, worn lobby with a cobwebbed chandelier. An old woman with hair dyed red, round rouge smudges on her cheeks, a black dress, and pearls, doubled as ticket seller and candy clerk. Beyond her, near the curtained entrance to the theater, lurked a tall, slim, silver-haired man with a white moustache hugging his lip, who was apparently the ticket taker and usher. He was dressed in an old, exquisitely tailored white linen suit. Together, he and the candy clerk resembled the couple pictured on the poster outside, but fifty years later. Willie wondered if they were indeed those same people, but living in exile now with their past, their memories, their movies.

Willie bought a ticket from the woman for the $2.50 matinee price and ordered a bag of popcorn, even though it looked about as old as the movies that were playing. She shoveled it up and charged him for everything at once.

"The movie began a half hour ago," she said in Spanish.

"That's no problem, *señora*. Tell me, is Mr. Del Rey, the projectionist, still here?"

"Of course," she said. "He's been here for thirty-five years."

"Where would I find him? I want to say hello to him."

She couldn't conceal her interest. Mr. Del Rey apparently didn't receive many visitors. Her scrutiny of Willie increased and she got a lively look in her eye. He wondered if she and the cadaverous-looking gentleman taking tickets might not be deep-cover Cuban agents. If they were, he hoped the Cuban government provided them with health benefits. This was a seriously aging spy network.

She pointed with a trembling finger to the back of the lobby, up red carpeted stairs.

"Between the two entrances to the balcony you'll find a narrow closed door. Knock there."

Willie handed his ticket to the gentleman and went up, feeling the eyes of both of them on his back. The stairs were dark, probably never lighted, because no one much used the balcony. If the clientele was as old as the staff, they probably couldn't climb stairs anymore.

He reached the balcony level, which was warmer, duskier, and even mustier than the lobby. He found the narrow door and knocked softly. From beyond the door, in the theater, Willie could hear the passionate strains of a female singer wringing every drop of despair from an old bolero.

Then the door opened a crack. A mulatto man with a narrow face and startling gray eyes—cat's eyes—gazed out at him.

"What is it?"

"Mr. Del Rey?"

"Yes."

"I'd like to have a word with you, if I can."

"About what?"

"Some people I'm looking for."

The door stood open just enough for Willie to see the man frown. "What people?"

A knowing, expectant look entered the man's eyes, much like the response Willie had gotten from the rouged lady in the lobby. That made Willie take a chance.

"It concerns some visitors who have recently arrived here from Cuba." Willie put a little spin on the word "visitors."

Del Rey didn't speak, but behind his eyes interest flickered. He examined Willie up and down and then opened the door.

"Come in."

Willie stepped into a small, dark, low-ceilinged room with two very narrow, rectangular openings looking down on the theater. Del Rey closed the soundproof door behind him. An old projector ran, pointed through one of the openings, its spools rotating slowly. It beamed a grainy black-and-white movie onto a large screen below. Through the other opening, Willie saw a handful of people scattered around the theater, all of them old, given their hunched outlines.

Del Rey offered him the one chair in the cramped space and pulled out a stool from under a table for himself. Covering most of the narrow wall behind him was an old color poster of Varadero, the most famous vacation beach in Cuba. Since almost no light reached it, its deep blue waters and snow-white sand hadn't faded, like a memory that didn't change.

On the table sat the empty tins for the film that was running. The waste paper basket overflowed with styrofoam coffee cups and the strong smell of tobacco suffused the room. Del Rey sat smoking a cigarette, the trace of a smile on his lips.

"Excuse the cramped conditions," he said. "Such is the life of a projectionist."

Del Rey was lean, with a narrow, straight nose and those startling eyes the gray color of cobblestones. He wore black pants and a white shirt that had stenciled on its pocket a filigreed monogram, VDR, but was also a bit frayed at the cuffs. He had to be in his midfifties at least, but he hid it well. His hair was still jet black and combed straight back, his face smooth, unlined, except for fine cobwebs around the eyes. It seemed that there had come a moment during all those years in that cramped room when he had stopped aging, just like the characters on the screen below. Either that, or he dyed his hair.

His diction was very precise. An aged, tattered elegance marked him, and Willie could easily picture him as a stylish, extremely handsome young pit boss in the casinos of old Cuba.

He asked Willie to wait a minute while he prepared the movie reels so that they would not be interrupted. While he did so, Willie watched the movie that had been made in that same old Havana. The screen was alive with the scene of a young couple walking down a cobblestoned boulevard between street lamps and large old buildings constructed during the Spanish Conquest, with wrought-iron balconies and studded doors. The girl wore a low-cut white summer dress and the young man, a striped zoot suit. A horse-drawn cart passed them in one direction and a beautiful old Buick in the other. A friend emerged on a balcony, called to them, and they waved. Then they reached a plaza where a band played and couples danced the mambo. It was beautiful, sunny, spirited, sexy, and you knew why losing it had pissed off the people who had lost it.

Del Rey finished, sat down before him again, and lighted another cigarette. He spoke now in a husky whisper.

"So you're here to talk about the visitors who have just recently come." He gave "visitors" the same knowing inflection Willie had.

"That's right."

"I wonder if we're speaking of the same visitors."

"They arrived by boat, power boat, last night."

On the screen laughter burst out. Del Rey focused on him.

"I assume these are ones who came from Havana."

Willie nodded. "Yes, directly from the island. How did you know?"

"Because it's my job to know, isn't it?"

The older man pulled on his cigarette and the orange ash glowed. He acted as if he knew who Willie was, as if he expected to be contacted about the visitors. Willie didn't dissuade him.

"Have you seen them yet?"

The other man shook his head. "No, not yet."

"But you know them."

"Oh, yes. I know all of them."

Willie frowned. "All of them?"

"They are coming in all the time now. Constantly."

"From Cuba?"

"Of course. Where else? That's where the operatives are, isn't it?"

"Yes."

"Well?"

"I'm just surprised there are so many."

"Well, they have various operations to organize. Missions that form part of the new plot designed by the leadership. You know about it, don't you?"

Willie nodded, but said nothing.

Del Rey leaned forward, staring dramatically into Willie's eyes. In the background, the Cuban music played.

"Then tell me about it."

Willie hesitated. "What do you mean?"

"Just that."

"I don't understand."

Del Rey said nothing. To Willie it became obvious that the projectionist had mistaken him for someone else and realized that he'd been tricked. Willie was sure there would be trouble. Maybe violence. The man might have a blade concealed somewhere on his lithe body.

Then Del Rey's demeanor changed completely. His gaze softened with amusement. He pulled on his cigarette, crossed a leg, and laughed dryly. Willie was confused.

"Why are you laughing?"

Del Rey exhaled and tapped Willie's knee with a long, elegant finger. "Every few years, a policeman like you or some federal agent appears in this projection room. I know then that something has happened that involves Cuba, or at least people here are worried that something is happening. I have no idea what these things might be. But some policeman like you will ask me these same questions about secret agents, the shady people who I am supposed to know."

"I'm not a policeman. I'm a private investigator."

Del Rey shrugged. "Same thing. Same questions."

"And why do they come to ask them of you?"

"Because they believe that I am a spy, of course. That I am some kind of agent for the enemy, the Cuban government. That's why you are here too, isn't it?"

Willie didn't answer. The other man smiled and spread his arms, almost scraping the opposite walls of the narrow room.

"If I am a spy, what am I going to find out sitting in here all day and night? I can tell you who eats the bad popcorn here and who doesn't, but not much else."

He reached into the drawer of the table and brought out a bottle of cheap rum and two paper cups.

"Let's have a small drink together. I always like to do this. These visits from people like you mark the passage of time for me . . . my time in enemy territory."

He winked, poured the rum, and they touched cups. Willie watched him sip and tasted his own. He felt as if he'd found the cave of a hermit, or one of those Japanese soldiers they used to discover hiding on Pacific islands, not knowing that World War II was over. Except this was Miami.

"So you're saying you aren't an agent of the Cuban government, that no other agents have contacted you, and not to come bothering you."

The mulatto man smoked and shook his head. "No, I'm

not saying that. It wouldn't do any good to say that because people will believe what they want anyway. What I do say is I live like this, in this theater and in my hotel room at the Ponce de Leon Hotel downtown, so who can I possibly be spying on? I know what some people used to think when I first got here more than thirty years ago, but many of those people are dead. The rest think *I'm* the one who is dead because they haven't seen me in so long. Or they have just forgotten about me. The only people who remember me are people like you, who have my name in some file."

During his time in the Intelligence Unit, Willie had performed surveillance of supposed Cuban spies. He had tailed people who were allegedly deep-cover agents, who had worked as cab drivers or short order cooks for so long that they were really only cab drivers and short order cooks anymore. Willie figured that if the call ever came from Havana, they would simply hang up, blow it off, and go back to watching the Spanish-language TV. Was Del Rey one of those or something different? A spy working at this theater might serve as a contact for all kinds of individuals who came to the movies. Maybe they left messages hidden in the seats.

"Do you deny you were an agent of the Cuban government back in Nineteen sixty?"

The projectionist shook his head. "Of course not. Everyone knows that. But let me tell you this—many people live here who were on the other side in those early days and turned against it later. They don't talk about it, but there are many of them. And being an agent back then meant that you kept an eye on anyone who was suspected of being untrustworthy. Following them around. Nothing more."

"And who did you watch?"

"Whoever I was told to."

"And were you asked to watch Carlos Player, your boss?"

Willie's knowledge of Player surprised Del Rey and made him suspicious.

"What if I did?"

"Why were you watching him?"

"I was surveilling him and his wife because I was told they might try to smuggle money from the country that they had accumulated from the hotel and casino operation. That was the concern of my superiors."

"And you reported back to those superiors on the movements of the Players."

"Yes. But in the whole time I watched them I never really reported anything that might be damaging to them."

"Is that right?"

"Yes it is. The truth is I was in no hurry to do any harm to Carlos Player. I had nothing against him. In fact, I liked him."

"Did you?"

Del Rey exhaled luxuriously. "Player was a man of great style. Not just outer style, but a graceful, fair-minded man. His wife was also an enormously attractive person. Very kind and good humored. A person of my color didn't always encounter that."

"I can imagine."

"And they ran a very stylish operation. They always had a good word for everyone. Carlos would drift through the casino in his white dinner jacket with a glass of Pernod in his hand. He spoke impeccable French and English. Many diplomats and journalists frequented Casino Cuba in those days because it was a nest of political gossip. It was a very interesting time. The place was full of people gambling for either money or power, and Carlos always attended them with style. Even Castro and his people would sometimes come."

Willie's eyebrows went up. "Into the casino?"

"Not in the gaming room, but the restaurant. It was near their offices and they would sometimes come to eat. Carlos he had to play host for them as well."

Willie watched him. "And you say you never reported anything damaging about the Players. Nothing that would have made the government come after them?"

"I had nothing to report."

"Did you ever hear that they were part of the underground?"

Del Rey drew on his cigarette and nodded from behind his cloud of smoke. "Yes, but that was only later, after they were dead. Some people whispered that the Players had been killed because they participated in the resistance. If they did, they covered their tracks very well. I knew nothing about it."

His smoke drifted before the lens of the projector and turned a swirling, milky white. Willie wondered if Del Rey's answer was also murky. If Del Rey had passed to the State Security, the G-2, information that had helped them eliminate two members of the underground, he wouldn't breathe a word of it to anyone in Miami. Never.

"What was the relationship between Carlos and Maria Player and their Mafia partners?"

Del Rey thought a moment and shrugged. "It was mostly a business relationship. Carlos, I know, did not like some of them. He didn't care for thugs."

"Like Rico Tuzzi."

Del Rey looked impressed. "So you know Tuzzi."

"We've met."

"Then you've seen why Carlos Player didn't care for him. Tuzzi was a very rough sort of human being, not at all polished. He spoke no Spanish so he could not communicate with many of the customers. Carlos Player, as I said, was highly refined. He had minimal contact with Tuzzi. He had a better relationship with Mr. Cozy Costanza."

"Did he?"

"Yes. Costanza was a man of refinement. He dressed tastefully, distinctively. He was not visibly a gangster, like Tuzzi. Before the change in government, Costanza would escort important guests who came to gamble. They included American politicians and businessmen, and Carlos would also spend time with those special guests. Of course not long after the communists came to power, those guests stopped coming and many of the Mafia left as well. Like Santo Trafficante, who was very important in Cuba, and Meyer Lansky, who built the Riviera Hotel.

Mr. Lansky and Mr. Costanza used to play cards next to the pool at the Riviera, until the government took over the hotel and Lansky left. That was in late 1960 and it was clear Cuba was turning communist. Costanza, he stayed a few months longer because he just loved Cuba, I think, and because maybe he hoped the situation would change. It didn't."

"Did you get any sense there was trouble between the Mafia and Player, just before he and his wife died?"

Del Rey thought and then shook his head. "No, but in those last days I wasn't really watching anyone too closely. By then I had made up my mind that I was no longer meant for Cuba or government service. It turned out I was not a terribly loyal revolutionary and I wanted to get out myself. I made reports on my surveillance assignments, routine movements, but I made them up."

Again Willie wondered, but he had no way of confirming if the former croupier was telling him the truth.

"Have you had any contact with the old Mafia chiefs since you came here?"

Del Rey shook his head ruefully. "No. The Italians are just like the Cubans here when it comes to my past service with the Cuban government. I haven't exchanged a word with either Costanza or Tuzzi in over thirty years."

"Did you ever hear talk tying them to the deaths of Carlos and Maria Player?"

"I don't remember that. I know the government claimed it was bandits."

"Did you believe that?"

Del Rey shrugged. "I didn't believe anything anyone said back then. But I recall they arrested a man for it."

That surprised Willie. "They did? Who was it?"

"A ruffian, a common criminal."

Willie's squint deepened. "What was his name?"

Del Rey suddenly became cautious. "Why?"

"Because I saw a man get off that boat last night who seemed to fit the bill."

"What did he look like?"

Willie described the man he'd seen. When he got to the

scar under the eye and the tattoo on the hand, Del Rey tensed perceptibly.

"Was his name Miguel Angel Matos?" he asked.

"I don't know. They didn't give me their names. Why? Who is this Matos?"

Del Rey's sudden nervousness had forced him to get up. He opened the door and stepped into the dark hallway as if he were afraid someone were hiding there. Willie followed.

"Who is Matos? What did he have to do with all this?'

Del Ray studied him, his cat's eyes even more vivid now in the darkness. He shook his head.

"I'm sure I've made a mistake. There's nothing else I can tell you that will be of any help. You should go now and it would be better if you don't come back."

The elegant ex-croupier then wheeled around and disappeared back into his projection room, laughter ringing from the screen beyond.

Chapter 11

Willie stared at the closed door. Was the man he had seen get off the boat the night before named Matos? If he was, Mr. Del Rey would not be happy about it. Not at all. More than thirty-five years after the events, he was still scared. Willie wanted to know why. He could try to lean on the projectionist, but he sensed that wouldn't produce anything at the moment. Del Rey was spooked. Willie would have to give him a chance to calm down.

He was descending the worn, red carpeted stairs when someone he recognized came into view. Olga Tuzzi was carrying a bag of popcorn and reading a poster at the foot of the stairs. He wondered if she came simply to see the film or to speak with Del Rey, with whom she had worked at the Casino Cuba all those years ago.

Either way, she apparently hadn't heard yet of the shooting at the *Treasure Coast*. She wouldn't be munching popcorn if she had. Willie decided to break it to her slowly.

"Hello, Mrs. Tuzzi."

She looked up with a start, her full, glossed lips opening in an "O." Today, she wore a red toque, a matching red pantsuit, and a string of pearls.

"The detective," she said.

"That's right. How are you?"

She rolled her eyes. "*Comme ci, comme ça.* Getting older every day."

"I didn't notice you looking any older today. In fact, for someone who danced at the Casino Cuba all those years ago, you look very young and fit."

The hint of a smile tugged at her pursed lips and quickly disappeared, like a small wave passing through the water.

"Thank you. You are a nice boy." Her face went serious. "Do you find Bobby yet?"

"No, not yet. I'm still looking."

"I'm very worry about him."

"I'm doing my best. And you? You're here to see the film?"

"Yes. The old Cuban and Mexican films, they are my favorite. They remind me of when I was young."

"You could have been in the movies yourself, it seems to me."

Her hand went to her hip. "I was. I begin in the chorus line for two movies of a very good director," she said propping her other hand on her other hip, popcorn and all, as if she were about to break into a Folies Bergères leg kick. "Then I went to work for another director in the movie *Moon Over Havana.* I dance a tango, me and the leading man, a very handsome, passionate *muchacho* named Jorge. Later he died, still very young."

She closed her eyes and swayed just a bit as if she were being dipped by her long dead tango partner.

After a few moments she opened them. "Another director he told me that dance it was the most sexy moment in all of the cinema Latina. He told me I would be the star in his next movie."

Her eyes flared momentarily with promise, but the enthusiasm faded again. "Then all the trouble it began and he leave the island. I went back to work in the clubs and I don't see him again."

For moments she said nothing after providing Willie that short history of her very short movie career. At the center of each account was a man and Willie knew by the naked look in her eyes each one had been her lover. Olga Tuzzi was not the kind of woman who could hide that connection, even if she wanted to.

Willie sensed that all those men had lavished praise and promises on Olga Tuzzi, while enjoying her pleasures, and had then cast her off. Behind her deep brown eyes you made out the memory of pain. But you also saw that she refused to give up her romantic vision of those times, or of the men. She seemed a woman who would not give way to bitterness. Maybe it was because her past was all she had. Or maybe she had witnessed what bitterness had done to her husband.

"I just came from talking to Rico," he said.

Her nostalgia dried up completely now and she returned to the nervous present. Her red-painted fingernails went to her pearls.

"What did he say?"

"About what?"

She thought a moment. "About Bobby."

"He told me the government had killed Bobby's parents, and that maybe I should come and ask a man who works here named Del Rey."

Her glance shot to the top of the stairs and ricocheted back to Willie's face.

"You know him, don't you?" Willie asked. "He used to spin roulette wheels at Casino Cuba."

She nodded reluctantly, but said nothing. Her silence told him much more than words would have.

"Mr. Del Rey must have been a very handsome young man in his day," Willie said. "A dashing pit boss."

She nodded again, looking into his eyes with trepidation as if he had nabbed her at something. Willie wondered if she and Del Rey had been lovers somewhere along the line. In fact, he wondered if they still were. Her fear seemed that immediate. He wondered if that was how she had survived years of living with a thug like Rico Tuzzi. And maybe she was the answer to how Del Rey had dealt with years of isolation. They were about the same age and Willie could see them together. Two human artifacts of high-rolling, sensual old Havana, clinging to each other and their memories. Maybe.

"Did you know that Del Rey was working for Cuban State Security back then?"

She shook her head with a broad sweep, but not taking her eyes off him. "No. I didn't know nothing about that."

Willie wouldn't have shared anything like that either

with Olga Tuzzi. She was an open book with her secrets printed in large type.

"If Del Rey was snooping for State Security, shadowing Carlos and Maria Player, then Bobby might come here to find who killed his parents."

That idea worried her. Her eyes darted up the balcony stairs again and back to Willie.

"Did he come here?"

"No, not yet."

"I don't think Mr. Del Rey he would hurt Carlos and Maria."

"So he claims. Is there anybody else Bobby might visit? Anyone his parents knew in those last days who is still around?"

Olga Tuzzi gazed reluctantly into her past, as if she were afraid what she would find there. She apparently encountered something or someone who registered. You could see it in her eyes, although she bit her lip as if she didn't want it to escape her.

"Who was it?" Willie asked.

She spoke as if she were confessing a crime. "I remember one man, he used to come to the casino to talk to Carlos. I would go to the office to see Maria and he would be there. He was an American, tall, hair blond, with skin very red. The sun it was bad for him. He would always look at me like he wanted me."

Willie watched her. The man she described sounded like the former diplomat Willie had met at Cozy Costanza's place.

"Was his name Clancy? James Clancy?"

Her eyes opened wide. "I forget the name, but I know I see him there talking to Carlos. They seem very serious."

What would have taken Clancy to Carlos Player's inner sanctum? Willie wondered.

There was a burst of laughter from the movie.

"Mrs. Tuzzi, have you talked to your husband in the past couple of hours?"

"No."

He told her what had happened at the *Treasure Coast*. Her mouth fell open.

"Do you have any idea who that could have been or why it happened?" Willie asked.

Again she rummaged through an inventory of shadowy, dangerous characters she obviously had in that head of hers. This time she shook her head mutely.

"Are you sure, Mrs. Tuzzi? Could it have anything to do with Bobby?"

"I don't know anything. I better go now."

Before he could ask her anything else, for example about those old rough clubs she had danced in and who she might have rubbed elbows with there, she hurried away. She didn't climb the stairs to see Del Rey or head out the door to find her husband. Instead, she crossed the lobby into the lower level of the theater, in a rush to disappear into her fantasies and into her past.

Chapter 12

Willie watched the door close behind her. For a few moments he thought about staying and watching the movie himself. He could use a jolt of old Cuba right then; a taste of rumba, some heavenly Havana nights, a dose of old fantasy instead of new trouble. He thought about it, but he had things to do, so he left. That turned out to be a mistake.

He slipped out of the theater and crossed the street. He was almost to the LeBaron when suddenly a black Cherokee with tinted windows came speeding in his direction. It veered at him, almost pinning him against a parked pickup truck.

He had been shot at once already in the day and that was enough. He was reaching for the .38 at the small of his back when the power window of the passenger seat slid down and a man in camouflage shirt, cap, and dark glasses stuck his head out and spoke with an accent.

"Mr. Cuesta, can you get in please?"

Willie had his hand wrapped around the gun when he looked into the back seat of the car. Another man in full camouflage uniform with a white ascot around his neck sat there. He wore mirrored sunglasses, but Willie recognized him.

That same man reached over and opened the back door. Willie released his gun, fixed the back of his shirt, glared at the guy in the front seat, and got in.

The Bronco took off with a squeal of tires into the barrio. Willie turned to the man next to him. "Practicing your political kidnapping, Mando?"

The man shook his head. "If we were, you wouldn't have been asked so politely, Willie."

His name was Armando Capitán, better known as Mando, and he had served for decades as the leader, or *comandante,* of a Cuban exile commando group called Delta-5. Everybody in Cuban Miami knew of Mando. He was a symbol, a poster boy of the Cuban exile battle against Castro.

Mando's cellular phone sounded just then and he answered it. Willie watched him as he talked. Many Cubans had undergone amazing metamorphoses in the wake of the Cuban revolution. Over the years Miami had crawled with generals who had become janitors, bankers who had worked as bank guards, and small tradesmen turned into tycoons. It was as if the voyage between the island and Florida had taken them through a force field that warped identities, scrambled genes. Mando's evolution was radical. He had gone from wastrel to warrior.

Before the revolution he had been famous as one of the most decadent playboys in Havana, heir to a sugar fortune, a far-grazing womanizer and gambler. Willie had leafed through copies of the old Cuban society magazine *Bohemia* and seen photos of a young Mando dressed in evening clothes at the Havana Country Club or in the casinos, always supporting starlets on his arm.

When the revolution came, Mando's world collapsed and he lost everything. Unlike other sugar barons, Mando failed to smuggle his fortune to Miami, and unlike those others he remained on the island. He fell out of sight for a time and when he re-appeared he did so as a counter-revolutionary leader, a sybarite turned saboteur. Mando, who had made many a champagne cork pop, started making dynamite go off all over Havana. Miraculously he had managed to escape capture. He eventually fled to the United States, later joined the Bay of Pigs invasion, and was taken prisoner along with most of the members of that exiled army. He was sentenced to Cuban prison, but was released two years later with the other captured invaders.

Mando then settled in Miami, where he maintained his

new persona, his camouflage uniform, and his new cause. For more than thirty years, he and his aging general staff had trained battalions of Cuban refugees in guerrilla tactics in preparation for an invasion of Cuba that had never come. Every weekend they marched out to a camp on the margins of the Everglades and practiced shooting, sabotage, and surprise attacks. In all these missions, the trainees were magnificently successful, but, of course, the real enemy was almost three hundred miles away in Havana, about two hundred miles to Key West and another ninety from there.

Occasionally Mando sent real commando teams down to the island. A few had managed acts of sabotage in Cuba. But his last landing team had been captured when it was still in the surf. People who didn't like Mando joked that he should include suntan lotion and beach towels in his field kits because his men didn't make it off the sand.

But Mando didn't quit. He was, in his way, a fascinating individual. He retained as many of his old playboy affectations as he could afford—the ascot, a taste for martinis, which he sipped in his command tent, a bit of gambling at the jai alai.

Exile, Willie had learned, could be an anxious, strange, sometimes surreal experience. People were suddenly unable to find the streets they'd once walked in Cuba, unable to locate the friends they'd known all their lives. A person's life became someone else's life from one minute to the next when he or she stepped on the boat or plane to leave. It was like falling down the rabbit hole, a form of madness. Many people endured by never relinquishing the idea of returning to Cuba. For others, survival became a matter either of vivid religious distraction, or, in more extreme cases, the creation of a fantasy existence. Mando was an example of the latter category, except for one important detail. The guns he and his friends played with weren't fantasy. They were real. If the cause were at stake, Mando was capable of killing. Willie was sure of that.

While working in Police Intelligence, Willie had kept track of Delta-5. He had even helped bust some members for gun running. Despite that, he and the *comandante* maintained a kind of relationship. That was largely because Willie's family and Mando's had known each other for years. They bumped into each other at weddings, funerals, *quinces,* Mando always in full uniform.

Willie looked at him now with his immaculately pressed camouflage, a pearl-handled pistol on his hip, the matching white ascot at his neck, his mirror shades, and his MacArthur-like composure. The older man finished his call and turned off his phone.

"If this is a recruiting mission, Mando, I still work weekends," Willie said. "I can't make it."

Mando nodded. "I understand you will always be a worthless civilian, Willie, but I also understand from a mutual acquaintance that you may have some intelligence we can use. Something to do with a possible infiltration by enemy agents."

Willie's eyes narrowed even further. So this was Cassandra's doing. She hadn't put his name on the radio, which was good, but had leaked it to Mando instead. This was to be expected in the scheme of things. Mando was a heavy hitter in the community. Passing along a tidbit like this one about possible infiltrators would purchase Cassandra much goodwill and was too much for her to resist.

"I saw two people get off a boat down at Matheson Hammock. They had just come from Cuba."

"I understand they were smuggled on a pleasure boat. I have checked with certain sources at immigration and around the community. None of the legitimate boat captains who engage in such rescues knows anything about this. And the ones who arrived haven't contacted anyone about political asylum. We believe these aren't legitimate refugees."

"You think they're agents for Castro."

"Possibly."

"That's quite a leap, Mando."

"We have our informants."

Willie didn't believe any of it. He thought Mando was just being Mando.

"You don't know who these passengers were?" Mando asked.

"No."

"What were you doing there when they disembarked?"

"Fishing."

Mando glowered at him. "This isn't a time for jokes, Willie. Believe me."

"I was doing some troubleshooting for a client."

"Which client?"

"I can't tell you that and it doesn't really matter."

"So you tripped over the operation by accident, is that what you're saying?"

"In a way, yes."

"What can you tell us about the agents?"

"One was a man near sixty. He was trim, hard, scar above the eye. Had the look of a gangster."

"And the other person."

"A woman."

"What did she look like?'

"About as good as it gets. Thirtyish, black hair, dark eyes."

"Where did they go?"

"I have no idea."

Mando's eyes narrowed into bayonets. "I don't believe you. Somebody must have met them, taken charge of them. Some contact person."

"Possibly, but I don't know where they went. I thought, given your intelligence capabilities, your sources, you would know exactly where to look next."

Mando scowled at his sarcasm. "I'll tell you this, Willie. The underground is still alive here. If we think enemies are being smuggled in we will respond. That is clear."

"I'm sure you will, Mando. Speaking of the underground, I heard some names mentioned recently. Two people who were cadre in the underground in Cuba and got killed."

"Who were they?"

"Carlos and Maria Player."

Mando winced slightly. Willie thought he saw recognition in the old soldier's eyes, but then Mando's thoughts ducked for cover.

"I don't remember them. But many brave people fought in the underground, all divided into different cells for the sake of security. What is your interest in them?"

He tried to make the question sound offhand.

"Nothing, really," Willie said. "Like I said, just names that came out of a conversation."

Mando turned and met Willie's gaze for several long seconds, as if he would ask another question, but he didn't. Here was another person who, for some reason, refused to expound on the charming, romantic, murdered Carlos and Maria Player. Instead he changed the subject.

"If you hear anything else or see these two people smuggled in, we trust you will be in touch with our headquarters."

Willie said nothing and Mando tapped him lightly on the cheek. "I have put up with you all these years, even though you have insisted on being a neutral. I've maintained that discipline mainly out of affection for your widowed mother. But now is no time for that. You don't want to get caught in the middle. This time it could be extremely dangerous. And I wouldn't want your mother to suffer."

"I'll tell her you're thinking of her."

Just moments later they pulled up again outside the theater and the Bronco stopped. Willie got out. "Thank you for the tour of Little Havana, Mando." He saluted the *comandante*. Then the command car took off and went wheeling back into the barrio.

Chapter 13

Willie made it home this time. He pulled into his parking space just off Calle Ocho and climbed the stairs to the apartment. On the machine he found a message from his mother, as if she had sensed Mando and Willie discussing her.

"It appears you have forgotten that you have a family," she began in a dolorous tone. "It's been three days since I've heard a word from you."

In truth it had only been two, but neither mathematics nor the exact truth were in his mother's repertoire when she was angry with him. He could picture her now propped behind the cash register at the *botanica,* surrounded by her potions and her religious images.

"I don't even know if you're alive," she said. Melodrama was also part of her arsenal, although Willie knew she would already have spoken with Tommy, who had seen him just the night before.

"I don't know how or where you are, but right now I'm preparing a flan. I thought you would want to know that." She hung up then, knowing she didn't have to say more. Willie's mother made a flan in which she used cream cheese and evaporated milk. It was rich beyond description. It was also smart bait to dangle before Willie. He couldn't resist his mother's flan. He would get there as soon as work allowed.

He was just erasing the message when the phone rang. It was Ellie Hernandez and she sounded under more strain than she had the day before.

"Mr. Cuesta, Bobby just called me."

"Where was he?"

"He wouldn't tell me that."

"What *did* he tell you?"

"He warned me that you should stay away from him. You could end up dead and it would be my fault. That's what he said. His voice sounded so cold. I've never heard him talk like that before."

Willie had grabbed a watering can and was dousing a potted banana plant on the back porch. "Well, quite a few people have talked to me like that, so don't worry. I'll be all right."

"How did he know you were looking for him?"

Willie hesitated. He didn't want to recount for her the scene at the marina the night before. She wouldn't want to hear about the gun-toting hood with the scar. That would only scare her more. And obviously Player hadn't told her.

"I went to his condo last night. I guess he knows I was there. What else did he say?"

"He said I shouldn't do anything else to try to stop him. He says he's close to finding who killed his parents. He has names now of people who were around them in those last days."

"Did he mention any of the names?" Willie was thinking of Costanza or Tuzzi, some reason that would have made Bobby or his nasty looking accomplice shoot up the *Treasure Coast*. Willie figured it could have been them, although he wasn't going to tell her about that little incident either.

"No. He didn't tell me that or anything else. I told him he could get killed. He says he would be better off dead than not finding the people who killed his folks."

She went silent. Willie could see her biting her lip, trying to spare him her worries, as she had the day before.

"Don't worry, I'm following my own leads," he said finally.

"Sam Suarez phoned me too. He's going to Bobby's condo tonight to make sure there is nothing there that belongs to the bank. He told me to have you there. He wants to know what you're doing."

Willie made a face. He was moving up in the world now. He was being summoned by one of the merchant princes of the city. Or rather he was being ordered around, which meant he probably wouldn't go. Ellie Hernandez seemed to read his mind again.

"Please come. Do it for me and for Bobby."

"Okay. I'll be there. You get some rest."

He hung up, finished watering the plant, and put the can away. He had told Ellie that he had leads, but that was stretching things. He looked up James Clancy, dialed the only number he found, but got no answer at all. The only other possible lead he had was the piece of paper he had found in Bobby Player's shirt pocket the night before. He took it out and sat at his computer.

Willie pulled up a program that matched telephone numbers to addresses. He had used it when he was on the police force. When he left, a friend of his, Officer Lawanda Brown in the Research Sector, arranged for him to plug into police databases from home. Willie had once helped her younger brother out of a scrape.

He punched in the number from the slip of paper, 305-555-2117. The screen went dark and then a list of telephone numbers appeared, all starting with 555-2. He ran the cursor down to 2117. The name Richard Preston stood next to it. Service had been connected just three days before. Willie read it again. Richard Preston—RP—just like Roberto Player.

The address listed was an apartment in the northwest corner of Little Havana. Not far away.

Fifteen minutes later Willie was turning onto the block. He found the place, a two-story, whitewashed apartment complex that made the shape of an L, with all the doors facing a grass courtyard. In the garden grew a dazzling, blood-orange *flamboyan* tree in full bloom and about a dozen different kinds of palms. If you had to hide out, it was best to duck into a place with thick foliage.

Willie parked across the street and down a little ways, got out, and crossed to the mailboxes on the near wall of the building. Latins made up most of the tenant roster, but he spotted the name Preston in new stencil tape on box number 9. The landlord had glued it there certainly, not Bobby Player.

The box took a key. Willie looked around, saw nobody, pulled out his Café Bustelo pick again, and opened it in a moment. The box was empty except for some junk mail, including a special offer from a new Cuban restaurant. These people had just arrived from Cuba. They probably wouldn't want to eat *vaca frita* or *pollo rostizado con maduros,* but he left it for them to decide.

He closed the box, then climbed the stairs to the second floor and walked past number 9. He slowed as he did and heard a radio playing inside. He could make out a news commentator speaking in Spanish. He lingered a moment, but heard nothing else. The blinds were pulled closed and you couldn't see in at all. So he walked back down the stairs, got into the car, and waited for Mr. Miguel Angel Matos, or whoever was staying in there, to come out.

He sat for a half hour and saw the sun move just a bit across the sky, but not much else. An old woman with bright red hair, very tight toreador pants, and a red parasol emerged from number 5 on the ground floor. A few pedestrians passed by and two dogs—one of them a pit bull—were walked. Neither the door to number 9 nor its blinds opened. Willie polished his shades, listened to an Albita Rodriguez CD on the player, danced a little *guaguanco* in his seat, polished his shades some more, and watched. He turned on the radio and heard an ad about the new club out near the Everglades. "Come to the New Casino Cuba—dining, dancing, gambling, a floor show. Just like the Cuba of old." So Sam Suarez had named his joint for Carlos Player's old club. That was interesting.

Willie waited some more and started to get jumpy. Maybe they'd just left the radio on. Maybe nobody was in there. He could use the phone number and hang up if anyone answered, but he didn't want to risk tipping them. He was thinking he'd leave and come back later.

But right at six o'clock the door to number 9 opened and the young woman he had seen on the dock two nights before emerged. She wore a short sundress, white with a red-and-black floral print, very young, very tropical, and very sexy. She also wore sunglasses and black sandals, and carried a black purse.

She locked the door behind her, descended the stairs, looked both ways—so that her long, dark brown hair swung one way then the other—and then walked away from where Willie was parked. He gave her a half block, got out, and trailed her discreetly on the opposite side of the street.

Tall and leggy, she walked with long, smooth, strides. Willie still carried the rhythm of Albita's *guaguanco* in his head and the woman seemed to move to it. She traversed the first cross street and kept going. In the middle of the second block, a young Latin guy dressed in a blue guayabera and jeans came toward her on the sidewalk. Whether out of modesty or operative caution, she averted her face the whole time. As the guy passed her, he said something to her. She didn't stop or even look at him. The guy swiveled and considered her appreciatively as she receded. Then he glanced at Willie walking on the other side of the street and rolled his eyes. Willie didn't respond.

That block was long and Willie started to wonder where she might be going. Was she headed somewhere specific, to make a contact, or was she simply exploring? As she walked, she looked all around her, at the houses, the gardens. In one driveway, several young girls were jumping rope, keeping several lines spinning at the same time. She slowed and watched them bouncing inside the helix they'd created and listened to their chants. For a moment he thought she would jump in herself, in that short dress of hers, but then she moved on.

She reached the next corner, turned, and went temporarily out of sight onto Flagler Street. Willie muttered, *"Mierda,"* under his breath and ran to catch up. He turned the corner and didn't see her. The sidewalk was crowded with after-work shoppers and bus commuters and she had disappeared into that pedestrian traffic.

He started to weave through the crowd and then stopped. Two storefronts down he saw her standing in front of a window staring at women's clothes. He pulled back, stood near the curb, and watched her out of the cor-

ner of his eye. She took off her sunglasses and pushed her
hair out of the way. A sign in the window advertised de-
signer names she'd probably never heard of. In Cuba
there were no such windows these days, no such clothes,
not for Cubans. She stared at the clothes wide-eyed, as if
they were a kind of temptation, something dangerous.

She stayed there for several minutes, then started walking up the street again only to stop in front of a jewelry
store. If she had been on her way to make a contact, she
had gotten distracted, Willie thought. She stayed trans-
fixed several minutes and then moved again, but only to
stop at the next window. Over the next twenty minutes
Willie lurked within forty feet of her. She advanced from
store window to store window, looking in every one methodically. Fabric shops, furniture, housewares. Her fa-
vorites, decidedly, were clothing and jewelry. She might
have been a Cuban operative snuck into the country
solely to study American consumer society in detail. She
was window-shopping and Willie, like a fool, was following her.

The whole time she wore an expression of wonder mixed
with trepidation, the look a little girl might get if she were
doing something forbidden. And after a while that nettled
Willie because it reminded him so much of his former
wife. Her name was Natalia and she too had sailed across
the water from Cuba. Not on a pleasure craft, but on a raft
constructed from wood and inner tubes, balanced with
bottles of fresh water hanging at the sides and equipped
with umbrellas for shade. She and a handful of other people traveling on three such rafts had been picked up by a
fishing boat off the Florida Keys. The boat was headed
home to the Miami River, the crew radioed ahead, and
Willie was dispatched by patrol to guard the rafters until
immigration agents arrived.

Willie recalled approaching the fishing boat and spot-
ting her right away, standing on the deck with a white
shirt knotted beneath her breasts and sunbleached jeans,
thick dark hair tangled by the sea wind and full of salt,
cheekbones burnt by the sun. And in the midst of that sea-
scalded face, two lustrous dark eyes that, despite a long,

tiring ordeal at sea, were full of emotion. They were eyes you knew had been pegged to the horizon for days, not only in search of salvation from the sea, but in hopes of a new life. Even though she was safe now, she still wore that searching hopeful gaze.

As Willie approached he saw her and she saw him too. Over the next hour, he did the work he had to do, but felt her eyes on him all the time. It was as if he were the Statue of Liberty and she had just sailed into New York Harbor. Her eyes said, "You mean a new life for me, don't you?" Whenever he returned her look she would stare at him with that same intense gaze, the slightest smile on her lips as if she knew him and knew that he would help her. Before he left Willie simply asked her name and wished her luck.

But the next day, as he made out his reports, he'd had to call the immigration guys and he asked about her. Unlike almost all other Cuban refugees, she had sailed from Cuba with no other family member and she had no relatives in Miami. She would be turned over to a social service agency and would end up, temporarily at least, in public housing. Willie found out where she was being held and that day, after work, he went to see her. His idea was to give her a bit of money to help her get through those first days, one Cuban to another. At least that was what he told himself. The truth was that he had become bewitched by a sea creature in the same way the ancient Greek sailors fell under the spells of the sirens.

When he arrived, she greeted him with that same enigmatic smile, as if she had been expecting him, as if he *were* her family, the person she could count on. She was an orphan sent floating from the coast of Cuba, not in a basket but on a raft, and she had floated right up to Willie's feet. In the end he signed for her and she was released in his custody. She spent the next two weeks at his mother's house. It was Willie who helped her with the immigration procedures and assisted her over the other refugee hurdles. It was Willie who took her shopping for the first time and saw the kind of childlike,

Christmas-morning expressions that he was seeing now on the face of this other Cuban woman.

And, in time, it was Willie who brought her to live in his house and who became her lover. She was a wonderful lover, tempestuous at moments and beautifully calm and happy afterward. Willie, who had always had too many girlfriends to live with one woman, was calm with it too. Because of the way they had met, he had come to feel that the relationship was fated, predetermined by the gods, the gods of the sea, so to speak. He didn't say that, but he didn't fight it either. Eventually, they married.

Meanwhile, she remade her life. The courage she had shown in taking to the water was borne out in the way she found work and struggled with the strangeness of Miami. The city was both heaven and hell to her, blessed with comforts but also violent and frightening. She watched the nightly crime news in Spanish the way some people would watch a horror movie. Each day when Willie came home from the police department she greeted him desperately as if he had made it home alive after another day of hunting vampires. She worried about him because, after all, he was both lover and father to her, the person who explained the world to her.

But in time that changed. She became more polished and self-assured. Willie, to a degree, felt he had formed her, but now the need for a guide and protector diminished. She made friends and went out on her own. Willie told himself this was good, that her strength was welcomed, but he increasingly found himself in waters he wasn't used to. She was making her own discoveries and chafed at his influence. In time, they began to argue and she pulled farther away from him. For a while distrust lived with them like a third person in the house, a skulking, largely silent presence all its own, until finally she left.

The whole relationship had lasted less than two years. Willie had known anger and frustration, foolishness and denial. One night he had dreamed about her: crossing a bridge he had looked over the edge to see her floating down the river beneath him, hands folded on her chest,

eyes closed, maybe asleep, maybe dead. He knew she
was gone for good. Eventually he understood that you
could provide safe harbor for another adult only for a
time and then they had to face the elements on their own,
no matter what *you* wanted. He also realized that the
gods wouldn't be the gods if they didn't screw with you
from time to time.

Willie thought of Natalia as he watched this other
woman who'd come on the same current from Cuba, but
maybe for different reasons. As she drifted on to the next
stores, Willie followed and watched her even more closely
than he needed. She reminded him of his former wife in
another way as well. She was beautiful. To begin, her face
was unusual—long, deeply tanned, and dark for a Cuban,
the cheekbones very high. Her mouth was wide, maybe
too wide for her face, but her lips were thin and delicately
shaped. Her eyes were dark and expressive. The angles
and color of her face made it look like it had been carved
from tropical wood and sanded by hand, until it was
smooth. Her long, dark hair softened it even more.

And then there was that long strapping body and the
way she moved. Surveillance always became, to a degree,
obsessive. You watched one person to the exclusion of
everyone else. But this was different. After a while he
realized he was no longer watching her solely because of
the way she had been smuggled into the country or because of Roberto Player. He was watching her just for the
pleasure of watching her.

But that didn't last long. She suddenly looked at her
watch, turned, and hurried down the street, as if she were
late for an appointment. He tailed her three blocks, all the
way to the Catholic church on that same side of the street.
She ran up the front steps and disappeared through a
thick, carved wooden door. Willie sped up, scaled the
stairs, and entered through another door.

The inside of the church was shadowy, the light seeping
through the stained-glass windows a deep blue. It wasn't a
large space, but at first he didn't see her. He thought she
had slipped out through the side door. But then he spotted
her, kneeling all the way up front, before a rack of red vo-

tive candles. They were alone in the church and Willie stood in the shadows at the rear, watching her. She lit a taper and used that to light one of the votive candles. She stayed kneeling for a time before the candle. If she were a spy for the Cuban government then either this was a show or she had a few eccentricities the Cuban Communist Party maybe didn't know about.

She got up and sat in the front row, staring up at the plain wooden altar and a large wooden crucifix behind it where Christ hung, a pale blue. Several minutes passed and then a man entered through the side door of the church. Willie didn't see his face until the man reached the altar rail and turned toward where the woman sat. He recognized Victor Del Rey, the former croupier and Cuban government agent, the projectionist whose theater operated just a few blocks from the church.

Gazing around the church warily, Del Rey sat in the first pew, just a few feet away from the young woman. They turned to each other and began to talk. Willie could see them clearly enough, but could hear nothing. It was clear that Del Rey was surprised and unsettled by something the woman said to him, but she proceeded to calm him. She spoke, he answered her, and finally he nodded reluctantly. Then the meeting was over, having lasted no more than two minutes. Del Rey rose and headed right out the side door again without looking back, hurrying to get away from her.

The young woman got up then, walked up the center aisle of the church and out the doors. She led Willie back the way they had come, but this time walking the opposite side of the street. She stopped only once, outside a lingerie store. She stared at what she saw in the window. Some of the negligees barely covered any part of the full-bodied mannequins and again Willie doubted there was anything like them in any shop window in Cuba.

She stayed staring, but then her expression changed and you could tell clearly what she was thinking. She was imagining herself wearing one of them. A look came over her that was both coy and challenging at the same time, totally womanly. It was the look she would give the man

who saw her dressed that way. Standing not more than
thirty feet away, Willie had to take a deep breath.

Before he could exhale she had headed down the street
again. She led him quickly back to the apartment. From
across the street he watched her climb the stairs and put
the key in the door. He expected her to open it and disappear again. Instead, she turned and looked right at him.
She stared into his eyes for at least ten seconds over a
limb of the *flamboyan*. It was clear what she was saying.
She knew he was following her. But did she know why?
Did she recognize him from the boat dock the night before? Did she realize that he knew who she was or at least
how she had arrived in Miami? Or did she think he was
just another guy who couldn't take his eyes off her? There
was that question in the way she looked at him. How
much should she worry about him? Then she turned the
key in the door and disappeared inside.

Willie waited, but no one else came to the door or the
apartment window. He thought it over, then got back in
the car and waited some more. He wondered if Player and
the other man were in the apartment. If they weren't,
would she try to contact them? He had his answer ten
minutes later.   •

The same black Mercedes he had seen at Matheson
Hammock wheeled up and parked right across the street
from him. Roberto Player and the man with the scar jumped
out. Scarface had changed his clothes, Willie noticed, and
now wore a spiffy tropical shirt patterned with bright blue
parrots. Before Willie could move, he ran across the narrow street, pulled a gun, and stuck it through the open
driver side window and right under Willie's chin. It felt
cold against his skin. Twilight had set in and the street
was empty, no one to notice what was happening.

"Give me the keys to the car," the man said in Spanish.

Willie had no choice. He did as he was told.

"Now get out."

Willie did and the man frisked him quickly, finding the
.38 in the small of his back and pocketing it. Then the
man turned to Player. "Go get Aurora."

Roberto Player climbed the stairs to apartment number 9 and, along with the woman, started to bring out baggage. They loaded it into the trunk of the Mercedes.

"Who are you?" Willie asked the man next to him.

"It's no concern of yours who we are," he said. "This is private business."

"Let me guess. Your name is Matos. Miguel Angel Matos."

Even a face as hard as his, a gaze as veiled as his, couldn't conceal his annoyance now. Del Rey had hit it right on the head. There were several moments when Willie expected the gun to go off. He expected to take one in the belly right there. But the gangster apparently thought better of it. The corpse of a former policeman would draw the kind of attention he obviously didn't want.

"Del Rey, who you're in touch with, worked for Cuban State Security back in the old days," Willie said. "Is that who you work for these days? Did they turn you in jail?"

"You don't know what you're talking about. I've told you this is a private matter."

Willie studied his eyes, trying to find the truth. But now Bobby Player had stashed the last of the luggage in the trunk and crossed to them. He shook his finger at Willie as he had the previous night.

"You stay away from us. You don't understand what's going on here and neither does Ellie."

"You're the one who doesn't understand, Bobby. These people aren't interested in the Mafia or anyone else who you think killed your parents. This man was jailed for it."

"I know that, but he didn't kill them."

"Is that what he told you? Well, he's still here on his own business and not yours. They're using you and you could end up dead."

Willie put out a hand to grab ahold of Roberto Player. Mr. Matos didn't like that. The gun suddenly came up toward Willie's head. As Willie sank to the ground, the last thing he saw was the flock of blue parrots on Matos's chest. Then they, too, faded into darkness.

Chapter 14

Willie opened his eyes and stared into the twilight. The sky hadn't changed much since the last time he'd looked at it, which meant he hadn't been out for long—unless it was already the next day. He was slumped in the driver's seat of his car, an act of kindness or at least discretion on Matos and Player's part, rather than lying in the street in full view. He looked out and saw the black Mercedes was gone.

He rubbed the side of his throbbing head. A welt was growing and a bit of blood came off on his finger. He got out gingerly, went to the front bumper, found the magnetized metal box that held his extra keys, and started his car. He drove straight home, climbed the stairs slowly, daubed the wound a bit with a wet cloth, and took a pain killer. Then he poured himself a double rum, put on a CD of some chanting monks from Spain, turned it low, and lay down on the sofa overlooking the backyard and the bougainvillea.

In his early twenties, Willie had briefly considered becoming a monk. A television documentary he'd seen seduced him: a beautiful old monastery tucked into green hills, its quiet corridors, the resonance and harmony of the hymns, a life of peace, totally devoid of the ugly and the unexpected. Willie was a rookie patrolman then, and his new life was full of the violent, the unpeaceful, the ugly, and the unexpected. For about a week, he had flirted with the idea. But his girlfriend at the time, a second-shift barmaid named Tina, had finally talked him out of it, one way or other. He had to agree that certain aspects of the monastic life might not work out. But there had been moments since when Willie had regretted the decision. The monks were calling to him right now as he prodded the welt on his head.

But a minute later the phone rang right near his head, making him wince. He let the machine answer and heard Ellie Hernandez's voice. "We're at Bobby's condo and we expected you to join us here," she said. She sounded disappointed in him, but Sam Suarez would have to wait to meet him.

Or at least that's what Willie thought. Before the monks had made it through three numbers someone rang his front doorbell. Willie was on his second rum by then, still flat on his back. He got up, took his spare handgun from the closet, and eased his way down the stairs. He parted the curtains and saw Ellie Hernandez and Mike Suarez on his top step with two older men behind them, one being Sam Suarez. He wanted to say that office hours were over, but he didn't have office hours. So he tucked the gun away and opened up.

"Sam wanted to talk to you," Ellie said by way of apology for barging in on him.

Willie stepped aside, let the four of them in, and then followed them up the stairs. The place was crowded with five people standing in the cramped living room. Willie brought a chair from the kitchen so everyone could be accommodated. He put the rum bottle on the table with some ice and mismatched glasses.

The one man he didn't recognize wore a clerical collar. Mike introduced him as Father Quentin Perry.

"Father Perry was a founder of the Peter Pan program," Mike said. "He helped smuggle me and Bobby over here." Willie shook hands with the priest, a tall, slope-shouldered man with watery blue eyes.

Then Mike introduced his father, although he didn't have to. Willie recognized Sam Suarez from photos in the newspaper. Suarez was gazing around Willie's digs—the aged rattan furniture and potted banana plant, the faded Wilfredo Lam posters on the walls, the four-poster bed with mosquito netting visible in the bedroom, a cobweb here and there. He didn't look too impressed with it, but he turned and shook hands. Willie found that Suarez had a hard grip. Willie didn't return it. He was having enough trouble just standing up.

In the newspaper, Sam Suarez was usually pictured at some business function or social event, smiling broadly. He wasn't smiling at all now. Willie realized how extremely short he was, not much bigger than Ellie Hernandez, something that had not been obvious in the newspaper photographs. The small body was sleek, his silver hair so fine and slicked back it looked as if he'd just gotten out of water. His business suit was steel gray like his hair and beautifully tailored, with gold cuff links peeking out at his wrists, each embedded with a diamond.

Suarez's eyes were dark, almost black. He had a way of tilting his head back and looking along his nose up at you as if he were deciding where to bite you. Legend held that he had taken bites out of lots of competitors on his way up. In fact his detractors had a name for him—the Piranha—which reflected both his small size and his ferocity.

Suarez was one of the greatest success stories of the Cuban exile. A banker in Havana when the revolution arrived, he had escaped to Miami in the mid-sixties without a dime. The story was that he had first worked scrubbing toilets, then bought the janitorial company that employed him, then the building where the toilets were found, and finally the bank that owned the building. His rise had been meteoric.

He owned a reputation for being smart and very sensitive to the business and political currents around him. Sam Suarez knew everybody and everything you needed to know, not only in the exile community, but in Washington and even in Cuba. He was said to be very well connected to the CIA and to several foreign governments. He also had a reputation for being brutally efficient with people who wandered into his pond, his field of influence. This was a case where the little fish—the Piranha—ate the big fish.

All that and Willie just wanted the great man to swim

home and let him go to sleep. But that wasn't what Sam Suarez had in mind.

"Roberto Player was at his condo this evening," he said now, his voice raspy and guttural. "Did you know that?"

"No I didn't. How do you know?"

"Because I left fifty dollars with the security guard there yesterday. I told him to call me if he saw or heard from Roberto and he would get another fifty. He telephoned me earlier, but Roberto was gone by the time we got there." So now Willie knew where Matos and Player had been coming from when they showed up at the apartment complex in North Little Havana. But Suarez was still in his face, or just below it. "What have you been doing with your time?"

"Me? I've been talking to people who knew his parents."

Suarez's cold gaze grew even colder. "His parents? His parents have been dead for thirty-five years. He's the one we're trying to find."

"What can I tell you. He's interested in his parents, the people who knew them and the people who had reason to kill them."

"So you haven't seen him at all?"

"Oh yes, I saw him all right." Willie fingered his welt, poured himself a bit more rum, and sat down.

"Where did you see him?"

"At an apartment in Little Havana. But you won't gain much by going there. I'm sure they won't go back."

"They? Who are they?"

"He's traveling with a man and a woman, the same two Mike saw him with last night."

Willie shot a glance at Mike. It was obvious the younger Suarez had kept quiet about the ruckus at the marina. He rolled his eyes, resigned to what he knew was coming.

So Willie told the story. When he had finished, the older Suarez glared at his son, his small teeth bared in anger.

"He's sneaking money from the bank, smuggling people

in from Cuba, which is against the law, and you're protecting him."

"He's going through something hard right now," Mike said.

"He's always been going through something. He's always been unstable, soft."

The priest's bass voice filled the room. "Take it easy, Sam."

But Sam Suarez was hovering over Willie, who was slumped in his fan-back rattan chair. "Who are these people he's smuggling in from Cuba?"

"I don't know their names for sure. They didn't exactly check in with immigration. But Bobby swears they know who killed Carlos and Maria Player and that the people who did it are living right here in sunny Miami." Willie sipped his rum. "You knew the Players. Is that possible?"

Sam Suarez studied the question and Willie studied him.

"I don't know what you're talking about," Suarez said, in very much the same way Rico Tuzzi had said it.

"What I'm talking about is this. Bobby believes his parents were killed by their partners in the casino business, members of American organized crime, or maybe someone else they were involved with in Havana. I understand you knew people like Cozy Costanza and Rico Tuzzi back then?"

Suarez's face looked as if he had smelled something unpleasant. "Yes, I knew them. What about it?"

"You handled their money?"

"I'm a banker. I handle the money of any legitimate interest and they were legitimate businessmen."

"I understand you still do their banking."

"What about it? They're not in jail are they? And what business is it of yours?"

Willie shrugged. "Well, it's my business because today at about noon a couple of guys with automatic weapons tried to shoot holes all through one of Costanza's gambling barges. I was there looking for Bobby. I saw it happen, but I couldn't tell who it was doing the shooting. I figured maybe you hold the lien on the boat and you'd like to know. And maybe you'll know if Bobby has reason to punish those people."

"Why would I know something like that? And why would I know who killed Carlos and Maria Player?"

"The Players had stashed away a large amount of money, a treasure chest. And when they were disposed of, that money disappeared. Their partners would have known about that stash. Since you were Carlos Player's banker, Mr. Suarez, I figured you might have known about it too."

Suarez tilted his head back again with that "where do I bite you?" look. "Everybody knows that people with money stopped taking it to the banks because they were afraid the government would take over everything. The Italians hid their cash and so did Carlos Player."

"I'm told Player had a half million dollars put away. I wonder where he kept it."

Suarez hesitated, as if the Players were still alive and he would be violating a confidence. But, of course, they were long dead. "The cash was in a safe in the master bedroom of their house," he said finally. "It was under one of the Cuban tiles on the floor. What about it?"

"Who knew it was there besides them and you?"

"I don't know."

"I understand they were talking of leaving Cuba soon and I was wondering how they were going to smuggle themselves and that money off the island. I assumed Carlos might have discussed it with you."

"He did at one point."

"Really? And what did he say?"

"He said he knew someone who could move large amounts of cash to the United States. He said he was going to do it and asked me if I wanted to do the same."

Willie made his eyes flare with interest. "And what did you say?"

"I said no."

"Why was that?"

Suarez sneered. "Because I'm a banker and I don't take risks like that, giving large amounts of money to someone I don't know."

"He wouldn't tell you who would be carrying it? I thought you were good friends."

"No, he didn't tell me and I didn't ask him. You didn't ask something like that, not at that time."

"Did he say it was someone in the Mafia?"

"I told you, I didn't ask."

"But maybe the Mafia had figured out a way to do it and figured it would be a waste to leave it behind. Did your Mafia clients ever discuss the matter of smuggling with you?"

Suarez didn't like the reference to his "Mafia clients." "The Italians? No, they didn't."

"Did Carlos Player ever discuss his undercover political activity with you?"

"No. If he had I would have told him he was foolish. In the end he just ended up dead. He ruined his son's life."

Ellie Hernandez let out a gasp. "You shouldn't say that. Bobby's parents were heroes of the underground."

Suarez stared into nothing. "That's what people say. Who knows?"

That sounded strange to Willie and to everyone else in the room apparently. Dead silence followed. Willie broke it.

"What do you mean by that?"

Suarez peered at him from the corner of an eye, as if he would explain himself. But then you saw the thought pass behind those eyes, circle, and dive again out of sight. He shook his head.

"I don't know what they were involved in. They didn't discuss it with me."

Sam Suarez was someone who had been at the center of events for a long time. Willie would bet that he knew a lot about what had happened thirty-five years ago in Cuba, what Carlos and Maria Player were mixed up in, and maybe what had gotten them killed. Suarez also had the drop on what was happening these days in Miami, whether it was the Costanza family or Cuban exile commandos. But Sam Suarez had made his fortune keeping information for his own use, not spreading it around for free. Willie sipped his rum.

"I still think it's strange that you were talking to Carlos

Player in those last days and he never mentioned that money," he said, his voice full of skepticism. "What were you talking about then?"

Suarez, even more pugnacious now, pointed at Mike. "We were talking about our sons. They were both in an orphanage far away. We promised each other that the first one to escape from Cuba would take care of the other one's son as long as necessary. That's what we were talking about, exactly what any decent man would discuss at a time like that."

Suarez was glaring at him imperiously now. The mood in the room swung suddenly. Everyone had been staring at Suarez. They weren't accustomed to hearing him cross-examined by a lowly commoner like Willie. Now they were looking at Willie as if he'd overplayed his hand. They felt his weakness, his vulnerability, as the Piranha peered along his nose and sized him up for the kill. The monks chanted in the background, calling to Willie.

Willie was still slumped in his chair with one hand shoved in a pocket. He brought it out now, holding the jagged half of a red poker chip that Ellie had given him.

"What's that?" asked Suarez.

"It's what Carlos Player gave his son Bobby when he put him on the plane to Miami. He kept the other half and when they were together again, it would be whole. That was the plan. Right, Ellie?"

The small woman nodded, staring red-eyed at the chip almost as if it were a communion host at mass. Willie held it closer for Suarez to see.

"He never showed it to you?"

Sam Suarez shook his head.

"How about you, Mike?"

The younger Suarez nodded. "Yeah, Bobby used to show it to me when we were in the orphanage, but I haven't seen it in years."

"Ellie found it on the dresser at Bobby's place. We're not sure why."

Sam Suarez's temper flared again. "So what does that have to do with anything? All that matters is that we find him before he causes trouble for the bank and for himself. Before he brings everything down around us."

Suarez closed in on Willie. "I want you to find Bobby. Do whatever it takes. I'll pay you."

Willie glanced at Ellie and back at him. "Ms. Hernandez has already contracted me. She's my client."

Sam Suarez frowned. What Willie was saying had nothing to do with the highest bidder and that threw him.

"It's the same thing," he said. "We both want you to find him."

"Yes, but if I find him, what you want done and what Ms. Hernandez wants done may be different."

Ellie looked from Willie to Suarez and back to Willie and he knew it was true. Her concern for Bobby Player was governed by love. Suarez's, seemingly, by fear of embarrassment and lost business. And, just possibly, given his reticence to discuss certain details, by fear of what Roberto Player would find out.

The Piranha showed his teeth again. "You have it your way. But I have influence with many people here, including the police. This is a small pond." He turned to his son. "You drive Ellie and Father Perry home. I'll go on my own."

Sam Suarez glanced at Willie but didn't offer his hand. He muttered a reluctant "good evening" and then he swept out.

Chapter 15

The four of them were left in silence for several moments. Willie felt he had failed as a host. What could he do but pour himself just a bit more rum?

Mike Suarez met Willie's eyes. "My father is angry with Bobby, but he didn't mean what he said about Bobby's parents."

"He didn't say much." Of course what Sam Suarez had implied was that Carlos and Maria Player weren't the heroes they had been cracked up to be.

"My father was good friends with them," Mike said. "They helped each other during the roughest times. My father even doctored the ledgers in his bank to help people who were taking their money to try to smuggle it out of the country. It was a very dangerous thing to do. He could have gone to jail for a long time, but he did it anyway for friends like Bobby's parents. My mother told me the stories, how she was afraid all the time that the police would come to the house and drag him away."

The priest was listening. "And we have to remember how good Sam has been to Bobby all these years."

Willie sipped. "You helped bring Bobby Player and Mike here out of Cuba, Father?"

"Oh yes. And thousands of others, with the Lord's help."

"You smuggled them?"

The priest got a mischievous glint in his eye. "That's right."

"How?"

The other man sipped his rum. "Well, to get out of Cuba they needed entry visas from other countries. But

foreign diplomats and their dependants never needed
such visas. Governments extended an international courtesy to each other in this respect. All that was required
was to present a form called a visa waiver and they
waltzed right through the immigration lines. What we had
to do was get those waivers printed in the names of the
Cuban children."

He held his hands out like a magician about to make an
egg appear out of nowhere.

"And how did you do that?"

"We counterfeited them. We borrowed waivers from
diplomats willing to help us, copied them, then we smuggled them into Cuba in diplomatic pouches and circulated
them through an organized pipeline." He looked very sat-
isfied with that bit of intrigue.

"And these kids just got on planes in Havana and flew
here by themselves."

"Just like Peter Pan."

"And the Cuban government didn't catch on?"

"It took awhile. They eventually stopped the flow. But
only after fourteen thousand came out."

"And later the parents started coming."

"Yes, several years later, but we didn't have to sneak
them out." He appeared disappointed, as if he would have
enjoyed a bit more skullduggery. "The U.S. government
cut a deal with Castro and many were allowed to fly here.
By that time, the Peter Pan children were spread all over
the country in foster homes and orphanages. It was amazing what changes they had gone through in the meantime.
Cuban kids lived in the snow and ice of the north, something they had never dreamed of." He sipped his rum, as
if he himself were fighting off the cold. "But they were
well cared for and well educated and had learned to speak
English. Many of their parents couldn't speak the language and for the first years the kids were leading their
mothers and fathers around, teaching them what they
needed to know to survive, their roles totally reversed. It
was an unusual experience."

"But Bobby's parents didn't make it."

The priest lost his look of mischief. "No, they didn't.

God in all His mystery decided they shouldn't reach here. We made contact with the Cuban government and were told they had been found murdered, killed by thieves. We confirmed their deaths through independent sources. Telling Bobby was one of the toughest things I've ever had to do."

An expression of suspicion came over the priest's face, as if he were hearing a confession in which the sinner was leaving something out.

"You had your doubts about the Cuban government version," Willie said.

The other man shrugged. "Well, just because a political revolution and armed struggle sweep a country, that doesn't mean the common crime stops. Sometimes criminals take advantage of the confusion, but at a distance there was no way of being sure what the truth was."

"You knew they had been involved in the underground, right?"

"Not until later. There were very, very few people who knew of their involvement, it turned out. Even now I can't identify anybody who knows exactly what their roles were."

"Do you have any idea what Sam Suarez was hinting at? He seemed to have doubts about their patriotism."

The priest shook his head. "No, I don't."

"Do you have any idea who Bobby is hunting for?"

The priest looked pained. "No. But revenge is a malignant thing even in an instance like this. It's a way of playing God, and men are never good at that." He drained his rum. "And I have to play priest in the morning so we better be off."

He and Mike shook hands with Willie and headed down the stairs. Ellie lingered a minute. She hesitated to speak and had to struggle to look him in the eye.

"The woman who got off the boat, what was she like?"

"What do you mean what was she like?"

"What did she look like?"

"She's tall, dark hair."

"I mean, is she beautiful?"

Willie knew he couldn't lie to her. "Yes, she's beautiful."

Ellie considered that, staring past him out the window. She had been sure of Roberto Player before. Now she was having her doubts.

"You were right in the first place," Willie said. "That's not his reason for running away from you. It does have to do with his parents."

"Yes, but he isn't talking to me about it, is he? He's talking to her. It's very important to him and he is keeping me on the outside while she's on the inside."

"Because he knew you would try to stop him, protect him."

She nodded, but you could see she wasn't convinced. You could see the images inside her head—Roberto Player with another woman. There was nothing Willie could do for her but find him as fast as he could.

"Thank you for not selling out to the highest bidder," she said. "Sam could have paid you a lot more."

"That's all right. I make brilliant business decisions like that all the time."

He escorted her downstairs and gave her a kiss on the cheek. "Don't worry, *mi amor.* Everything's going to be all right," he said, although he wasn't at all sure that was so.

He watched her climb into the car and then he headed for the mosquito netting.

Chapter 16

As it turned out, he was right. Things weren't going to be okay.

It was about five A.M. that morning and Willie was dreaming. At the center of the dream, for some reason only the dream gods know, was a stylish Panama hat, white straw with a tasteful black silk band. It lay in the middle of a poker table. Willie and a cast of faceless dream characters sat around the table and played, apparently for the hat. Tropical darkness and a steamy heat crowded the room around them. It was the middle of the night on some Caribbean island. A wooden fan revolved overhead, the surf whispered and the windblown palm trees thrashed. For some reason the hat had become of tremendous importance to all of those gathered at the table. Maybe a secret was tucked in the headband. Winning it was a matter of life and death. The cards were dealt suddenly, the way it happens in a dream, and it became clear that Willie had won. He reached for the hat and found underneath it a red poker chip. He didn't have time to inspect it. He knew the others would try and kill him. They started to come in his direction. The darkness broke over him like the surf outside.

And then the phone rang. Willie sat bolt upright and the darkness pulsed around him. His head pulsed too, where Mr. Matos had given him that love tap. Maybe that was why he had been dreaming of a hat. Willie was surrounded by mosquito netting as if he were in the midst of a cloud. He never used air-conditioning. He kept the windows open, the ceiling fan turning, and netting draped around his old four-poster bed. Through the gauze he read the digital clock. It said 4:55 A.M. The air was full of the odor of gardenia that always floated up from the garden at that time.

Willie went groping through the netting for the phone. The voice on the other end was muffled, a disguised voice of a man speaking Spanish.

"If you want to find the people you're looking for, go to the Delta-5 headquarters now, *amigo*." Then the connection was broken.

Willie lay back a minute watching the fan turn above him. Then he dragged himself from bed and pulled on a yellow guayabera and white linen pants. His sandals were just a bit cool on the soles of his bare feet. He was still half asleep as he went out the back door and headed for the parking lot, stepping into the atmosphere of gardenia.

He walked down the quiet side street. Some of his neighbors kept roosters in their backyards, despite city ordinances. But not even the birds had begun to make noise yet. He could remember the peace of this hour, which he had always enjoyed during his days on third shift patrol.

He made it to his car, got in, and headed north. Little Havana was quiet and stifling. Willie drove the familiar streets on automatic pilot. The alleyways, which he looked down from habit, stood empty. The strains of another old bolero ran through his head, this one a nocturne about "people among the palm trees, let them rest in peace."

The Delta-5 headquarters were located on Twenty-seventh Avenue in a two-story commercial complex called Havana Plaza. It rose out of the urban landscape like some kind of vision. The architects had designed the structure with a colonnade, archways, studded wooden doors, black wrought-iron balcony railings, and a lime-stone facade, like Spanish colonial structures in Cuba. It was not so much a building as it was a memory carved out of stone. Delta-5 had moved in there many years ago, along with other Cuban businesses. In Miami, after all, fighting Castro was an industry.

Willie parked across the street from the headquarters. No lights were on and no noise escaped it. The commandos were home dreaming of victory, which is where Willie should have been. He crossed the street and the narrow parking lot and looked in the window. Willie had visited the headquarters many times before when he was working for the Intelligence Unit. It was a strange place, a kind of clubhouse and museum for a war that, except for that one decisive battle at the Bay of Pigs more than three decades before, had been fought largely in people's imaginations, very rarely on any battlefield. It featured life-size mannequins dressed in the uniforms worn by commando trainees over the decades, some of them outfitted in camouflage, the others in wetsuits. In their hands they gripped actual weapons wielded in training—old M-16s and newer Ak-47s. Other similar weapons hung from the ceiling on wire filaments so that it appeared to be raining rifles inside the one-room headquarters, like a surrealist painting.

The rear wall was covered with a large mural of Cuba. Every day, aging men gathered there to drink pots of Cuban coffee and discuss the Cuba of old. They created verbal murals of the island, which disappeared every night when they went home and which they created anew the next day out of caffeine and nostalgia, a kind of drug experience. But no one was there now and even the mannequins looked asleep.

Willie rapped on a window and waited. He knocked again and then a door leading to a rear office opened right in the middle of the mural, a piece of Cuba swinging open weirdly. Light spilled into the front room and an older man shuffled toward Willie, dressed in camouflage pants, which he had been apparently using for pajamas. He appeared to be sleepwalking. Willie recognized him as the aging commando riding shotgun in Mando's car the day before. He was pulling guard duty, or maybe he lived there.

He stood squinting between the mannequins. "*Quien es?*"

"It's me, Willie Cuesta."

The old man frowned, shuffled over, and opened the door. He scratched his hair sleepily, his eyes still closed. "What are you doing here at this hour? I'm asleep."

"I was told to come here."

The other man looked confused. "Told? By who? It's the middle of the night, *hombre*."

It sounded strange to Willie as well and he started to explain. But then he heard a sound in the street and he turned. A car had driven silently up Twenty-seventh Avenue. It had reached the entrance to the parking lot, when suddenly the driver turned and pointed it right at the building and gunned the engine. The car swerved as it approached, the lights sweeping over Willie. A moment later, automatic-weapon fire peppered the facade of the headquarters.

Willie still felt he was moving slowly, as if in a dream. But he managed to jump inside, knocking over the old man, then slamming the door behind him and laying on the floor. Shots destroyed the windows on either side of the door and toppled several of the mannequins, the first casualties of this battle that seemed to be happening in a nightmare. The hanging weapons rotated on their filaments wildly so that Willie felt trapped inside some brand of arcade game.

Willie grabbed the old man and pulled him toward the thick front wall so that they were both pinned to it. He reached for his back holster and realized he had been so asleep he hadn't remembered to bring the spare gun. The old man had picked up one of the weapons dropped by the mannequins, but he found the banana clip empty of bullets. He tried to fire it but all that came out was silence. He looked befuddled. Still, pressed against the wall, they would be safe unless the attackers could make it through that thick door.

The firing started again, two more mannequins biting the dust without cries of pain, and then it stopped. Willie edged toward the nearest window. He could see that same old green Chevy that had rambled out of the past and attacked the *Treasure Coast*. Then a face appeared in the window. It was that same melting hangdog face he had seen the day before. Another one just the same materialized next to it. They were the perfect faces for this particular nightmare.

They gazed into the headquarters, then stepped back

and a match was struck. Willie saw the reflection of a larger flame dance on the far wall. The next thing he knew a firebomb had come through the window and had landed in the middle of the floor. It exploded with a shushing noise and a wave of heat broke over Willie. Flames spread across the floor and reflections danced on the walls all around.

The old man jumped up and groped for the door. Willie grabbed him.

"No. They'll shoot you down." Willie hauled himself to his feet. Staying close to the wall, he led the other man to the far edge of the flames, where they were the least intense. "Cover your eyes!" He took a breath, raised his free arm over his own eyes, and then ran around the very edge of the fire. The flames seemed to reach for him, kissing his exposed skin and whispering at him with that breathy sound that flames make. Willie took one, two, three long strides and got beyond them. He stopped, looked back, and saw the military mannequins melting. He smelled the rubber of the wetsuits.

He dragged the old man through the doorway in the mural and into the backroom, where he had been sleeping. Willie saw a rumpled bed, a desk, another large Cuban flag hanging vertically on the wall. But no back exit. There *was* none. No door, no window leading to the back alley. No nothing. He whirled on the old man. "There's no way out?"

The other man, addled by fear, didn't react at first, only gaping around in confusion. The flames had reached the doorway and were flicking their tongues at them. The sound of it was loud. The air was thinning and the smoke was thickening. Willie figured he would meet the same fate as the mannequins. He would be remembered as the leader of a commando unit made up of wooden dummies.

He stood at the back of that room, the smoke starting to envelop them. Strangely it reminded Willie of his mosquito netting, a gauze curtain that had to do with sleep. But then the old man finally moved. He strode right at the Cuban flag that hung on the back wall as if he were going to walk right through it. He reached out toward it and suddenly the back wall swung open, the same way the mural had. The flag had been nailed up to cover a door. It swung out now into an alleyway. The old man walked right through that flag door to the outside.

The air that rushed in only excited the fire more and Willie had to jump out before the flames grabbed him. A moment later he was standing in the alley, the door slammed behind him, and the sound of the fire came through the walls as if a large, talkative crowd were inside.

The old man was in shock now and Willie dragged him down the alley out of danger. Embers floated in the air. Willie eased his way around the edge of the building. Both the ancient Chevy and the men in hangdog masks were gone, as if they had never been there.

Sirens were approaching in the distance. Willie went back, sat with the dazed old man, and waited for help.

Chapter 17

It arrived a minute later. A hook and ladder and two other fire trucks wheeled up. By then the fire had spread to the entire roof of Delta-5. The firefighters began to scramble.

An ambulance came and Willie delivered the old man to the attendants. He had been holding Willie's hand in a desperate grip and only let it go at the ambulance door.

The rising sun was clouded by smoke. A half hour after dawn geysers of water finally controlled the blaze. Delta-5 was gutted. All that remained was a studded door hanging in front of a large charred cave, like the gate to the Inferno. The warrior mannequins had been transformed into distinct piles of ashes.

Willie stood to one side watching it all, too tired to move. The Cuban bakery next door was also burnt out. The smell of charred sweet bread hung in the air and made Willie hungry. When a fireman came out carting an unburned tray of buns, Willie nabbed a couple.

Cops were everywhere. They kept neighbors from blocks around from getting too close. The babble of excited Spanish filled the air like the smoke. A news helicopter hovered. It passed, turned around, and passed again. A radio reporter on the ground spoke mile-a-minute Spanish into a microphone. He asked nothing of Willie. Neither did the police. In the confusion no one realized Willie was an eyewitness. The old man in camouflage had been taken away in shock without being questioned. Willie didn't offer any information. He had nothing much to offer. He would wait until someone asked him.

Suddenly Mando was standing right next to him, as if he had stepped out of the smoke. He had apparently been helping haul hose and his normally spotless uniform was soiled with soot, although his ascot remained unsmudged. His look was a bit crazed.

"Did you come to see what your friends from the boat were up to, Willie?"

Willie flicked a piece of debris from Mando's shirt front. "They aren't friends of mine and you shouldn't be running your mouth that they are, Mando."

Mando squinted as if sighting down a rifle barrel. "I tried to tell you yesterday that this was coming. I told you our enemies were here. I doubt you paid me much attention."

"That was one of the first things I thought of, our little outing in your jeep. Your predictions and that impressive intelligence network you have."

A news helicopter flew right overhead, its blades thwacking. Mando's head jerked and he looked up as if he were being attacked again. He realized he wasn't and he fixed on Willie.

"You think we did this ourselves?"

Willie shrugged, but said nothing.

"You think I would injure one of my own men, destroy my own center of operations?"

"Stranger things have happened in so-called wars, Mando."

The *comandante* quivered with anger and for a moment Willie thought the old man would strike him. "Now, I understand why you aren't in intelligence anymore Willie. You don't have any intelligence. You're a fool. If you know anything about these people you better tell me now. If we find out later that you were in possession of important facts and didn't tell us, we'll consider it treason. And you know how long you'll last around here if you're found guilty of being a traitor to the freedom of Cuba."

Willie gave Mando his extra cynical squint, the one he reserved for mugs who tried to muscle him, even old men in altered states of mind, like Mando.

"Will you give me a blindfold and a last cigar?"

Mando smoldered but said nothing. The old man carried a look in his eye as if the explosion had genuinely taken him by surprise. The fact was Mando had perpetuated this dream of war for decades and now, seemingly out of nowhere, a real bomb had been thrown at his headquarters. His imaginings had suddenly come true. That would certainly startle and alarm an old man—if he hadn't thrown the bomb himself. Willie picked another bit of soot off the uniform.

"Okay, let's say someone is out to get you, Mando. Why wouldn't it be your old Mafia buddies? Somebody shot up their gambling boat yesterday at the Port of Miami and they must think it was you. Everybody has heard the rumors over the years about their going back to Cuba and everybody knows what you guys would do about it."

Mando stared disconsolately at the ruins and considered that possibility. For several years a rumor had persisted that Castro might reopen casinos in Cuba. The Soviets had disappeared into the mists of history and taken their aid with them. A little roulette might resurrect the economy. Whenever that rumor raised its head, speculation would follow that the Mafia might be interested in once again helping guide the enterprise. That they would recreate the high-rolling days of the past. That Santo Trafficante's soul would not rest until the dice were tumbling once again in Havana.

Of course, if the Italians did go into business with Castro, they wouldn't be able to live in Miami anymore. A bloody war between the Cosa Nostra and the exiles would be inevitable. Willie recalled now what Cassandra had mentioned two nights before about rumors concerning the Italians. Maybe she hadn't been fabricating. Who knew? Maybe the mob had gotten tired of waiting for Castro to fall. Maybe they were doing the unthinkable—talking to the bearded one. Maybe Mando had attacked the *Treasure Coast* and Cozy Costanza had gone out, bought the same ghoulish masks, and struck back. In Miami, all was possible.

Mando, for one, didn't like the idea much. He didn't need old friends suddenly being transformed into enemies, or at least he didn't want Willie to know about it.

"They have no reason to do that," he muttered at the rubble. "We have done nothing to them."

"Then the only thing it can be is old scores being settled."

The *comandante* frowned. "What do you mean scores?"

"Maybe it's payback from the old days in Havana. Maybe it has something to do with the deaths of Carlos and Maria Player."

Mando tensed now. "I don't know what you're talking about. I told you that."

"How about Miguel Angel Matos? Do you know him?"

It took a moment for the name to penetrate the armor of Mando's dissimulation. Once it did, he couldn't keep the recognition out of his eyes. Willie closed in on him.

"You know who that is, don't you, Mando? Is there reason for someone to come after you now? What went on back then that had to do with the Players?"

Firefighters ran all around them, but Mando didn't notice. He wore that same haunted look Del Rey had worn, as if something long imagined had suddenly materialized for real. His thoughts were far away in both time and space. "Why are you asking me about this man, Matos?"

Willie studied him and considered telling Mando what he knew. But Mando wasn't telling Willie anything *he* knew. Not even close.

"If you know nothing about Carlos and Maria Player, then I don't think Mr. Matos will be of interest to you, *comandante*."

Mando glared at Willie, but said nothing. "What is it about Carlos and Maria Player that no one wants to talk about?" Willie asked "Tell me that. They've been dead more than thirty-five years. What difference can it make?"

Willie could see Mando plotting possible answers. In the end, thirty-five years of silence won out. The *comandante* decided to make no move, not at the moment.

Suddenly, the firemen came charging out of the building. A moment later the ceiling of Delta-5 caved in with a deafening roar and much smoke. Mando watched it as if his life were caving in. Finally, he turned again to Willie and was suddenly back in the role of warrior.

"I don't have time now to discuss this foolishness with you. This was perpetrated by our enemies. If you know anything about who did it you'd better let me know. I told you before. The old underground still operates here. We still have the ability to strike and we will be constantly active now. We will defeat this enemy. And if you are with them, you'll die with them."

He swiveled on a heel and walked away to huddle with his junior officers. Willie watched the commotion a few more minutes and was about to leave, when he noticed Mando drift away from his colleagues. He went to speak with a man standing by himself just outside a strip of yellow crime-scene tape. Willie recognized James Clancy. Clancy was wearing a golf outfit much like the one he'd worn the day before, except this time the shirt was red and the pants were blue. The shoes were still white.

Willie watched them talk. Mando was extremely agitated. Clancy shook his head in commiseration. Finally, they shook hands and Mando headed back to his men.

Willie jumped over some firehoses and got to Clancy just as he was about to disappear into the crowd.

"Excuse me, Mr. Clancy."

Recognition came into the tall man's eyes.

"Ah, Mr. Cuesta. You sure do get around."

"I might say the same about you. I didn't know you were acquainted with Mando Capitán. How did he fit into your work as a cultural attaché in the old days?"

Clancy smiled. "I knew Armando back then, just as I knew Cosimo Costanza. They and others were part of the social whirl in Havana. I turned on the radio on my way to the golf course and heard about this insanity. I came to make sure Armando was all right."

"Do you have any idea who might have done this?"

Clancy shook his head. "As I told you, my field was culture, not politics. Especially not this kind of politics. I'll tell you this much. No chorus girl did this."

"I was talking to a chorus girl yesterday who remembered you from Cuba," Willie said.

Clancy brightened. "Oh, yes? Who was that?"

"A lady named Olga Tuzzi. She used to dance at

Casino Cuba. She recalled seeing you in conversation with Carlos Player, serious conversation, in Player's office just days before he died."

The other man shrugged. "Well, I guess bar tabs and gambling tabs can be considered serious business. I was there to pay mine off. Rumors were running rampant that Americans were going to be expelled, and days later it happened. One doesn't want to leave bad debts, Mr. Cuesta."

"No, I guess one doesn't."

"And one doesn't want to be too late for a tee time either. I should be on my way."

They shook hands and he turned and strode up the street in search of the first tee, an extremely strange apparition on the streets of Little Havana.

Willie watched him go. He thought about heading home and climbing back into bed, renewing the dream of the hat. Instead, he decided to go clean up and then visit Victor Del Rey again. It was the ghostlike old croupier who had first mentioned Miguel Angel Matos and who had met with the beautiful Aurora the day before. Maybe he would be willing to enlighten Willie more about Mr. Matos. Now that things were beginning to blow up.

Chapter 18

Willie showered and shaved and slipped on a sea-blue guayabera and dark gray linen slacks. He downed a *café con leche,* locked up, climbed back in the LeBaron, and drove downtown to the Hotel Ponce de Leon, where Victor Del Rey had told him he lived. He parked down the street from the hotel and walked to it, a narrow white stucco place not far off Flagler.

The Ponce had seen more prosperous times, at least Willie hoped so. Despite the bright morning sun, the faded pink lobby was still dusky, as if night never quite left it no matter what time it was. A couple of spindly potted palms propped against one wall needed water bad. And the elderly, liver-spotted man slumped in a rocker wearing a narrow-brim Panama hat needed water too. He was staring at dust suspended in the air before him. The hotel bore the name of Ponce de Leon, the explorer who had come to Florida looking for the fountain of youth. Neither he nor anyone else had found it in this place, not lately.

Willie crossed to the front desk. Behind it, an older woman wearing a flower-print shift in day-glo colors sat at a table sorting mail. Her hair was dyed a strange shade of orange, thin on top. She didn't notice Willie standing just a few feet away and didn't respond when he said hello, so he tapped the bell. She looked up and tried to focus on him through bifocals, as if she would recognize him any moment. She stared several seconds, but then gave up trying to place him. She got up and hobbled to the counter. It seemed to bother her that she didn't know who he was, as if strangers never came to the place.

"Can I help you?"

"I'm looking for a Mr. Victor Del Rey. I'm told he lives here."

"Yes, he does live here, in 408, but he hasn't come down yet today."

"I'll go up and see him, if it isn't a problem?"

She still didn't like the looks of him.

"Mr. Del Rey doesn't get visitors."

"That's all right," said Willie, heading for the elevator. "He knows me and I'll only be a few minutes."

"You'll be longer than that if you wait for that elevator. It isn't working."

Willie thanked her and headed up the stairs. They reminded him of the stairs that led up to the balcony at the Mirage Theatre where Del Rey worked—worn and musty. As he got to the second floor he heard someone down the hall and behind a door yell something, but it was incoherent, unintelligible. Maybe it was a warning shouted in a nightmare, or at least uttered before the teeth had been put in.

He continued up, allegedly closer to the sun, but the stairway and halls grew darker. On each landing hung a framed photograph cut out from an old color rotogravure magazine featuring palmy scenes of Florida. They were faded from age almost to invisibility.

He found room 408 at the end of the fourth-floor hallway. Del Rey was serious about being out of the way. The rest of the rooms were quiet, but Del Rey had his radio tuned into a Cuban oldies station. The old romantic favorite *"Solamente Una Vez"* sounded from behind the door.

Willie knocked and waited. There was no answer, so he knocked again. Maybe Del Rey was totally absorbed in the song, an anthem of his youth.

Willie tried the door and the knob turned. It was only halfway open when he saw the projectionist. He lay on the bed in the small, desolate room. Del Rey looked right at Willie, as if he had been expecting him. Unfortunately, this time Willie hadn't arrived soon enough. Victor Del Rey had hidden from his past for years, but he hadn't hid-

den well enough. Despite the open eyes, Willie knew he
was dead.

Willie closed the door behind him without a sound and
crossed right to the bed. Del Rey was lying on his side.
The cause of death was visible. Around his neck was tied
an alligator belt, pulled to the tightest notch and then beyond. The buckle had left an indentation on the side of his
neck that was now black. His bulging eyes were still the
color of cobblestones, and now they were as dry as stones
too. Willie touched his hand but it was cold. He had been
dead for hours. His shoes were off but he was otherwise
fully dressed in the same monogrammed white shirt and
black slacks he had worn when Willie had spoken with
him the day before and when Willie had seen him in the
church.

The phone rang then, at least six times. Willie thought
of answering it, but he figured it was the desk clerk checking to see that Del Rey was all right. Well, he wasn't.

He looked around quickly. It was one of those old hotel
rooms with so many layers of paint that it was now a
smaller room than it had once been. The paint, in this
case, was flesh colored. The walls were decorated with
more old posters of Cuba and a small blue pennant that
said HAVANA. The space within those walls was sparsely
furnished—an old rattan rocker, a dresser, a table with a
cooking ring. A wallet sat on the dresser. Willie looked in
it and found thirty dollars, which meant Del Rey probably
hadn't been killed for his money. Also lying on the
dresser was half a coconut, the kind you bought out of the
back of pickup trucks in Little Havana for the coconut
milk. It had apparently been Del Rey's last meal.

The mirror attached to the dresser was discolored and
chipped. Taped to it were several snapshots. Two in particular caught Willie's attention. One in black-and-white
had apparently been taken decades earlier along the old
seawall in Havana, with the port in the background. The
other, in color, was set in downtown Miami, probably
twenty years later. They were both of Del Rey and Olga
Tuzzi. Willie had been right. Olga Tuzzi had been a
bombshell. Given the barren room, and the barren nature

of his life, Olga had apparently acted as Victor Del Rey's lifeline, his only passion. Like the song said, *"Solamente Una Vez."*

Nothing else caught Willie's eye. The drawers hadn't been rifled or the closet, where he found an old gray linen suit hanging, some beautiful basket-weave shoes, and a few other articles. There was hardly anything in the place, but what there was hadn't been disturbed. Willie checked everywhere. He uncovered no code books or any other evidence to incriminate Victor Del Rey, the alleged spy. The only radio was Del Rey's console job, which was now spewing news of the Delta-5 explosion. Willie listened and figured he was the only one who knew that blast and this dead man he was looking at were connected. Or almost the only one.

Just then the door swung open and two uniformed cops stood staring at him, two guys he didn't know. They glanced at Del Rey and then looked back at him.

"You better call Homicide, *amigos,*" Willie said. "This guy's dead."

The whole time they waited for Homicide, Willie didn't budge. He propped himself on the corner of the dresser and looked at Del Rey. The old lady with the hair dyed orange showed up. When no one had picked up the phone she had summoned the police. Nobody else had visited Mr. Del Rey all day, she told anyone who wanted to hear. It couldn't have been anybody but Willie who had strangled him.

Lieutenant Bill Compton of Homicide showed up a half hour later. He was a square-headed, heavy-set, red-faced guy, whose shirt collar didn't close all the way because his neck was too big, and whose dark blue suit jacket was small on him. Willie knew him from his own days on the force. They'd worked together on a case or two and had gotten along.

Compton shooed the onlookers away and closed the door on them. He examined the body the same way Willie had.

"Well, you didn't kill him, unless you did it a good ten hours ago and then came back."

"I didn't kill him any time."

"I can't imagine you did, Willie. At least you'd be smart enough not to come back."

"Thanks for your belief in my moral character."

Compton nosed about as Willie had, without much evident hope of finding anything. Willie picked up the coconut and sniffed it. You couldn't lift prints from a shaggy coconut. He liked the smell of coconut. Compton turned back to him.

"So assuming you didn't come here to kill him, what did you come here to do?"

"To have a few words with the gentleman."

"About what?"

"A murder."

That raised Compton's interest. "What murder was that?"

"One that happened more than thirty years ago and it didn't happen in your jurisdiction either. It happened in Cuba."

"Why would that interest you?"

"Because it interests a client of mine."

"Was there a chance that this dead gentleman here committed that crime?" he asked, crouching down and taking a closer look at Del Rey's neck and the belt wrapped around it.

"I can't say for sure. He told me he had nothing to do with it. I don't think he did, but I can't be sure."

Compton eyed Willie. "So you did talk to him before he died."

"Yes, very briefly, yesterday afternoon at his place of employment. The Mirage Theater."

"And?"

"And what? He didn't say he was going to be killed, if that's what you mean."

"What did he say?"

"Nothing that would make any sense to you or any difference."

"Did it make any difference to your client?"

Willie frowned. "I don't follow you."

"I mean if your client was interested in this murder

thirty years go and maybe this guy did it, maybe we wouldn't have to look too far to find who did this. Maybe it was an act of revenge."

"My client didn't have that kind of motivation."

Since his client was Ellie Hernandez, what he was saying was true. He didn't bother to mention Roberto Player.

"Maybe you could give me the name of your client and I could ask these questions directly," Compton said.

Willie shook his head. "I don't think I can do that. My relationship with my client is confidential. Just trust me, she doesn't know Del Rey or anything about this."

"She?"

"That's right. Anything illegal about having a female client?"

"No, nothing." Compton came around the end of the bed, went to the window, but didn't touch it. He looked out on the fire escape.

"Except that a neighbor down the hall said three people were here last night. Two men and a woman, a very nice-looking woman. Long black hair, even longer legs."

He looked at Willie, who didn't say anything.

"They apparently came up the back stairs and through the fire door. They stayed a short while, after which nobody heard a peep from this fellow here."

"My client doesn't have long black hair or long legs either."

Compton didn't buy that at first. He had to search Willie's eyes a while. In the end he didn't find the lie he was looking for. So he crossed the room and peeked into what Willie knew was the almost empty closet.

"I couldn't help but notice you at the scene of the explosion this morning. I was called in on it briefly. Did that have anything to do with this?"

"Not that I know. In fact, I don't know anything for sure about this killing here."

"Anything for sure?"

"That's right. If I did, I'd tell you. If you keep me here or take me downtown I won't be able to tell you anything more than I have. But if you let me out of here I may be able to hunt up something to help you. When I do, I'll be in touch. I don't care for murderers any more than you do."

"I'd rather have the name of your client so I can ask her."

"And I can't tell you that. Just believe me, she can't help you."

They watched each other. He could see Compton weighing his options. Hauling Willie down to the shop and having him give the same answers again and again would just be a waste of time. After all, Willie knew the drill. He had been on the other side lots of times.

Finally Compton nodded. "I don't think there's anybody who knows the Cubans the way you know them, Willie. And the way I remember, you're way smart enough not to have a murderer for a client, because if you did you'd have to withhold evidence. That's still a crime."

"I remember."

"And you still recall where the station is and how to find me."

"That's true."

"If not, I know where to find you."

"I assume."

Compton opened the door. "I also figure you don't want to be here when the TV vans show up."

Willie said he wouldn't. He thanked Compton, took a last look at Del Rey, walked past the other police without saying a word, and headed down the stairs. The two men and a woman had obviously been Bobby Player, Matos, and Aurora, but he didn't want to clue Compton to that. Not right then.

Willie hit the street just as the first TV van arrived. They took no notice of him and he went to his car without getting hassled. He mulled over where to go next. It didn't take long. If Matos and his gang of two were going from suspect to suspect, their next stop might be Rico and Olga Tuzzi.

Chapter 19

He was already downtown so it took Willie only five minutes to reach the port, not that it did him much good.

The *Treasure Coast* was locked up. The Latin maintenance man Willie had seen the day before was waiting outside, but neither Tuzzi nor his wife had shown up. The guy had no idea where they were at the moment.

"But Mrs. Tuzzi told me she would be dancing at a new club that's opening out the Tamiami Trail," he said.

"The New Casino Cuba."

"That's it. I don't know if she's still going to do that."

He stared at the bullet holes the length of the boat as if whatever had happened there would alter Olga's plans. Then he decided he didn't want to be there either. He bid good-bye to Willie and took off.

So Willie climbed back in the LeBaron and drove over to Miami Beach, to Cozy Costanza's place at the Coral Arms. Maybe Tuzzi and Olga were holed up there.

Wrong again. Not only weren't they, but Cozy Costanza was gone too. Willie found an elderly, thin-haired reception clerk in the lobby, taking the place of the feisty Salvatore. The man's steel-rimmed glasses were a bit fogged, due to spray from the grotto.

"You missed him," he told Willie. "He and his associates left very early this morning on a little excursion."

"An excursion."

"Yes, they were carrying overnight bags. Mr. Costanza said they might be gone for a couple or three days. He said they weren't going far, right here in town, and there was no need to water the plants."

It sounded to Willie as if Cozy and his boys were tak-

ing to the mattresses. If you had thrown a firebomb into
the headquarters of a commando group early that morning, it might be a good idea. Of course, if you hadn't done
it, but somebody thought you had, you might decide to
take cover anyway.

"Do you know where they went?" he asked the desk
clerk.

The little man with the misted glasses shook his head.
"No I don't, and even if I did, I didn't get this old giving
out information about people like Mr. Costanza."

"Gotcha."

So Willie headed home. He didn't know where Rico or
Olga Tuzzi, Cozy Costanza, Bobby Player, or Mr. Matos
were. He was starting to feel very unpopular, which wasn't
good. A few minutes later he felt even more unpopular.

He was almost home when his Sky pager went off. On
it he found the number of his brother Tommy's club. So
he kept going and drove there.

The side door was unlocked as always during the day,
and the public area stood completely empty. The waiters
cleaned up before they went home at night, and the tables
on all levels waited for the next night's crowd, with bright
white tablecloths and fresh candles. Only music stands,
microphones, and speakers stood on the bandstand. The
bars gleamed, fully stocked. When he saw the place like
this it always reminded him of a movie set waiting for the
actors in a major production number.

He crossed the dance floor to the hallway next to the
stage and entered his brother's small office. Windowless
and square, it was papered with promotional photographs
of the musicians who had played there: Willie Colon, Ray
Barreto, Celia, Joe Arroyo. You couldn't name a big-time
act that wasn't pinned up there. It was like a cramped,
funky Latin Hall of Fame.

Tommy sat in the middle of it at a scarred wooden
desk. He was dressed in a black silk shirt and faded jeans,
his daytime duds. He had a cigarette going, burnt almost
to the nub, balanced on the edge of a full ashtray. A bun-
dle lay in front of Tommy, wrapped in butcher paper. The
room was milky with the smoke, but even so Willie could

smell the distinct odor of rotting fish. Tommy didn't look happy.

Willie stopped in the doorway. "What's up?"

"Come 'ere. I'll show you."

Willie went to the desk and Tommy undid the butcher paper from the package. Inside Willie saw an old, tattered Cuban flag, same colors as the American flag, but the stripes were in white and blue with one white star stitched onto a red background. Tommy unfolded that too until Willie was gazing down at a fish. It was a cod—what they called in Cuba a *bacalao*—and it was about a foot long. It stared up at Willie with one very dead, very dry eye. From the smell, it had been dead a day or more.

"Where'd you find this?"

"Right at the side door. The butcher paper had my name written on it."

"Anybody see who left it?"

"No." Tommy pointed at the phone on the desk. "But just a few minutes ago some guy called. Didn't give his name. He said if my brother Willie didn't stop poking his nose into business that he shouldn't poke into, and if he didn't stop associating with certain people who have come here to cause trouble, the man was goin' to do something to you. He was also goin' to bomb my club and ruin my business."

Willie didn't move. He stared at the phone as if by looking at it he could see who had said these things.

"Who was this? What did he sound like?"

"Like a guy who isn't happy with you. That's what he sounded like."

"Did he speak English or Spanish?"

"Spanish. And I think he had something wrapped over the phone to disguise his voice."

"Old or young?"

"I couldn't tell. All I know is what he said and I didn't like it. A bomb or even a few bomb scares and my business goes to hell. You know that. My kids don't eat."

And maybe worse, Willie thought. If it was like Delta-5 and it wasn't just a scare, people got hurt.

"Who are you messed up with, Willie?"

Willie shrugged. "People."

Tommy ran a tense hand through his thick hair. "Oh, good. I'm getting dead fish at my door. My place is going to blow up and I'm not even gonna know why. Does it concern the Cubans who got smuggled into the country?"

"Probably, but I don't know for sure."

Tommy fired up another cigarette and added to the haze in the room.

"You know I don't scare easy. But at least I gotta know who and what I'm up against. Who is it that might be bringin' a bomb to my club?"

Willie knew he was right. So he filled him in quickly on his meetings since the night before.

Tommy rolled his eyes. "So that means I only have to worry about some Cuban gangster, a guy who is maybe with Cuban G-2, Delta-5 commandos, and the Mafia. I don't need this right now, Willie. I got enough I'm up against."

He was probably talking about the New Casino Cuba, the big new competition.

"I'll take care of it. Don't worry," Willie said.

"How you going to do that?"

"I don't know yet, but I will. But tell Billy Blanco to hire a couple of his cousins for extra security the next few days, at least when you have customers in the place."

Tommy got up and crossed the small space between them. He wrapped an arm around Willie's shoulder and made his brother look at him.

"It's like I said, just don't keep me in the dark. And don't do anything asinine, anything crazy."

Willie took a last look at the dead fish, then left without another word. He climbed into the car and drove straight and fast to his mother's *botanica.*

The shop was right on Calle Ocho about ten blocks west of Willie's office. He parked in front and hurried in, making the bell over the door jangle.

Just inside, flanking the entranceway, stood two life-size statues—one of the Catholic St. Lazarus and the other of the black female Santeria spirit named Francisca,

her hair tied in a bandana and a cigar clenched in her
teeth. They were each as tall as Willie. If you had prayed
to either of these two spirits for a cure and had received it,
you might buy one of the statues for your home. People
did it all the time. Right now the two hulking *santos*
served as bouncers who worked the door for his mother.
Few stickup men or other *malditos* in Little Havana
would dare the wrath of the *santos* in order to rob the
place. At least in theory.

Willie went by them and through the store. Half of it
was filled with wire bins piled high with roots, vines,
branches, leaves, and dried animal extracts. Other herbs
hung in clumps from the ceiling. Each was labeled with
its common name and the malady it would cure. Nerves,
heart problems, aches in the bones, madness. You name
it, his mother could prescribe a treatment. Behind the
counter she kept squirreled away some of the more popular cures that people might try to shoplift. These included
ground-up bull penis to cure impotence.

The second section of the store was dedicated to traditional oils, potions, pommades, incense, and bath addi-
tives that fended off evil spirits and augmented a person's
chances at love and good luck. Willie's mother also
stocked the most up-to-date products—aerosol sprays that
increased your desirability, your cash flow, your general
good fortune.

"This is very modern and it works almost as well as the
traditional methods," said his mother, who kept a can of
moneymaking aerosol next to the cash register. "The spirits are moving into the modern world," she would tell her
customers. Willie agreed, except he was worried that too
many were evil spirits.

He found her sitting behind the counter in front of her
small television. As she watched the tube, she strung special spell-breaking bead necklaces, which were another
big item of hers. She was a broad-shouldered woman
with a full chest. Her hair was black, thick, and long, and
her face was striking—the forehead wide, cheekbones
pronounced. But her most memorable feature was her
eyes. They were deep set, dark, and piercing and con-

veyed an air of clairvoyance. She turned them on him as he came behind the counter.

"I had a feeling you would come today. Before that I was starting to think you had lost your memory and forgotten how to get here," she said.

Willie bent down and kissed her on the cheek.

"I didn't forget, Mama, but I've been busy."

"When you're busy, you forget you have family."

"That's not true, Mama."

"Your brother Tommy, he doesn't forget. He comes every day."

"That's because he has more time."

His mother strung the beads and shook her head.

"It's because he has a normal life and a wife and children. He isn't a *vagabundo*."

Willie said nothing. This was his mother's eternal incantation. Ever since he had divorced years back and then later left the police force and a weekly paycheck, she had plagued him. Willie knew that concern and love, not malice, lay at the root of her words.

"Has anyone called for me here today or come looking for me, Mama?" He asked it in an offhand manner so as not to worry her.

"Why would anyone look for you here? You never come here."

Willie went to a small refrigerator under the cash register and took out one of the beers she kept there for him. His mother watched him.

"I have a root that is good for memory. Beer isn't good for that."

"I don't need it, Mama, but maybe some of the people I'm working with right now could use some."

"Which people?"

"I'm looking for a man who was one of the Peter Pan children."

His mother paused over her beads. "That's a very long time ago."

Willie told her the tale of Roberto Player and his parents. She shook her head.

"The poor man sounds haunted."

"Right."

"It is impossible to forget one's parents, especially if you have not been able to bury them. Then they'll haunt your dreams."

"I guess."

"Even people who left Cuba and later had their parents die on the island, they get woken up at night by their ghosts. This boy, who doesn't know what happened to his mother and father, it must be worse."

"It seems like it."

"If he or you find who killed them, maybe he will find some peace."

"Maybe."

"But you have to remember to be careful, Willie."

"I know. Some other men are mixed up in this too."

He told her about Armando Capitán of Delta-5, Tuzzi, the death of Del Rey, and everything else. But he didn't fill her in about the menacing call to Tommy. That would worry her. And he didn't tell her to be careful herself because he knew that would do no good. When he'd been on the force and received threats to himself and his family, his mother never responded. She always said she had the spirits to protect her. Willie knew that if anyone ever did anything to her they wouldn't live to stand trial.

"This man Del Rey, the hermit, he sounds like another haunted one," she said now.

"Very."

"The Mafia, that is a demon I've never dealt with. But Armando I've known a long time and he's possessed. Some say he's possessed by a sane spirit, others by a crazy spirit. I don't know, but he is driven by something beyond him."

"You met Mando soon after he arrived, right?"

She nodded. "Yes. I worked many years aiding the new arrivals."

"Did he show up here as broke as they say?"

"I know Mando had money because he used it to start his commandos here. Where he got the money I don't know. Some people said the CIA gave it to him. Others said somehow he had brought money out. I don't know.

But after a while, he had none. People don't know it, but it is his wife who works. She supports him all these years. She is the *comandante* at home too. I think that is hard for him."

Willie told her he had to go home and get some sleep. After all, he had slept only a few hours the night before. She paid him no attention. Instead, she closed the front door and took him by the hand into the back room, where she warmed him some *picadillo* for lunch and found him another beer. When he finished that, she put a large serving of her flan before him. The room was suffused with the smell of Cuban food and incense, because this was also where she had installed her private consulting room. In the corner of the room stood another life-size statue, this time of Santa Barbara, who did double duty as a Catholic saint and a Santeria diety.

Willie's mother sat with him at the small table with the embroidered tablecloth and talked about the clients who came to her for the reading of the cards and other spiritual consultation. She was a cheaper version of a Santeria priest and specialized in *abuelas,* grandmothers. She performed no animal sacrifice, no cleansings with magic stones or ritual baths. But she possessed a reassuring bedside manner and a soothing voice, combined with the experience of exile and an intuition about individuals.

She was telling him now about an old woman who was having visions of her past life in Cuba, visions so strong she was losing her lease on reality.

"She walks down the street here and asks strangers how to get to the Prado, one of the big beautiful boulevards in Havana. Or she asks which way it is to the Havana Hilton, which hasn't existed for decades. They tell her she'll have to walk on water to get there. The woman is lost in her past, more than most people here."

"So what do you tell her?"

"I tell her I understand. Havana was like heaven. It is natural that she wants to be back there. But when she feels one of these spells gaining control of her, she should get off the street and call me. We'll reminisce together. That way she won't get hit by a bus on Flagler Street when she believes she's crossing the Prado."

Willie chewed the last piece of Cuban bread soaked in garlic and told his mother he had to get home to bed. On the way out, she handed him the beaded necklace she had been making.

"When you see the woman again, the one who loves the man you're looking for, you give this to her. She sounds like she has a bad spell on her right now and this will help. And remember to be careful. I don't like what the spirits are saying to me right now. They are very agitated."

Willie gave her a kiss and then walked between St. Lazarus and Francisca out the door.

Chapter 20

At eleven that night Willie headed west on the Tamiami Trail toward the Everglades. He'd slept until sunset and woken to a balmy night. He'd phoned Ross to fill him in on the day's events, but had only reached the machine. The old man was certainly out fishing for snapper. Willie would fill him in later.

Now he had the top down, the sky was full of stars, and he was driving head-on into that fresh, sweet, tropical wilderness smell of the Glades. Houses gave out and a couple miles later he passed a sign that told him he was entering Miccosukee Indian tribal lands. Above the trees Willie spotted the beams of klieg lights scanning the sky, marking the new club. That was just in case you couldn't stay on the two-lane blacktop, the only road leading there, the only road that cut across the Everglades from Miami.

Tommy had warned him months before about this new competition. The Indians had cut a deal with a group of Cubans to open up a Havana-style club and casino. The Miccosukees brought to the table an old and abandoned Mediterranean style mansion built on their lands decades before. More important, they put up their onshore gambling license.

The *cubanos* would lay out everything else—the money for the renovation, the personnel for the dining room, casino, and nightclub, and the historical memory of Havana. In short, the Cubans would provide the style. It was a big idea and big investment, just the kind of project that had always appealed to Sam Suarez.

Willie followed a slight bend in the road and saw the entrance now. It was a blue neon sign that said THE NEW

CASINO CUBA, nestled in a stand of transplanted royal palms. A few more cars were just turning in and Willie fell in behind a silver BMW.

They veered off the Tamiami onto a narrow, newly-paved driveway that ran through thick vegetation. Willie had been up that road once years before. Out of curiosity he had traveled there to see the old mansion built by some fat-cat northern industrialist who had fallen in love with the Everglades back in the 1920s. He had lived there as a near hermit the last twenty years of his life, amid the Spanish moss and wild flamingos. After his death from old age, his family had sold the place, but the buyers had eventually abandoned it. The place Willie had seen back then was a palazzo, something out of a past century, but it had been choked with underbrush, overrun by lizards, snakes, rats, and who knew what else, and crumbling, seemingly held together by cobwebs and air plants.

Willie followed the BMW as the driveway curved and suddenly the mansion came into view. Willie took his foot off the gas and slowed down just to get a good look at it. The crumbling wreck on a dirt road that Willie had visited those years back was no more. The new black pavement he was on became a long, looping, semicircular driveway lined on both sides with royal palms, beautifully lighted and separated by lush plantings of white roses. It led up to a colonnaded entryway and a spot-lighted fountain with sylphs dancing around it, which Willie knew to be a replica of a famous fountain in Havana. The mansion itself, a two-story Mediterranean villa with long wings stretching off to either side, was now a dazzling white. It featured tall arched windows through which you could see large chandeliers and brocaded walls and from which came orchestra music—nostalgic mambo music. From gargoyle-faced planters on the roof, tropical vines grew down the facade. Parked right in front sat a big, shiny black Buick sedan built about 1955, its chrome glinting in the sweep of the kleig lights. Surrounded by the dark edge of the Glades, the whole dazzling scene seemed to float like something in a dream, a dream of Cuba past.

Willie drove up to the entranceway now. Before he could stop, a valet, outfitted all in white, had the door open. Willie thanked him, climbed the marble stairs in front, passed through the colonnade and walked in. He passed under an antique crystal chandelier into a spacious lobby area. On the domed ceiling above him was painted a colorful mural of Spanish conquistadors landing on a beach, the beautiful blue Caribbean behind them. The walls were wainscotted in rich tropical wood. The floor was pink marble.

Before Willie, at the entrance to the dining room, stood an old, silver-haired man wearing black tie. He was the maître'd and looked like he had probably held a similar position in Cuba almost forty years ago. He had the age and the polish.

Willie stuck his head into the room. It was lined floor to ceiling with mirrors, separated by cascading lush red drapery. The tables were covered with bright white table-cloths and the whole room was candlelit. The tall white candles were reflected in the mirrors into infinity. It was beautiful.

"Will you be dining, *señor?*" the man asked Willie in Spanish. "The chef is very good. He used to be at the Hotel Nacional in Havana."

Willie told him he might eat some other night. "Right now, where can I find Sam Suarez?"

The maître'd pointed off into the wing to the left. "His office is at the rear of the casino, *señor*. You will see a red carpeted staircase in the back."

Willie thanked him and headed that way. But first he stopped in at the bar, a mahogany room, as cozy as a wooden chest, with cane-back chairs and new bright brass rail. Black-and-white photos of old Cuba—its beaches, its plazas—lined the walls. He ordered a daiquiri, the traditional lime daiquiri invented in Cuba—in a place called Daiquiri—and got it done perfectly by the red-coated barman. The other people at the bar were extremely well-dressed; men in Italian suits and women in clinging evening gowns. They were, in general, older than your average club crowd, but here and there he saw a pair of young porcelain shoulders. The conversation was a gabble of Spanish mixed with English. Willie paid and drifted on.

Right next to the bar he found the nightclub. It was a dusky ballroom at the rear of the building. An orchestra of men in white dinner jackets played the mambo music he had heard from outside and some of the early dancers— early for a Cuban crowd—were using the dance floor. Behind the orchestra stretched a large, curtained stage, which was still empty. A sign next to the door advised that the show started at midnight.

Willie kept going and drifted into the casino now. This was not the shrunken space of the *Treasure Coast* gambling boat where he had been two days before. A full-size gaming room, high ceilinged, lit by dozens of chandeliers, it was packed with gamblers all dressed to the nines like the people at the bar. The place hummed with the sound of roulette balls spinning around wheels and the ka-ching of slots. In one corner, a craps player had a hot hand and there was a big commotion as he blew on the dice and tried to win for everyone. Willie passed a blackjack table where the dealer in white shirt and black bow tie called out the numbers, first in Spanish, then in English. Cigarette girls drifted around in skimpy bodices and net stockings, their trays hanging just under their full breasts. The costumes were old, but the girls were quite new. Waitresses in equally skimpy costumes maneuvered through the crowd with trays full of rum and other drinks. The mambo music from the ballroom was piped into the casino, giving it all a Latin flavor Vegas couldn't have. It was dazzling and it was sexy. The whole rakish, tropical scene might have been warped through time from Havana in 1958, with people standing where they had forty years before, only a bit grayer now.

Willie found the red carpeted staircase the maître d' had mentioned. It led to a mezzanine level, the outer wall of which consisted of mirrors. Willie climbed to the top of the stairs and found a door there marked PRIVATE. He knocked once and then went in.

He stepped into an office three sides of which were

wood-panelled. The fourth wall was made of mirrors, except these turned out to be two-way mirrors and you could see right down onto the gaming floor as if you were looking through regular glass. Casinos often had such devices so that owners and managers could watch for croupiers or customers running scams on them. This would be where Sam Suarez might sit during the night to keep an eye on his investment.

Except none of the people sitting there was Suarez. One of them was a middle-aged man who had to be a member of the Miccosukee tribe. He wore what looked to be a new pinstriped gray suit, a blue pinpoint shirt without a tie, and alligator-skin boots. He wore his long black hair in a pony tail. He was obviously overseeing the tribe's investment.

Next to him sat Cozy Costanza, along with the two young goons Willie had seen at the Coral Arms—Blondie the maid and Salvatore the doorman. Salvatore jumped up the moment he saw Willie and got brawny. "What are you doing, following us now?"

He started toward Willie but then Cozy held up a hand and he stopped. The Miccosukee, exercising the great discretion of a race that has already had enough trouble, took that pause as an opportunity to excuse himself and descend to the casino floor. The door closed behind him and Cozy was left staring at Willie with distaste, as if Willie were the U.S. attorney.

Tonight the capo was dressed all in black—a black blazer, black silk shirt, black linen slacks, and black Gucci slip-ons. Willie was closer to him than he had been the day before. He could more clearly see the age in his face, the capillaries that ran through the skin of his sunken cheeks and through his prominent nose. They looked like the pattern you might find in fine Italian marble.

In his left hand Cozy held a rubber ball, which he was squeezing methodically, apparently as some kind of therapy for his hand or arms. It was about the size of a tennis ball and pink in color, the kind of ball once called a "pinky" and used in stickball. Willie had played with them in Little Havana and he imagined that someone like

Cozy Costanza had also used them decades earlier when he was a boy in an Italian American ghetto, like Little Italy. It was hard to find the kid in Costanza now, the child in striped T-shirt and shorts running out a hit on some city street. It was hard to see any innocence in him.

On the other hand, it was a good thing for Cozy he was so old. If he hadn't been Willie might have lifted him off the ground by his jowls. If it was Cozy who had sent that package to Tommy the night before, Willie wanted to know. He wanted to know if he smelled of fish. But, of course, doing anything like that at the moment would only get him killed, so Willie bided his time.

The old man was still scowling at him. "This is the second time in two days you've barged in on me in a place where you weren't invited," he said now. Cozy's diction was precise, no discernible accent, the gentleman gangster Willie had read about.

"I didn't expect to find you here tonight. I must say I'm surprised. I didn't know you were involved in this enterprise."

Cozy looked down at the gaming floor. For a moment he appeared like a Roman god gazing down on the human beings below, deciding who would enjoy good fortune and who wouldn't. He shook his head.

"You're leaping to conclusions," he said. "I'm not involved in this. Except for giving my old acquaintance Sam Suarez some advice, I never have been involved. You and I both know that if I had been, this project would have drawn immediate attention from state and federal law enforcement authorities."

Willie wasn't sure he believed Cozy, that he didn't have a stake somehow in the New Casino Cuba. After all, this was Cozy Costanza, who avoided the truth as easily as he evaded taxes. But Willie couldn't argue with his logic.

"They'd be on you in the blink of an eye."

Cozy nodded. "Exactly the kind of attention one never wants. I mean I can run a small gambling boat, but this size operation would be seen differently. No, I'm here tonight only because Sam invited me as a courtesy. I came in the back door and nobody saw me. When I'm done looking I'll leave the same way." His eyes hadn't left the floor below. "It reminds me very much of Casino Cuba in Havana."

"The old days."

"Yes. Unfortunately those days are long gone."

The old man was lost in his memories for several moments before Willie brought him back. "What happened at your gambling boat yesterday?"

Cozy turned back to Willie. "What are you referring to?"

"The guys who shot up your boat."

Cozy shook his head. "What guys shooting at my boat? I don't recall anything like that happening."

Cozy looked around at his thugs. They both shook their heads and Cozy looked back. Willie shrugged.

"I guess news travels slowly. Or maybe Rico Tuzzi didn't bother to tell you."

"And possibly it never happened," Cozy said.

Willie shrugged. "Maybe I'm seeing things. I'm having visions. I wonder if I imagined Delta-5 being burned down this morning."

"No. Everybody knows that happened. The fire has been on television, but the shooting up of the *Treasure Coast*, that never happened."

Cozy was giving Willie a course in history, current events, Cosa-Nostra style. Willie checked to see if he was getting it right. "What you're saying is, 'Yes, somebody blew up Delta-5, but it couldn't have been you, because the Cubans never did anything to you. So why would we blow them up?' "

"Your logic is correct. You're a smart *muchacho*."

"Which, between us, means you *did* have reason to bomb Delta-5."

Cozy shook his head, again not too happy with Willie. "No, I never said that. What I said was we don't want anyone to think we had reason to do that, even if somebody did shoot up the boat."

"So you don't think Delta-5 did the shooting?"

Cozy shrugged. "Why would Delta-5 people do that to my boat? We've always had the best relations with our

Cuban friends here. Italians and Cubans are very much alike. Loyalty is of prime importance to us."

Cozy reached for his drink, a martini with three baby olives in it. He stared at it suspiciously a moment, as if maybe there was a listening device in one of the olives. Then he sipped it and put it back down.

"I'll give you an example. When certain law enforcement agencies decided to make scurrilous accusations against me and my associates a while back, it was our friends in the Cuban exile community who spoke right up for us. They told the authorities that we were good, patriotic Americans. I had very respected members of the Cuban community vouch for me, people who I'd been in business with back on the island."

Willie remembered that. Former Cuban government figures swearing what a lovely guy Cozy was. Of course, it was because of the Mafia's strong position against Castro over the years. The endorsements had caused a stir at the time, but that had been at least twenty years before.

"That was a long time ago," Willie said. "Things change."

"In this case, they haven't changed, not between us and the exiles."

"So your organization is not thinking of doing business in Cuba."

Cozy looked at Willie as if he was crazy. "We both know the moment I or any one of my associates go into business with Castro we might as well be dead. Every Cuban in Miami would want to be the first to shoot me. They could sell raffle tickets for the privilege. I'm an old man. I no longer need that kind of trouble."

"So who do you think shot up the boat?"

"Maybe you can tell me. You seem to know more about what's going on here than I do."

Willie doubted that. "Do you remember that Carlos and Maria Player had a son?"

"Yes, of course. His mother would bring him to the casino some mornings before it opened. He would spin the roulette wheels and play with the dice. He was a nice boy." The words fell from his lips without emotion.

"Well, that son is forty years old now. He has some questions about how his parents died."

"Is that right?"

"You knew that Carlos and Maria Player worked in the underground against Castro, didn't you?"

Cozy looked at Willie the way he would examine an opponent across a poker table, an adversary he had never played before. His hand had stopped squeezing the ball. "Yes, I knew."

"Did you approve of that? It seems to me that activity might draw the kind of attention from Castro's government which you wouldn't want."

Cozy shook his head. "This time your logic is incorrect. You see, what Carlos Player and I both knew was that communism and the gambling business could never co-exist, no matter what the government happened to do or say at the moment. In our business, each individual is dealt cards, maneuvers the best he can, and then he takes what comes. Communists do not subscribe to that world view. We also knew that Castro was saying that he wasn't a communist, but that he was lying, cheating so to speak, and that eventually he would break the bank, all the banks. We knew betrayal was coming, as it always does."

Costanza shook his head ruefully as if he were disappointed in human nature. Like Tuzzi he had spent his life in the gambling business. It was a world dominated by the odds. Some people won, some lost. The only thing that made life more than a matter of playing the odds was good character and that, in his experience, was in short supply.

"So the Players joined the underground," Willie said.

"Yes."

"That was a very risky thing to do."

Cozy considered that and nodded. "Carlos Player didn't gamble for money. He was a conservative man in most ways. But he knew that moments came when you had to take certain risks. Moments of fate when you had to push your chips into the center of the table and let the dealer hand out those last cards. That was the situation for Cubans right then. You either put up, or you folded and left the game. You left Cuba." He shrugged. "He didn't want to leave. He had too much to lose. So he shoved his chips in."

"And he lost."

"That's right. Neither he nor other people involved knew just how completely Castro had fixed the game. The situation was hopeless. And when Castro discovered what they had tried to do, he killed Carlos and his wife and killed them brutally."

"So you're convinced that Castro had them murdered."

"Of course."

"You know that for a fact? I'm told that Cuban state security didn't even know the Players were in the underground." Willie was remembering what Del Rey had told him.

Cozy didn't like that. "Is that right?"

"Yes. That means that maybe someone else might have murdered them and stolen their money. Of course, anybody who did that would want people to think that the Players were killed by the communists. The Castro government wiped out lots of other members of the underground. It is a theory that would be very easy to peddle in Havana back then, and today in Miami as well. In a way, it's a bluff that nobody around here would ever call."

Cozy looked at him stonily. The capo didn't like the implications.

"I don't know what you're talking about," he said finally.

Willie shrugged. "It's like you said, Mr. Costanza. One, the situation was hopeless, and two, betrayal is always a possibility. Why leave a half million dollars behind, even if it does belong to your partners? That's not good business."

Cozy's bodyguards bristled again. Costanza had become immobile, looking even more now like fine Italian marble. "You should be careful what you say," he muttered.

"I told you yesterday that I was just trying to warn you. Bobby Player, Carlos and Maria's son, thinks you and your associates, like Rico Tuzzi, may know what really happened to his parents. He might show up to ask you some questions."

Costanza got to his feet. "I appreciate your concern," he said "Now we have to be going." The old man put the "pinky" away in his pocket, drained his martini, and then shuffled toward the back door. Salvatore and the maid both glared at Willie. Then they all disappeared into the night.

Chapter 21

Willie left the office right after Cozy, except he exited out the front way. He walked downstairs to a bar at the rear of the gaming floor and refilled his daiquiri. The bartender was liberal with the Bacardi. Then Willie drifted out of the casino and back to the nightclub.

It was after midnight and the show was about to begin. The place was packed now with hundreds of people who had poured out of the dining room or had momentarily left the roulette wheels.

Willie was led to a very small table for two against a far wall. He had just sat down when the white-coated orchestra swung into the overture for the show. The music was right out of the fifties; lots of rumba led by rumbling conga drums and a dazzling horn section that played and danced at the same time. They went from one throbbing melody to the next. Lights of different colors came up behind them on the main stage and on two curved staircases sweeping down out of the heavens. A mist seeped up through the floorboards.

The first dancers appeared out of that mist. They were young, both men and women, and decked out in what dancers might have worn on the Cuban stages of the fifties. The men wore bright green shirts with ruffled sleeves and pants to match, with straw *guajiro* hats. They were barefoot.

The women danced in long crimson skirts slit up the side as far as they could be. Above that they wore the very skimpiest of halter tops, silver in color. Their hair was wrapped in crimson bandanas. They began to spin so that their skirts flared out revealing silver G-strings.

They whirled about the stage for a time and then the

men and women broke off in pairs into scorching rumbas. First the women approached, hips in rocking, yearning rhythm to the music, until they made the men bend over backward beneath their onslaught. Then they pulled away, only to come back again. The men descended slowly, melting under the seductive powers of their partners, until they were bent back over their knees with the women dancing above them, their hips moving in double time or triple time to the cannonading music of the drums. Finally the men jumped up and grabbed the women close so that they danced like one undulating body. Slowly the men bent the women back until they were both almost parallel to the floor, still in rhythmic motion, the seduction complete. There remained only the act of love.

And that was when the stage went dark, the music was transmuted with a blare of brass, and another contingent of dancers appeared. A half dozen women wore brief silver bottoms with just scatterings of rhinestones sprinkled over their breasts. The costumes were topped with headdresses hung with glass pendants and mirrors that looked like chandeliers. In their hands they held large fans made of peacock feathers. The men danced in white zoot suits topped by Panama hats. Neon signs flashed all around them. La Habana—Farandula—the Nightlife.

If the first dance had been about the sensuality at the root of Cuban life, this one highlighted the heyday of Havana before the revolution, when it was the toast of the world. The Paris of the Caribbean. They danced mambo, chacha, rumba. They were glitzy and sensual. They danced and gambled the night away, within reach of the stars that hung just above them on the ceiling of the stage. At the end of the dance one of those men reached up and picked a star, an illuminated rock, right out of the sky, and held it in his hand as if he were the owner of the night. All the other lights were dimmed, leaving only that starlight.

That was when Olga Tuzzi suddenly appeared, descending slowly from the rafters, suspended by invisible wires. She was dressed in a super-tight blue sheath dress that sparkled with rhinestones and she wore a headdress to match. Wrapped in dark blue and shimmering with starlight, she was like the night itself.

She descended into the arms of those male dancers in the white zoot suits and began a medley of boleros about the night—moonlit nights, tropical nights, nights at sea, nights full of love.

All the time she was handed from one man to another, glamorous and elusive. Her voice was seductive, her dancing tantalizing. She finished a half hour later with a song called only *"Noche."* She pleaded that the Havana night always have the heartbeat of a person in love and that it remain forever wrapped in the silk of her song. As the last notes left her mouth, the lights went out and night enveloped them all.

The nightclub exploded in applause. The entire crowd jumped to its feet, Willie included. Olga had been spectacular. Through the glitz and glamour of it, she had embodied a real sense of yearning, a sense of loss—lost island, lost loves. She had hit hearts throughout the ballroom with her arrow. She spent the next five minutes taking curtain calls and blowing kisses and then she disappeared.

The orchestra swung into more music and the dance floor filled right away. Willie wove through the crowd and found a door that led backstage. He picked his way through the girls in G-strings and boys in ruffles and finally found Olga's dressing room. A small crowd of admirers, mostly older people, had gathered and he waited about fifteen minutes for them to disperse. Olga was sitting at her makeup table just beginning to take off her greasepaint and smoking a cigarette when Willie knocked on the open door.

She looked up, surprised to see him. "The detective. What are you doing here? I think you are too young to remember me like those other people."

"You deserve fans of all ages. You were wonderful."

She exhaled luxuriously. "You are always very nice," she said, but then she frowned. "I hope you are not here to ask more questions. I'm too tired tonight."

She wiped off some greasepaint and Willie stepped

into the room. "I was hoping to speak to your husband if he's here."

She poked a finger between her breasts. "Me too. I want to speak to him. But I don't know where he is. These last two days they have been very bad since I meet you."

Willie knew it would be even worse when he told her about Del Rey, but he couldn't break it to her yet.

"You have no idea where your husband is?"

"No. Maybe you tell me. After you talk to him yesterday and somebody shoot up the boat, he takes off."

Willie squinted at her. Maybe Rico Tuzzi *was* taking precautions. Maybe he was lying low. Either that, or maybe he was already dead. Willie couldn't tell Olga that either.

"That was the last you heard of him, yesterday afternoon?"

"That's right. I come back from the movie and I see the boat. He is packing to go. He tells me there will be more trouble."

"What's the trouble about?"

"He doesn't say. He makes a phone call and goes out and he doesn't come back."

"Who was the call to?"

She shook her head. "I don't know who. He just hurry up to go."

"Maybe he was going to see Cozy Costanza."

"I ask Cozy. He don't know. That's what he tells me. Rico he's gone and maybe I go too. I go find some other city, someplace else to dance."

She looked into the mirror that had a crack in it and scrubbed away at more of her makeup. Her age began to show. Given that age, she probably knew she wouldn't find another city where she could dance. As good as she was, it was probably only in Miami where she could cash in on the nostalgia for old Cuba. But Willie wasn't about to tell her that either. She didn't really need to be told. When she looked up at him it was clear she knew there were big problems brewing, not only for Tuzzi but for her.

"This trouble, where is it coming from? Why do you come here tonight?"

Willie could try and put it off, but it wouldn't do any good. "Victor Del Rey is dead. I found him this morning. Somebody strangled him last night."

Pain contorted her face as fiercely as if he had twisted her wrist or punched her in the gut. Her eyes went wide and a hand went to her mouth.

"Oh no."

Willie closed the door of the dressing room and gripped her shoulder, afraid she would collapse. "I'm sorry."

It was clear that she hadn't known. She sat blinking desperately into the past, as if searching for Del Rey, her eyes growing moist and then scared. A fear loomed behind the tears. Willie tried to read it.

"Do you think Tuzzi killed him?" Willie asked.

She seemed surprised that he would ask and shook her head vigorously.

"No."

"You're sure?"

"Why would he kill him after all these years? There is no reason."

"Then who would have killed Del Rey?"

She looked at Willie imploringly and shook her head silently.

"Did you speak with him at the theater yesterday?" Willie asked.

She nodded.

"Did he say anything to you then that would make you think he was afraid?"

"He said people came here now from Cuba and there could be trouble."

"The same thing your husband said."

"Yes."

"But what kind of trouble?"

Her face was full of sorrow. "He told me it has to do with Carlos and Maria Player and who kill them."

"Really? What else did he say about that?"

She shook her head vigorously again. "Nothing. We only talk a short time. I tell him what you tell me about the boat. Then he is more scared. But he don't want to speak more about it. I ask him but he don't talk."

"Did he mention a name? Miguel Angel Matos?"

She shook her head

"Do you know who that is?"

"No. Who is he?"

"I don't know for sure." Willie described Matos. "Do you remember anyone like that from your days in those cafés near the docks or from Casino Cuba."

"Many people on the docks, they were like that. You think maybe he killed Carlos and Maria?"

"I don't know. He says he's helping Bobby. And that could be why Victor Del Rey is dead."

Olga Tuzzi's mouth opened in shock. "But Victor he has nothing to do with killing Carlos and Maria Player. He tells me that a long time ago, but he tells me again yesterday. He knows I care about them very much. He tells me he watch who came to speak to them, but he never say nothing to his bosses to hurt them. He always promise me that."

"Did he ever tell you he knew anything about who did kill them?"

"He say he don't know who did it. He say many people come to see Carlos Player at the casino. And you can't tell who is on the side of who."

"What do you mean?"

She looked anguished, confused, as if she were being confronted by those people right at that moment. "I mean everything it was changing and everyone was changing. You don't know for sure who is with the underground and who is with the government. Maybe someone tells you they are with the new government, but they are really in the underground. Or maybe you think they belong to the underground, but they are really spies for the government. It was very, very dangerous."

"Infiltrators," said Willie,"

"That's right, *infiltrados,* on both sides. You don't trust nobody who comes to the casino."

Willie remembered what Del Rey had said at the theater. "Everyone then was a gambler, for money or power." He sat down right in front of her.

"What side were Carlos and Maria Player on, Olga?"

Her eyes went big with fear and she began to shake her head.

"Tell me."

"I don't know. I don't know."

"Why don't you know? Someone told you that maybe Carlos and Maria Player were infiltrators. That they were communist spies. Is that it?"

Olga Tuzzi looked at him helplessly.

"Was it Rico?"

She shook her head hard. "No. It was Armando Capitán."

Willie's eyebrows danced. "Mando?"

"He come to the house one night very late. He talk to Rico. After he leaves, Rico he asks me things about Carlos and Maria."

Willie frowned. "What things?"

"About what side they are on. He say some people think they are really communists because some of the government people they come to the hotel and the restaurant and Carlos and Maria serve them and talk to them in private."

"And what did you say to him then?"

"I tell him I don't think that could ever be true. Carlos and Maria they weren't communists."

"But Mando didn't trust them still? And didn't like them?"

She shook her head. "No, he didn't."

"Did he convince Rico not to trust them or to like them?"

She looked scared, just like the previous time he had asked her about the possibility that her husband had been involved in killing her friends. "I don't know."

Olga broke down and cried now. When she did, it was as if she weren't just weeping for herself, but for everyone she knew, for her whole country. Of everyone involved, she had lost the most. Her dreams could really only be accomplished in the Cuba of her past.

Willie held her trembling shoulder. She had been lovers with two men back then. One was Cuban and spied for the government. The other, an American gangster, was involved somehow with the underground. Her best friends in the world had ended up dead, caught between those two forces somehow. She was still carrying that around with her.

"You shouldn't stay at your house," he said. "Is there somewhere you can go where no one would look for you?"

She thought a moment. "I have a friend I dance with years ago. I can stay with her over in Miami Beach."

"Do that. Give me the address and telephone."

She did. Willie left Olga then, the old chorus girl staring into the cracked mirror that had already brought her years and years of bad luck.

Chapter 22

Willie cut back through the nightclub into the casino looking again for Sam Suarez. Standing near a blackjack table
he noticed an off-duty Miami detective named Luis Mar-
tinez whom he recognized from his days on the force.
Luis was apparently moonlighting as casino security. Willie
scanned the place and noticed a few more familiar faces
in plainclothes making believe they were high rollers. Security was tight.

Willie drifted over to Luis and they exchanged pleas-
antries briefly.

"Have you seen Sam Suarez recently?" Willie asked.

Luis gestured toward another door next to the rear
staircase, this one on the ground floor.

"He's probably over in the cashier's room."

"I need to speak to him. It's about a case he has interest in."

Luis led Willie across the gaming floor. A blond woman
wearing a white shirt and black bow tie sat behind a
teller's window dispensing chips and cashing them in as
well. Next to her was the metal door Luis had indicated,
with two surveillance cameras positioned about it, one on
either side. Luis pressed a button next to the door, then
waved at the camera. The door buzzed and they went in.

The room they entered resembled a small branch bank.
Five tellers, each with a flower in her hair as if it were a
uniform, sat behind what had to be bullet-proof glass.
Their customers were casino employees, pit bosses, change
boys for the slots, a croupier or two possibly going on
break. They were cashing in their banks, taking out more

bank money, etc. The slot machine employees, in particular, were changing bills for coins they could dispense to
the players. The tellers counted money not with machines, but the old fashioned way, with fingers that
moved faster than the eye could see. You could hear the
corners of the bills snapping so that they made a sound
like some of those insects out in the Glades.

Two uniformed security guards, packing big handguns
on their hips, stood on either side of the small room. Behind the tellers on the other side of the glass stood a
gleaming walk-in safe. It was closed. Two desks sat before it, which might have been for the bank officers at a
normal branch. But no small business loans were made
here. It had no mortgage department. Here there was only
the luck department.

Sitting at one of the desks, talking on the phone, was
Sam Suarez, dressed in a white dinner jacket and black
bow tie. He saw Willie, finished his conversation, and
came out from behind the bullet-proof glass through a security door. The banker wasn't happy to see Willie there.

Luis explained that Willie had said it was important.
Suarez dismissed him roughly.

"Is this where you look for Roberto Player?" the Piranha said to Willie. "Believe me, I don't think he'll show
up here."

"No, I was looking for you."

The little man's eyes narrowed. "More questions about
Carlos and Maria Player, matters that happened thirty-
five years ago?"

"No, it's about things that have happened in the last
two days."

"What things?"

"The shooting up of Cozy Costanza's boat and then the
big blow at Delta-5 this morning."

Suarez looked even less happy now. He took Willie by
the elbow and led him out of the cashier's office, with the
sound of the money-counting crickets behind them. He
led him through the casino and the dining room to a
smaller, private VIP dining room at the rear of that wing.

It featured walls covered in a red fabric that looked like

silk, no windows, a central chandelier turned on low, a few tables, but mainly private booths that could be closed off with curtains. In the Cuba of the past, a private room such as this might have also been equipped with safe deposit boxes where patrons would keep their cocaine. This would allow them to stay at the craps table, on the dance floor, or in one of those private booths making love all night long. Rooms like this had featured live sex shows as well, starring men and women of unusual proportions. It was said that American women of the 1950s were particularly big fans of these shows. Cuba had been ahead of the game in everything.

Right now it was empty, except for one booth where the curtains were closed. Low conversation came from it. Suarez sat down at one of the tables and Willie sat next to him. Suarez used a buzzer on the table to call a waiter and ordered a Pernod. Willie stuck with his daiquiri.

A richly dressed couple entered and Suarez got up to greet them. Willie watched and remembered a story he'd heard about the banker. An Intelligence cop had been assigned to follow him briefly because one of Sam's confidential contacts with a foreign government interested the department. Nothing had developed there. His business dealings were judged to be above board. But the cop had found that at least once a week Sam left his cushy office at South Florida Federal and drove to a rundown bar on a side street in East Little Havana. He parked in an alley, took off his jacket and tie, entered through a back door, and sat at a back table. There he met a woman, a slightly heavy-set woman, middle-aged, inexpensively dressed, still attractive. "She doesn't look like a whore but like a PTA mother," the report said. Sam was married to a lady who belonged to the exile aristocracy, with whom he shared a mansion in Coral Gables and a very public life full of business dinners and charity events. With this other woman in the bar he would leave the tie behind, have a drink or two, play old Cuban tunes on the jukebox, dance a bit, and talk. Then they would retire to a motel nearby, where the cop, who once took the room next door, said they engaged in relatively quiet sex, interspersed with more talk, some laughter, and cooing. The cop later found out that the lady had once worked with Sam when they both scrubbed toilets for a living. She was now a supervisor at the toilet scrubbing company, which Sam still owned and which was located nearby. She was a single mother with kids and Sam helped her with money. "They talk about old times and old friends when they both worked bathrooms," the cop wrote. "Later he kisses her on the cheek and they say good-bye. Sam, it turns out, is a sweetie."

The Sam Suarez who sat down now next to Willie did no cooing and didn't reminisce. When the Pernod came, he poured just a touch of water into it, making it turn cloudy. He sipped it.

"I told you last night I know nothing about shootings or bombings for that matter. I'm a banker not a soldier. Why come to me with this?"

Willie wondered if Suarez wasn't clouding more than his drink. "Yes, you're a banker who's done business with all these people for years. You've always known what was going on, first in Cuba and now here."

"So what?"

"So what's going on?"

Suarez sneered. "Someone is trying to ruin business in Miami, that's what's going on. They're trying to bankrupt all of us."

"Who would that be?"

"Ask Roberto when you find him. Ask his friends who you let come into this country two nights ago, when you could have called the police."

Willie flicked his eyebrows. "I thought you put a high premium on secrecy."

"I did, but that was before Roberto and his friends developed an interest in guns and firebombs."

"You're putting your money on them, I take it. Why couldn't it be the Italians and the commandos going at each other?"

Suarez shook his head. "Because neither of them have anything to gain from doing that and everything to lose."

"Maybe they aren't consulting their brokers or you on this. Maybe they just got pissed at each other."

Suarez was still shaking his head. "No, they haven't lost their senses. I haven't gotten where I've gotten making bad wagers and misjudging people. Find Roberto and his friends and you'll find who is doing this. You'll also find ten thousand dollars in your bank account. I'll pay you that to find them, even if you find them tomorrow."

Willie whistled. "Ten thousand per day is just slightly above my normal fee."

"It's worth it to me to keep from having my bank, my other investments, like this club, and myself damaged by scandal."

From inside the curtained booth came a woman's coquettish laugh and then the rustling of silk. Willie sipped his daiquiri.

"I just bumped into Cozy Costanza up in your office. I was surprised to find him there."

"He's an old man. I invited him here as a courtesy because he was a partner in the original Casino Cuba. Nothing more."

"Cozy was telling me how he thinks the communists murdered Carlos and Maria Player because of their involvement in the underground. But last night you said you weren't sure why they died."

"I wasn't involved with the underground. I don't know what happened to them. I told you that."

"Do you think they were working for the communists? I'm told that's what Armando Capitán thinks and Rico Tuzzi for that matter. Tuzzi had his gambling boat shot up and somebody threw a firebomb at Mando's headquarters. Is it because they thought the Players had betrayed the underground? Is it because maybe they were involved in killing the Players?"

"I told you I didn't know then and I don't know now."

"But could it have happened? Those communist leaders who would eat at the hotel, did they try to sweet talk Carlos and Maria Player? Did they try to recruit them? Did Carlos ever mention it to you?"

"He never talked to me about such things."

"I thought you were his friend."

"At that moment there was no such thing as friends, only potential enemies."

Suarez's vehemence took Willie by surprise. He leaned closer to the banker. "I know you didn't want to give Carlos Player any of your own money to smuggle from the country. You didn't want to risk it. But I wonder if that's because you no longer trusted him. You received some information about him and his wife that wasn't to their credit. Did you hear that they had cut a deal with Castro? Did you hear it from Tuzzi or Mando? You knew them both."

Suarez's Pernod had stopped halfway to his mouth. Willie pressed him. "And how did their killers know about the money hidden in the house? Would the Players have told anyone else about that money?"

"I've told you I had no knowledge of who they told."

"What did you have knowledge of?"

Suarez's chin came up and his fists clenched. "I had knowledge of the fact that my son was far away. And I had knowledge of the fact I was being destroyed. Everything I had built and my family had built was being torn away from me. Day by day, week by week, with each government decree. They were rewriting the laws and each time they did, something else you owned disappeared." He snapped his fingers. "Just like that. Businesses disappeared, buildings disappeared, employees disappeared. Until you started to think the floor under you would open and you too would disappear. It happened to some people—like Carlos and Maria Player. That's what I had knowledge about. And now Roberto is letting himself be used by communist conspirators who want to bring ruin on us again and kill more people."

Willie sipped his drink. Sam Suarez had escaped that world where everything disappeared. Now he was reconstructing the Cuba of old, and securing it so that no one could steal it from him again. That was Sam Suarez's mania. The banker finished his drink.

"I have to get back to business," he said.

He got up and Willie did the same. From the adjoining

booth came the rustle of silk again and then an almost inaudible gasp. They left the couple to themselves. Suarez escorted Willie back to the casino.

"Please don't contact me again unless you've found Roberto. My offer still stands. Ten thousand dollars. I'll put it in your hands as soon as you bring him to me." He turned on a heel and disappeared into the casino.

Willie watched him. Sam Suarez wanted Bobby Player "delivered" to him. Willie wondered what he would do with him then. He was still wondering that when he noticed Mike Suarez approaching. The younger Suarez, dressed in a tuxedo, spotted Willie too. They met near a roulette table. Mike searched Willie's face.

"Do you have news about Bobby?"

"Nothing fresh. I just had a brief chat with your father."

"About?"

"About this and that. Tell me something. Did Bobby talk to you much about his parents?"

"When?"

"Ever."

"When we were kids at the orphanage he would tell me he missed them, especially after he stopped hearing from them. But he wouldn't talk about them really. He was only six when he left. He didn't know much about them."

"And later when he was grown?"

"Yeah, he talked more about them then," Mike said. "Not every day, but it was something that would come up with him regularly. He wanted to know the facts of how they died. It's like Ellie says, he's been haunted by it forever."

"Had he learned more about them by then? Did he ask people about them, like your father?"

"Yeah, he did that."

"Did your father ever tell him that some people suspected Carlos and Maria of being traitors to the underground?"

Mike bridled as if he were the one being accused. "My father would never tell him something like that."

"Did anyone else?"

"I've never heard anything like that. Everyone has always thought of Carlos and Maria Player as heroes who were massacred by the communists."

"But when he came back from Cuba he didn't think that anymore. Did he tell you why?"

"No. I told you. He wouldn't talk to me about it at all."

"That's strange isn't it? You're his best friend. Why wouldn't he tell you?"

Mike's eyes met Willie's for a split second and then skittered away. "I have no idea." But Willie was starting to think that Mike knew more than he was willing to say, maybe more than he was willing to face.

"Do you have any idea where Bobby might go to hide?"

"No."

"You're sure?"

The other man nodded. "I'm sure. I better get back to the floor now," he said.

Mike shook hands and walked away then. If he knew where Bobby might be, he wasn't saying. Maybe he didn't want to betray his friend. But it seemed more than that. For the first time Willie wondered exactly whose side Mike was on.

Chapter 23

Willie watched Mike cross the gaming floor and then drifted back into the casino himself. He bought ten five-dollar chips from a cashier. Then he sat down at the end of a quarter-moon blackjack table with four other players and a tall redheaded lady in a black bow tie who did the dealing.

They said blackjack was the favored game of loners. In craps, if you had a hot hand, people would bet with you and win. In roulette, it was the same. Poker was a game of wits among players. But in blackjack, each individual went up against the bank. Since the bank played by certain established rules, you were basically playing against fate, each player on his own.

For the next ten minutes, Willie won. He came up with two blackjacks, automatic winners, and enough face cards that the redhead had no chance. He sipped his daiquiri and looked around. At any moment you might expect Carlos Player to come walking across the floor in his white jacket. Or maybe, if you glanced at a roulette wheel, you might spot the young Victor Del Rey spinning the little black ball, calling out the winners. The daiquiris and the advancing hour were making Willie sink into the past.

He sipped his drink, moved a chip into the circle before him and remembered a story his late father had told him many years before about Cuba. Back on the island the old man worked as a musician, a saxophone player, in a dance orchestra. He had traveled from the eastern end of the island to Havana for a series of gigs and was headed back home. He had partied heavily with other musicians

in the capital and now had only enough cash in his pocket
to buy a bus ticket home, with just a few pesos left over.
He decided to go into one of the big casinos and try his
luck with the extra money. If he won, he might make
enough to fly home on a new commuter plane to Santiago. He had never flown on an airplane.

His father bought a chip or two and headed for the
craps table. Just like Willie now, he began to win. His
hand had turned hot, making good on several passes.
Word spread around the gaming floor that the boy dressed
in a zoot suit, toting a saxophone case in his hand, was
magic. Soon he had a crowd around him, including a couple of almost naked showgirls who normally wouldn't
have given the time of day to a sax player from the sticks.

After seven successful passes in a row, Papa realized
he had won just enough for a plane ticket. "If I had raked
those chips up right then into my saxophone case and
taken a cab straight to the airport, I would have been
home in no time," he said years later. "Instead, I looked at
one of those showgirls pressed up against me with the
legs longer than mine, wearing nothing but rhinestones. I
had rhinestones for brains, *hijo*."

A half hour later, Papa went flat broke when he threw
boxcars. "When I lost the last chip, that showgirl she disappeared into thin air like a ghost," he said snapping his
fingers. "Then I hitchhiked all the way home to Santiago
playing tunes on my horn for ugly truck drivers. You
have to know when *La Senorita* Luck has answered your
prayer and not ask her for more, *hijo*."

Willie remembered the lesson his father had learned,
folded his cards, and scraped up his money. He was getting up when he heard a familiar voice at the table behind
him. He turned and saw James Clancy throwing his cards
face down and shoving his bet toward the dealer.

"Bust again!" he said.

Willie came up behind him. "Maybe you should quit,
Mr. Clancy. It seems your luck is no better here than it
was at the old Casino Cuba."

Clancy turned and looked at him. His face was even
more flushed than usual, probably from rum. "The ever-

present Mr. Cuesta," he said. The booze had not reached his tongue. He spoke clearly. He looked at the few chips remaining before him and then back at Willie. "I think you may be right. I'm starting to feel like a third world economy here. All debt and no earnings."

"Do you have a minute? I'd like to ask you a couple of questions."

Clancy picked up his chips, threw the dealer a five dollar tip, and bid her good night. "Let's go have a cigar in the smoking room," he said.

He led Willie across the floor to a small alcove just the other side of the dining room

It was called The Humidor, a dark space suffused with the aroma of expensive tobacco. A half dozen tables were spread about and a handful of men and two women enjoyed late-night smokes. Beyond them stood a walk-in humidor. Its cedar drawers stood open, their gold locks held keys, waiting for members to stash their costly tobaccos. The New Casino Cuba covered all the vices with style, just like old Cuba.

Clancy gestured Willie into a chair. Tonight the tall man was wearing a beautiful, white, elaborately embroidered guayabera and black pants. He sat down and proffered a leather cigar case.

"Have a Cohiba, Mr. Cuesta." He leaned forward and whispered. "These are real Havanas. The genuine article."

Willie accepted. They clipped the cigars and then Clancy fired up, first Willie's and then his own. "So how can I be of assistance?"

"I wanted to discuss your involvement with the anti-Castro underground back in 1960."

Clancy's cigar stopped an inch from his mouth and he smiled. "What makes you think I know anything about the Cuban underground?"

"Let's just call it a hunch."

"I told you I worked as a cultural attaché. The underground wasn't considered a cultural organization. Not by a long shot. I handled showgirls and musicians, not anticommunist guerrillas."

"Didn't you? We both know that a person's title at an

embassy may have nothing to do with his real duties. We both know that the CIA staffed the Havana embassy and that those agents had contact to one degree or another with the underground. I wonder what your true duties were."

Clancy's smile disappeared totally now. "That's an indiscreet question to put to a former foreign service officer. We're not always allowed to answer that one."

"I'm sure you won't tell me anything you're not supposed to, Mr. Clancy."

Clancy drew on his cigar and created a veil of gray-blue smoke and considered his answer carefully. "Let's just say I arrived in Cuba months before Castro took power. After a while we started to see the writing on the wall. I mean that literally. The people who didn't see eye to eye with the new regime said so by writing on walls and other clandestine acts of aggression. That was the beginning of the underground. From there they went on to form cells and plot more organized and serious antigovernment action."

"And it was part of your job to maintain contact with them?"

Clancy squinted. "If you're asking me what exactly my relationship was to the resistance, you may be getting into state secrets. Maybe you should tell me first what all of this is about."

Willie mulled that a moment. If Clancy really had served as an old "company" man, he would want a return for his information. Willie had dealt with the CIA often enough during his years in the Intelligence Unit. You didn't acquire anything from them free of charge. Knowing Clancy could get it all from Mando anyway, Willie gave him the full story of Roberto Player. He recounted Player's Peter Pan days, the rumors of his parents being traitors, the trip he'd made to Cuba, and his search in Miami for his parents' killers. Clancy listened and by the time Willie had finished all traces of his usual good humor had vanished from his face. He looked perturbed by the story.

"So this young man has doubts not only about who

caused the deaths of his parents, but their breeding, so to speak. He wants to know what side they were on."

"That's right. He's driving himself crazy, his fiancée, his employer, and his friends too. It's ruining his life and it's starting to ruin mine. You knew his parents and you maintained contact with the underground, unofficially of course. You tell me."

The tall man puffed on his cigar. He studied Willie a long time, as if he were trying to guess his exact weight to the ounce, only studying his face. Finally, he took the stogie from his mouth.

"You can tell Roberto Player when you find him that Carlos and Maria Player were two of the finest people I ever knew. You tell him two more courageous members of the Cuban underground never existed. There wasn't a drop of communist blood in either of them. I can confirm that."

Willie's eyebrows danced. "Is that right?"

"Yes, it is."

"And is that why they were killed, their underground work?"

"I don't have any doubt about it."

"By who?"

The tall man shook his head. "I don't know who it was exactly. We didn't know then and we still don't. If we knew, those responsible wouldn't be alive today, I'll tell you that much. We learned in the day or two before they were murdered that underground cells had been infiltrated. Those cells were being raided and rounded up, but it was impossible to warn them."

"Why?"

"Because by the end, all of us at the embassy who had any dealings with the underground were being followed day and night. Telephones were also tapped. We couldn't move from the embassy or call our contacts. You just had to hope that Cuban state security didn't know about certain people. We lost touch with all our underground workers. We couldn't do anything for them. Castro had ordered our government to reduce the size of the embassy to almost no one and that caused us to break relations

with Cuba. A few days after the Players died, all American diplomats had to leave the country, including me.
There was no way for us to know who had died and how."
He stared into his own marbled smoke and shook his head
bleakly.

"Did you ever hear of a Cuban named Miguel Angel
Matos?" Willie asked.

He could see a security check going on behind the
other man's eyes. "No, I don't remember anyone by that
name. Who was he?"

"I believe he was a gangster, a common criminal, arrested for killing Carlos and Maria Player. Now it appears
he's claiming he didn't do it, and he pretends to have information about who did. He arrived in this country two
nights ago with the help of Roberto Player. He's told
Player he'll help him find who killed his parents. Roberto
is convinced someone here did it, possibly some of his
parents' old colleagues in the underground. Rumors had
spread that the Players worked for Castro. People in the
underground may have heard those rumors. Could someone in the underground have turned against them?"

The expression on Clancy's face was one of pain. "I
don't think that happened. I've known the rest of these
people a long time and no one has ever mentioned to me
any doubts about Carlos and Maria. Things got tough
there near the end. And yes, in conspiracies people do de-
velop sometimes unreasonable suspicions about each
other."

"I can imagine."

"That has always been one of the dangers of entering
into any kind of clandestine endeavor, any conspiracy.
The pressures of it can lead people at a certain moment to
not trust each other. Especially if the moment is bad. And
the moment was very bad right then for the underground.
Since you have trusted so much in so few people, the danger of betrayal is constantly in the back of the mind. It can
become the explanation for any failure. In many cases
conspirators conspire against each other. Some, especially the amateurs, are killed by their own. Yes, it happens. But it doesn't mean it happened in this case."

"I understand that Armando Capitán suspected Bobby's parents of being communists, or at least in the service of the government. He may have convinced other people of the same. Did he eventually know, before they died, that they were really with the underground?"

Clancy shook his head. "They were in different cells and he would have known they were part of the resistance only if they were involved in an operation together."

"You yourself said the underground cells were being raided. They had been betrayed by someone. Could any of those other agents have believed that Carlos and Maria Player had betrayed them to government agents, to those same agents who would visit the hotel, who the Players spoke to in private?"

Clancy took his cigar from his mouth.

"Their contact with those communist government officials was part of their cover. They were encouraged to maintain those relations."

"But other people never knew that, did they?"

Clancy frowned. "No, they didn't. As I said, it was part of their cover. It was impossible to tell anyone."

"So other underground members might have suspected the Players."

"Hypothetically, yes."

"And since you couldn't make contact with them near the end because you were trapped in the embassy, you can't be sure what happened, if they were killed by their own people or not, can you?"

Clancy took moments to answer. It was Clancy and his organization who had encouraged the Players to court those communist officials and maybe it was for that they had been killed. You could see him examining the past in his head, maybe trying to remember movements, comments more than thirty-five years old, searching the possibility that Willie had presented him. Worry filled his eyes. They got a bit shaky and you could see the alcoholic in him now. Maybe he had become a drinker just to avoid questions such as these.

"Well?" asked Willie.

The big man stared at him. Anger and doubt and pain

battled in him. Finally, he shook his head. "I told you, I can't know for sure what happened in those last days. But if you knew the entire story of Carlos and Maria Player . . ."

He didn't go on.

"What do you mean the entire story?" Willie was reminded of what Rico Tuzzi had said about the Players being mixed up in something about which he would never know. "What are you talking about?"

But Clancy just shook his head. "I've told you all I can tell you." He studied those words a few moments, decided they were enough, and stood up. "Now I have to be going."

He nodded to Willie but didn't bother to shake hands. He hurried out, a man who suddenly seemed alone, and who had the past—a murky, secretive, and now troubling past—following close behind him.

Chapter 24

It was past two a.m. The competition had been analyzed and it was getting late. The time had come to head for his brother's club. Or at least he thought it had come.

He walked out of the Humidor and was passing the mahogany bar toward the exit when, out of the corner of an eye, he spotted someone he was surprised to see. She was standing near the entrance to the bar, apparently looking for someone. When her head turned he made out that same striking face he had last seen staring over that *flamboyan* tree in Little Havana, that high-cheekboned, sloe-eyed face. Tonight she wore not her red sundress, but a black, clinging number that barely reached her thighs, black stiletto heels, and she clutched a small silver purse. He was right next to her before she realized it.

"Hello, Aurora."

She whirled around, startled. Her expression said, "What are you doing here?" which was exactly what he started to ask her. She put a hand against his chest.

"*Aqui, no.* Wait until we are outside."

She slipped her arm through his and they hurried past the valets in the direction of the parking lot. That led them by the fountain and then across the empty garden. She stopped at a stone bench, sat, and Willie did the same. From there the club looked like a palace out of some glorious past.

"I'm surprised to see you're already part of the night-life," Willie said. "Where are Roberto and Mr. Matos tonight?"

"It isn't important where they are."

As she spoke her eyes drifted toward the cars parked in

a lot on the edge of the Glades. Willie figured Matos had to be waiting there somewhere, maybe watching them right now.

"Is Roberto all right?"

"Yes, he's fine."

"I'm working for someone who is very worried about him. Several people are very concerned for him. Those people are getting more worried all the time, especially with firebombs being thrown."

Her eyes flared. "We had nothing to do with that bomb this morning."

"Is that right?"

"Yes."

Willie deepened his squint. "You come into the country and a few hours later a firebomb explodes directed at one of your enemies and you expect me to believe that?"

"It's true. We were not anywhere near that place when that happened."

A couple walked toward them, heading for their car. She put her hand on his to quiet him, turned her face away from them, and waited until the people were out of ear shot. Willie turned back to her.

"I suppose you also didn't go to see Victor Del Rey, the old croupier, again last night?"

"Why do you ask that?"

"Did you or didn't you, *mi amor?*"

"Yes, we were at his hotel last night."

"What time?"

"About midnight. After he arrived from his work."

"And what did you do there?"

"We talked to him very briefly."

"About what?"

"About those last days when Carlos and Maria Player were alive."

"And what did he tell you about those last days?"

"What he saw. Who he saw. Not very much really. He said he was planning his own escape then."

"And then what?"

"And then nothing. Then we left."

"What time was that?"

"Maybe a half hour after we arrived."

"Really?"

"Yes. Why are you asking me this? We don't have time for this."

"Because this morning I found Victor Del Rey dead, strangled in his bed. That's why."

For ten seconds she searched his eyes for some sign of deceit, but didn't find it. "That can't be. He was alive when we left there."

"You, Matos, and Bobby Player were the only people seen going into or coming from that room all night."

"I'm telling you he was alive. Why would we kill him anyway?"

"Because he was a former Cuban agent, someone who betrayed the Revolution. And you left there and then went and threw a bomb into Delta-5, against your old enemy Armando Capitán. You tell Bobby Player that you are here to help him find who killed his parents, but from what I'm told, your friend Mr. Matos may have killed them and possibly in the service of the Revolution."

Her eyes went big now with disbelief and anger. "You don't know what you're talking about. We are not here as agents for the Revolution. Far from it. We have waited too long to waste our time doing what you say."

"Waited since when?

"Since Carlos and Maria Player were killed."

"But why would you care? You weren't even born then."

"I was born. I was a very small baby, but I was alive. And I care because my friend Mr. Matos, as you call him, is my father. He was arrested and blamed for the killings. He spent thirty years in prison and I had to go almost all my life without seeing him. That is why I care after all these years."

Willie stared at her and deciphered the resemblance. She was taller and darker, but it was there in the thin lips, the cheekbones, and more than anything in the serious demeanor, those dark eyes. They were even more serious now.

"Do you have any idea what it is to be a five-year-old

girl and be told your father tortured a woman to death. That he shot her husband too and left a little boy an orphan, all for some money. And at the same time your mother is swearing to you it isn't true. The world becomes a very treacherous place, a place full of lying monsters who have stolen from you your father, your own flesh and blood. All you do is plot your revenge, and then one day you find out that your revenge can't even be taken in Cuba. You will have to come here to find it."

"So your father has convinced you too that he didn't do it and somebody here did."

"He didn't. He was at our home with me and my mother when those people were killed. My mother told me over and over, before she died of anger and sadness."

"Did your father know Carlos and Maria Player?"

"Yes, he knew them."

"How?"

But she didn't answer. Another group of people were approaching them, several men. Suddenly, he felt her hand on his cheek, turning his head toward her. Then her lips were next to his, her hand still holding the side of his face, blocking him and her from view. With her other hand, she pulled him toward her, so that she was pressed against him. She wasn't really kissing him, but Willie saw no reason to waste the moment. He moved his mouth to hers and took a taste.

The men passed. She waited several moments, then slowly pulled away from him, looked over her shoulder and watched the men recede. She gave Willie a look that wanted to be reproachful, but didn't quite make it.

"We don't have much time," she said. "I need you to do something for me. We're looking for a person."

"Who?"

"Someone who we think may be able to tell us who killed Roberto's parents and who sent my father to jail for so long. A woman who was in Cuba at the time. We understand she is here."

"Who's that?"

"Her name then was Olga Moreno. She was a dancer at Casino Cuba."

Willie couldn't keep his eyes from dancing with interest. She was speaking of Olga Tuzzi. Aurora noticed.

"You've heard of her?"

"I may have. What is it you want to ask her?"

"I can't tell you that, but I assure you she won't be harmed. I came to talk to her tonight, but I was told she was already gone. Do you know where we can find her?"

Willie wasn't about to put them onto Olga Tuzzi. Given what had happened to Del Rey, that might be signing her death warrant.

"I don't know where she is, but if I find out where can I reach you?"

"We will call you in the next day."

She got up then, cast one last glance over her shoulder at him, and then walked toward the parking lot. Somewhere there, Mr. Matos and maybe Roberto Player would be waiting for her, but Willie didn't want another gun-wielding run-in with Mr. Matos. Not right then. He watched her until she was out of sight, then he headed for the valet.

Chapter 25

Willie arrived at his brother's club a bit before three. Despite the hour and the bombing at Delta-5, the parking lot was still crowded, just like the New Casino Cuba. You could sit home and worry or you could dance your fears away, love your fears away, and the Cubans chose the latter.

On the other hand, two off-duty cops stood out front and they hadn't come to dance. Tommy wasn't taking any chances.

Willie handed his keys to Esteban, the valet, and went in. He said hello to Big Billy Blanco at the door.

"How is it, Billy?"

"A few people staying home, but we'll stay out of the poorhouse."

Willie went right to the bar and ordered a daiquiri, this one definitely his last of the night. Around the premises he spotted two more cops, these in plainclothes. The customers wouldn't notice it, but Willie could feel that extra tension. He was just putting his daiquiri to his lips when he saw Tommy cutting across the dance floor toward him.

"Where you been?"

"Checking out your competition at the New Casino Cuba."

"And?"

"And it's elaborate. It may steal some people away from you for a time, but when they lose enough money, most of them will stop going. And the crowd looks older, a nostalgia crowd."

"I'll survive the New Casino Cuba. That's not my worry

right now. My concern is thugs sending me dead fish and threatening to burn me down."

"You get any more calls or any more fish?"

Tommy shook his head. "No fish. Just that bomb going off at Delta-5. I know you've been talking to those guys, so I figure you're out there dead somewhere."

"I'm way alive, *hermano*."

"Does the Delta-5 thing have to do with the people who called here?"

"I don't know for sure."

"Well, on the radio today I heard there are problems between the Mafia and the Cubans. And in case you've forgotten, we're Cuban."

Willie frowned. "What radio show?"

"It was Cassandra."

They both glanced up at Cassandra Vasquez's table.

"I'll be back," Willie said and he crossed the floor. He climbed the stairs to her table just as she was saying good-bye to two elderly fans who had dropped in on her.

"Hello, Willie," she called to him with her habitual leer. "Here to dance with me again? I couldn't fall asleep that night I was so excited."

She laughed wickedly and Willie sat down next to her. "I don't have time to dance tonight, Cassandra. I'd like to know where you got your information about bad blood between the Cubans and the Italians?"

She smiled lazily. "I told you I don't reveal my sources."

Willie shot her a skeptical glance. "You don't? So I guess Armando Capitán just happened to drop in on me yesterday. You never mentioned me to him."

"I didn't announce your name on the radio. I figure you should be grateful, Willie. And anyway, why do you want to know all this?"

Willie shrugged. "I'm just curious."

"Just like last time."

"And just like last time, I have some information to offer. Some information of my own."

"And what is that?"

"I was on Cozy Costanza's gambling boat when some-body shot it up yesterday morning."

That impressed her. "Is that so?"

"Yes. I can describe for you what the gunmen looked like, how they were disguised. I can tell you what happened from start to finish."

So Willie did, recalling the beat-up old car, the leisure suits, and the wigs and masks. Cassandra's eyes shone like transistors, heating up with interest.

"What were you doing there when that all happened?"

"Just a coincidence."

She didn't believe him, but she let it go for the moment. "You couldn't see their faces?"

"No."

"Well, the same story applies to one who contacted me. He called anonymously, a man speaking Spanish holding a handkerchief over the phone."

Just like the voice that had menaced Tommy, Willie thought.

"And what did he say?"

"He told me about the attack on the gambling boat, which no one had reported, and why it had happened."

"Why was that?"

"He said Mafia people from here might be returning to Cuba and going back into the gambling business."

Willie was about to sip his daiquiri but stopped it near his lips. "That rumor has been around a long time, Cassandra."

"Yes, I know. But he said he had details about secret meetings. And then he told me about the gambling boat being shot up. No one knew that. I sent someone to look at it and confirmed it happened. The next day, Delta-5 goes bang." She shrugged. "Whether the Italians are going back to Cuba, I don't know, Willie, but something is going on there, *mi amor.*"

Willie thought about it. Over the past two days, both Armando Capitán and Cozy had denied any problems between their camps. So either they were lying or the person who had called was trying to create trouble.

"That same person called me back this evening," Cassandra said.

"Is that right?"

"He told me something even more interesting."

"What was that?"

"The name of the person who had thrown the firebomb into Delta-5 this morning. An old Cuban gangster named Miguel Angel Matos."

Willie nodded blankly. "Really?"

"Yes. I'm told he's working for the Italians. That he worked with them in Cuba. I'll be putting his name out on my show tomorrow. If he is here, he'll be found."

Willie could just see the Cuban community and the police closing in on Matos and Bobby Player and he could see them dying in a hail of bullets. Mando Capitán just might get the war he was dreaming of.

For a moment Willie considered telling Cassandra the story of Roberto Player, about his own conversation with Aurora Matos, throwing Bobby Player and his accomplices on her mercy. But he knew it would serve no purpose. Cassandra would never keep quiet. The bigger story would prevail.

"Will you call me if this anonymous person phones you again, Cassandra?"

"Will you tell me what you were doing at that boat yesterday?"

Willie said nothing. Cassandra patted his cheek. "Be careful, Willie. We wouldn't want anything to happen to a good-looking boy like you."

Willie went back to the owner's table and sat next to Tommy.

"So what did Cassandra say?"

"She said she got an anonymous tip, maybe the same guy who called you."

Tommy said nothing. He didn't have to. Willie knew what he was thinking. That out of all the Cuban businesses in Miami, it was his club getting hassled, maybe by Italian gangsters, and the only reason was that his brother Willie was sticking his nose where he shouldn't.

That didn't make Tommy happy, but he didn't say it. He was being merciful.

"We made it through the night, so why don't you go home to your wife and kids," Willie said. "I'll lock up, make sure everything is all right."

Tommy took him up on the offer and cleared out. Willie sat nursing his daiquiri, listening to Chico Ruiz and his orchestra wind up their last set.

Chico was a Cuban who had built a raft several years earlier with the idea of leaving the island. Desperate, he had set off alone. All he packed with him was some water, lots of crackers to settle his stomach, and his trumpet, which he tied around his neck. After three days at sea, he figured he was lost, that the Gulf stream had taken a wrong turn and he had missed Florida altogether.

This happened to very unlucky rafters. Sometimes, ships hundreds of miles north of Miami would find empty inner tubes with empty water bottles and other pitiful belongings tied to them. The rafters, lost at sea, had run out of fresh water, drunk sea water, gone crazy, and disappeared under the waves. Or maybe they thought they'd seen the shore and had swum for it when there was no shore for miles and miles.

Chico Ruiz, alone on his raft, had been convinced that he would never see land again. That night, to soothe his fears, he had taken up his trumpet and played the graceful, solemn, plangent *Concierto de Aranjuez,* as a paean to his art and to his lonely end.

But the winds that night had wafted the music to the east and to a pleasure boat just over the horizon. Intrigued, those sailors had traced the music, as if they were following the sounds of mythical sirens, and found Chico just at daybreak, his lips cracking with thirst. He'd been on the verge of never playing again.

Now he headed a ten-piece orchestra. Chico Ruiz *y Los Siete Vientos*—the Seven Winds—it was called, despite the numbers. Cubans from all over came to hear Chico and Willie knew as long as Tommy employed him, business would be good.

Willie listened until the set ended and the musicians

packed up. CD music came on, but during the next half hour the place emptied out, couples clinging to each other as they swept out the door. The bar cashiers filled out their cash-drawer reports inside the office, Willie signed off on them and locked the proceeds in the safe. Meanwhile, waiters slapped fresh white cloths on the tables. The bartenders replenished the liquor from the secure liquor closet, which Willie opened for them and later locked again. Barbacks did the sweeping of the dance floor and the seating area. By 4:45 A.M. they had the club ready for the next night. Everybody bolted and Willie sent the security team home too. Big Billy Blanco was the last to split.

"*Mañana*, Willie."

"*Mañana.*"

Willie was left alone at the owner's table with a Tito Puente CD playing softly in the background. He finally drained his last daiquiri and walked around turning off lights and securing doors. He had to look in every nook and cranny of the place because every once in a while a person with a few too many in him decided he wanted to spend the night. Under the amphitheatre seating were tucked storage areas and more closets. Willie checked them all. Next to one such area he found a fire door open. Somebody had probably gone out that way and it hadn't swung shut. Willie peered outside, saw no one, and then pulled it closed.

He kept going, hitting the bathrooms. The stalls might hold someone who had dozed off. This night they didn't, but as he was coming out of the ladies powder room he thought he heard a noise in the club. He stood on the edge of the dance floor.

"Anybody there?"

He listened but no answer came and no other noise. Ghosts of dancers past.

He climbed up on stage and doused the klieg lights, leaving lit one small spot, which put out just enough light to allow someone to find the back door and get out. He was coming back through the curtain, when he thought he saw something move at the back of the club. He was standing next to a life-size cutout of a Tropicana dance girl that was propped on the edge of the stage. He squinted into the darkness and could see those bright white tablecloths faintly, but not much else.

"Anybody? Who's there?"

He waited, but again he got no answer. He turned to the cardboard showgirl.

"Nobody but us, *amiga*."

But not for long. As he stepped away toward the stairs, shots broke out. A burst of automatic-weapon fire shattered the silence, ripped the cardboard showgirl in half, knocked down a microphone stand just in front of Willie, thudded into the curtain behind him, and sent him sprawling behind a very large black speaker. He pressed himself against it, Tito Puente's tymbal music still playing softly.

Willie pulled his spare .38 from the small of his back, peeked around the edge of the speaker, and saw two bodies moving through the darkness toward the stage. He pulled off a shot, which sent them flying for cover. But they were working in harmony, heading for either side of the stage.

Willie looked up, took aim, and with his second shot busted the lone spotlight shining on the stage. His pursuers answered with a chorus of their own shots, but Willie rolled away from the speaker and under the curtain. He crawled to one side until he knew he was in the wings, jumped up and pressed himself into a corner. They couldn't get behind him there, but he looked around and realized that spot presented no door to run through. If he stayed where he was, eventually they would pin him in.

Willie heard one of them call to the other in a deep voice and then the sound of them running across the dance floor. They were closing in. With a solid wall behind him, the only possible way to go was to return the way he had come, cross the stage, and jump into the orchestra pit. They might not see him because of the dark, but the fall would be at least ten feet. They would hear him landing and drop him in seconds before he could get anywhere.

Then Willie's eyes fell on the sound system, tucked into the same corner as he, its small red lights shining in the darkness. Tito Puente was still jamming, just breaking into a solo full of rhythmic drum rolls spiked with rim shots. Willie peeked through the curtain. He couldn't see or hear his two pursuers. He couldn't see anything.

He waited for Tito to break into another solo. Then it came, a particularly wild riff including a rattle, two sharp raps, and then another long barrage of drumming. Willie suddenly raised the volume all the way. The sound filled the club. Tito's stick work sounded like gunfire, and Willie hoped it would send them ducking. He broke through the curtain, taking two long running strides on his toes like a male ballet dancer, just as Tito brought his sticks down hard. Willie launched himself into the pit. A blare of trumpets accompanied him, as if he were leaping into eternity.

Willie hit the wooden floor, rolled, and rose in a crouch. Tito unloosed another barrage and Willie used it to move to the very front of the pit. He ducked down there and waited, but no shots came. The music then shifted into a less raucous piano solo with a samba beat, and a vocalist was singing, something about the primacy of love, of all things.

But it was still loud enough to cover Willie's movements and he still had to move. He looked over the edge of the pit, but didn't see the two men. He timed his move with another loud lick, got out onto the dance floor, still in a crouch, and ran for the bar.

But he miscalculated where it was. Willie ran full tilt into a bar stool, knocked it over with a clatter, and drew shots that sent him scrambling behind the bar. He could feel footsteps approaching through the wooden floor. He quickly groped the wall behind the bar for the light switch, found it, crouched down as much as he could, and then flicked it.

The light spilled out onto the dance floor and illuminated a single man standing alone just twenty feet away. He wore

a red leisure suit and the same rubber hangdog mask and
Panama hat Willie had spied the day the *Treasure Coast* was
shot up. The face turned suddenly and the goon raised his
gun and fired. Willie hit the floor at the very end of the bar
and pulled off a shot. He heard the goon scream over the
music and then he saw the man go down holding his leg.

A spray of bullets from the second gunman riddled
the bar and sent Willie hugging the floor again. He
stayed there, heard nothing, and then crawled out from
behind the bar enough to see the dance floor. He found
the wounded man hopping toward a back door, which
was now open, meaning his accomplice had probably
already escaped through it.

Willie yelled to him to stop, but the wounded man, who
seemed to be dancing a solo hip-hop, kept going and disappeared behind a bank of seats. Willie got up and ran
toward the door. The injured man disappeared through it.
Moments later Willie heard a shot and then the sound of a
car peeling out.

Willie approached the back door, gun in hand, and
peered around the door frame. In the street, maybe thirty
feet away, he saw the body of the man in the red leisure
suit flat on its back. It wasn't moving.

Willie advanced carefully, looking into the darkness of
the parking lot and down the abandoned street. He eased
his way up to it and stared down at that rubber mask. A
round bullet hole had appeared in its rubber forehead.
The guy behind the mask, whoever it was, was definitely
dead. It hadn't been one of Willie's shots that had made
that neat a hole. The dead man had been dispatched by the
other shooter, his partner. The corpse would be one of the
two gunmen who had attacked the *Treasure Coast* and
used him and Rico Tuzzi for target practice. It had to be,
Willie told himself, even as he knelt down, peeled back
the mask, and found himself staring into the face of Rico
Tuzzi.

Chapter 26

It was seven a.m. when Willie finally got home. He had called the police from the club and several waves of them had arrived—patrol, crime-scene techs, and finally a young homicide detective named Johns who was working the lousy weekend third shift, had heard of Willie, and was deferential.

Willie told him a version of the truth. He had found two guys on the premises after he closed up and assumed they were there to do no good. They had fired at him, he had fired back, but he had not killed the man outside. He told Johns that he might have seen Tuzzi before, maybe in the club, but he wasn't sure. Johns asked him if he thought the "attempted robbery" of his club might have anything to do with other crimes in the neighborhood that night. Willie said he didn't know what Johns was talking about. He handed over his gun for testing and said he would be at the police's disposal after he went home and got some rest. Then he got out of there quickly before somebody more experienced, like Compton, showed up.

On the way home, Willie flipped on the radio news and learned exactly what Johns meant by other crimes in the area. Two other venues had been attacked in Little Havana overnight—the offices of a small newspaper had been raked with automatic weapons fire and a Molotov cocktail had landed at the doorway of another Cuban patriotic organization.

Willie knew all these incidents were connected—the firebombing of Delta-5, the shooting up of the *Treasure Coast,* the deaths of Carlos and Maria Player, and their son's search for their killers. Add to that the attack at the club, Rico Tuzzi as roadkill, and the other overnight events. They were all linked. Willie was sure of that.

He climbed the stairs to his apartment as the sun was rising and found a message on his answering machine. It came from Olga Tuzzi, recorded at three a.m., about two hours after he'd spoken to her at New Casino Cuba. Apparently she needed to talk to him as much as he wanted to speak to her.

"Mr. Cuesta. I remembered something that maybe it will help you. You call me please."

It was still too early to use the number she had given him. He would track her down later. Right now he had more urgent matters to attend to—he needed to get some sleep.

He did, about two hours' worth. Then he dragged himself out of bed, shaved, showered, and dressed, putting on an aquamarine guayabera, white linen pants, and sandals.

It was past 9:30 A.M. when he hit the street again and right away he felt the effects of the past two days. Word had spread about the attacks the night before. Instead of humming with the usual morning business, Calle Ocho lay quiet. A few cars were parked on the street, but many meters were empty. Across the way, Tomas Mesa had the door of his furniture store closed, but white-haired Mesa himself sat sentry out in front, propped in a cane-backed rocker, a pistol in his lap. He gave Willie a curt wave.

Next to Mesa's store was the Segura family's pawn shop. Through the window Willie spotted Segura, who also waved. Behind him Willie saw what appeared to be a shotgun leaning against the counter.

Willie strolled up the block. About the only business person with his door open was Terán the Santeria priest, on the far corner. Terán stood out in front of his office studying the street. He was an elderly black Cuban, bald on top, with a gaze so intense it seemed he had thought so hard his hair had fallen out. He always wore African dashikis in brilliant colors, tapping into the African roots of the Santeria religion.

He gazed on Willie with his deep-set muddy eyes.

"Things aren't good with you, detective."

"Things aren't good with anybody right now, *santero*."

"That's true. The saints aren't happy."

"Is that bad for your business?"

Terán shook his bald head. "My business is fine. Many people are calling me to do readings over the phone. It is a special service we offer in times of danger, when it is not safe to leave home. We do many of them during hurricanes. They put it on their credit cards. I'm also being called out to do many *limpias*."

Limpias were spiritual cleansings performed by passing holy stones, beans, flowers, or special branches all over the body to draw out evil spirits.

"People are worried about these violent spirits around us. The saints are worried about that too."

Terán was a hustler for sure, but a hustler who Willie had come to realize also did his clients some good. He was a cheap psychiatrist in a neighborhood where most people couldn't afford real shrinks. He was also plugged into everything that happened in the barrio.

"You look like you need a *limpia*," he said.

Willie had never been a believer. Terán knew that. But this time Willie had to think about it.

"Maybe you're right. I went to talk to some people yesterday and the place I went blew up. Then I decided to visit a man and when I got there he was dead. Then last night someone tried to shoot me."

Terán looked at him professionally now, checking Willie for telltale signs of possession by evil demons. Willie knew he had all the symptoms—black-rimmed eyes and a tremor, both from lack of sleep. He also had a history of involvement with the wrong types of people, even if it was to pay the bills.

"I can work you over with the special herbs, but it won't do any good if you don't believe," Terán said

"Well, if anything else happens, I'll probably start believing, *santero*. I'll see you later. Right now I have more people to talk to."

Willie got in his car and cruised west through Little Havana. As on his block, the streets were much emptier than usual. He spotted more sentries, like Mesa and Segura, guarding their turf. Supermarkets were super busy, people swarming them to buy food. As in the hurricane season, residents figured they might have to hole up for a few days. But this was a different kind of hurricane.

Willie drove out Calle Ocho, out of Little Havana, and through West Miami until the houses and strip malls gave way altogether and he neared the Everglades again. He passed the entrance to the New Casino Cuba, turned south and looked for the dirt road that led to the Delta-5 training camp. During his years in Police Intelligence, Willie had visited the camp often, keeping an eye on Mando Capitán and his troops.

Now he slowed as he saw cars parked on either side of the overgrown entrance. Two men in camouflage uniforms stepped from the bushes, each gripping an automatic weapon in his hands. The soldiers may have been make-believe, but the weapons weren't. Willie recognized one of the soldiers, a guy with a trimmed white beard. He was an old sidekick of Mando's. He sidled up to the driver's window wearing a snide smile.

"You finally come to sign up?"

"Maybe. I need to see Mando."

The soldier unhooked a walkie-talkie from his combat belt and drifted a distance from the car. A minute later he came back.

"The *comandante* says you can see him, but you have to leave your vehicle here."

Willie parked and walked up the dirt track. He walked slowly because on either side were posted more sentries with weapons. These commandos had waited decades to shoot somebody and he didn't want to make them nervous.

Beyond them on either side of the road, hidden by the vegetation, were constructed Delta-5's obstacle courses, trenches, and shooting ranges. In the past, Willie had watched mostly old men, and some women, clambering over and through those obstacles, spirited, breathless, and none too menacing.

Willie saw now that Mando had won new recruits. He

stopped and watched as a platoon of young men in camouflage, lying on their stomachs, took target practice with
their Ak-47s. The sound of it ripped through the swamp.
Willie kept going.

Mando's headquarters occupied a clearing about 100
feet wide carved out of the vegetation. It contained a large
field tent and a wooden tower about three stories high,
which looked like a guard tower in a prison. When the
commandos had first built it, you could see out to the
road. But over the years the surrounding vegetation had
grown and the armed guard in it couldn't see anywhere
but down at Willie.

Mando waited for Willie outside the command tent. He
wore full uniform, accessoried by his pearl-handled gun
on his hip and the matching ascot at his throat.

"Spying again, Willie, or reporting for duty?"

"Coming to see the enemy face to face, Mando, so I
don't get ambushed or shot in the back."

Mando's eyes narrowed. "As usual, I don't know what
you're talking about, Willie."

"No? I thought it had to be you who shot at me at the
port the other day, Mando, then shot up my brother's club
last night. I mean, the shots missed, so I figured it was you
or at least some of your Delta-5 commandos."

Normally, Mando would have flipped into a rage at
Willie's insults, but today he was playing it cool.

"I don't know what you mean by these comments, but
they don't matter, Willie." He pointed at his recruits traversing the obstacle course. "That is what means something. That our battle goes on and that we will find our
enemies and destroy them. There are too many real enemies around now for me to waste my time on you."

Willie glanced at the recruits. "And the day they get
wounded, you'll shoot them dead, the way you did Rico
Tuzzi. I wonder if they know that?"

The *comandante* frowned now with annoyance. "As I
said, I don't know what you're talking about."

"Rico Tuzzi is dead, shot to death last night."

Mando shrugged. "That does not surprise me. He was a gangster. They often die that way."

"You two were on the same side back in Cuba all those years ago. They say the Mafia used to even provide money for the underground. Was it Tuzzi who acted as bagman between your organization and Cozy Costanza?"

"What difference can that make now?"

"And you both came to believe that Carlos and Maria Player had turned traitors to the underground, didn't you?"

Mando's eyes narrowed to bayonets. "You don't want to ask these questions, Willie. This is not a box you want to open after all these years."

"Why not?"

"Because it will do no good. You'll never learn what you need to learn and you may only cause pain and trouble."

"Pain and trouble for who, Mando? For you?"

Mando shook his head. "For the person you're trying to help."

"For Roberto Player?"

"Yes. He has already suffered enough and knowing more will only make him suffer more."

"What does that mean? Does it mean his parents were executed by the underground for being communists?"

Mando didn't answer.

"And why do you say I'll never learn everything I need to learn?"

Even now the phrase reminded him of what the late Rico Tuzzi had said: that the Players had been mixed up in something about which he would never know.

Again Mando didn't answer. Instead, he swiveled and stalked into his tent. Willie followed. The command center was equipped with a cot, a table with a radio on it, and a map marked with red Xs. It was an ordinary street map of Miami like one you might buy in a gas station.

"Planning an offensive, Mando?"

"You are still a neutral and it's none of your business."

Mando stood over his map. He was in his glory now.

Willie came up next to him. "Maybe I'm not as much a

neutral as you think. I spoke to an old friend of yours last night."

"Oh yes?"

"I spoke to your CIA contact in Havana in the old days."

The old man turned suspicious. "Oh yes? Who was that?"

"Mr. James Clancy."

Willie's knowledge surprised Mando. "He told you he was our contact."

"That's right. And he told me he also served as contact with the Players."

"So he told you about Operation Espresso."

Willie's brows danced. "Not exactly. What was Operation Espresso?"

Mando became impatient. "Don't play with me, Willie. I told you I have no time."

"What is Operation Espresso? Did it involve Carlos and Maria Player?"

Mando shook his head. "If Clancy didn't tell you, then it's none of your business."

Willie didn't like his tone. "Okay, then let's talk about something that is my business. Let's discuss the fact that you suspected that Carlos and Maria Player were traitors, government agents, infiltrators in the underground. That you were involved in killing them and stealing the money they held. That maybe that bomb that went off at your headquarters is tied to those murders and not to Cuban government infiltration, as you claim. And that maybe you know that and are just trying to cover your tracks, *comandante*. You're hunting Mr. Matos because he knows what really happened to the Players."

Mando didn't react with his usual bombast. His eyes were steady, cold-blooded.

"In those days, traitors were executed, just as they are today, Willie. Be careful."

"Why do you think they were traitors? What did they do?"

"Ask your friend Mr. Matos, who is here working for

the communists. But you better not be with him when we find him because you'll be as dead as he is."

He threw open the flap of the tent and led Willie out. Willie marched back down the road without a word, feeling Mando's gaze pegged to his back.

Chapter 27

Willie drove back down the road until he found a pay phone, fished out Clancy's number, and dialed.

The old spy answered after several rings.

"Mr. Clancy?"

"Yes."

"This is Willie Cuesta."

"What can I do for you today?" His tone was icy. He hadn't enjoyed his conversation with Willie the night before.

"You can tell me about Operation Espresso."

Clancy hesitated. "Operation Espresso?"

"Yes. The one that involved Carlos and Maria Player. That Operation Espresso."

This time the other man fell into silence.

"Well?"

When he spoke it was with a voice that was tired, resigned.

"Where are you?"

Willie told him.

"Why don't you come here to my home? You're not far away. I'll be waiting for you." He gave Willie the address and hung up.

It took Willie twenty minutes to get there. The place lay a bit south and west of where he was. To get to it he had to pass through lime and orange orchards and tomato and strawberry fields where, on weekends, people picked their own basketfuls. The air was full of late spring heat.

He found Clancy's spread on a dirt side road. It was surrounded by a white brick wall and a tall, black, wrought-iron gate. Willie sounded his horn and seconds later a young

Hispanic man wearing a camouflage shirt emerged, apparently the gardener who doubled as a sentry. He checked Willie out carefully, then opened the gate.

Willie drove up the crescent driveway to Clancy's house. It was a medium-size plantation-style manse, white with green shutters, two floors, and large royal palms planted on all sides. Very tasteful.

Clancy was waiting for him on the porch outside the front door, like another tall palm. He was wearing a white guayabera and khaki pants. His usual sunniness had disappeared. He looked weary. In his eyes floated the same troubled look with which he had left the New Casino Cuba the night before.

He led Willie into the house. It was sunny, airy, with floors of red oak and wooden beams above, potted palms and paintings of the Glades. Clancy walked Willie into a book-lined library. Hanging just inside the library door as one entered was an old black-and-white photo of the streets of Havana during a parade of some kind. Clearly visible in the front row was a very young James Clancy.

Clancy sat down in one large easy chair, offering Willie another. Between them was a table with a coffee pot and he poured them each a cup. Then he got down to business.

"So you've stumbled on to Operation Espresso."

"Yes."

"What else have you uncovered since we spoke last night?"

"I uncovered that Rico Tuzzi is dead."

Clancy's sparse eyebrows went up, but he said nothing. Willie described the scene of the night before.

"You did know Tuzzi, didn't you?" Willie asked.

Clancy nodded solemnly. "As a matter of fact I did."

"Since the underground in Cuba."

"That's right."

"I guess it's like they say. War makes strange bedfellows."

"Yes, it surprised me as well at the time. Who would have expected that Mr. Tuzzi's organization would join forces with my own? But the fact is we had mutual interests."

"What could those have been?"

"Opposing the new regime in Cuba. Mr. Tuzzi's people and mine shared a desire to alter the course of Cuban history in a way we considered would be beneficial for its people. That was a moment when patriotism came from unexpected parties."

"Was it the patriotic Mr. Tuzzi who introduced you to Carlos Player?"

"Yes, as matter of fact it was. He was acting at the behest of his boss, Mr. Costanza. And it seemed at the time the perfect union because of what we had planned."

Willie sipped his coffee. "Just what was that?"

Clancy opened a humidor that was next to the coffee pot. Willie shook his head and Clancy clipped and lighted his own cigar. When he had created the requisite curtain of blue smoke, he answered Willie's question. "What we had planned, Mr. Cuesta, was Operation Espresso."

"And just what was Operation Espresso?"

"It was a strategy that existed back then under various names. Essentially it was a plan to eliminate members of the new Cuban leadership."

"You mean like sending Fidel Castro exploding cigars?"

Clancy nodded. "Yes, that was one of the more far-fetched plans. In this case, the idea was to poison them, and it was much more possible and realistic."

Willie hesitated, his coffee cup near his lips. "Was it?"

"Yes. And Carlos and Maria Player were recruited back then specifically for that purpose."

"Why?"

"Because in the earliest days of the new regime, top members of the government would sometimes go to the Casino Cuba restaurant to eat and to drink coffee. Even Castro himself showed up more than once. Carlos and Maria Player attended them personally when they showed up. They agreed to do the deed when the opportunity arose."

"So that's what Tuzzi meant when he said they were up to their necks in something big."

"Yes."

"So what happened?"

"The scheme never came off."

"Why?"

"Because Carlos Player and his wife were murdered."

Willie frowned. "Which means the plot was dis-covered?"

"Exactly. If it had worked, the history of Cuba over the last thirty-five years would have been quite different. We would never have had to leave, any of us."

"But it was discovered."

"Yes."

"How?"

"As I told you before, we never found out. We were forced to cut off contact with the Players and all our other operatives because we were being surveilled around the clock. We were trapped in the embassy or in our homes. Phones were suddenly out of order or tapped, including the Players' telephone. Our agents were on their own. Then the Players showed up dead."

Willie squinted at him through the smoke. "So how come nobody knows until now that the Players were mixed up in this?"

Clancy shook his head. "You hardly ever talk in public about assassination plots, Mr. Cuesta. And you certainly don't make them public if they fail. There has always been some journalistic speculation about such intrigues and Congress has heard testimony on other attempts, but none of us has ever volunteered information about this particular operation. You might say we adopted the policy of Mr. Tuzzi and Mr. Costanza's organization—*omerta*—complete silence."

"You did a good job. No one wants to talk about it even now."

"Exactly."

"Is that because maybe Carlos and Maria Player were killed by their own co-conspirators and nobody wants that known? After all, it's better for people to think that they were martyred by the communists."

Clancy fixed on him through the smoke. "I was up half the night thinking about what we spoke about at the club."

"And is it possible?"

Clancy hesitated and then finally nodded, as if he had been trying to keep from answering the question to himself all his life.

"Yes."

"Who could it have been? Armando Capitán?"

Clancy frowned, but said nothing.

"What was Mando's role in Operation Espresso?"

"He had no direct role. But as it was falling apart, he had to be told. People in his own cell were being detained. He was informed by other underground members so he could save his own skin. That was two days before the Players died."

"Plenty of time to kill them."

Clancy's expression turned hard. "But we don't know that he did."

"What are the other possibilities? How about the Italians? Tuzzi and Costanza knew. They both told me as much."

Clancy nodded. "Yes, they knew."

"And Sam Suarez was privy to that information too. I'll bet on it. Anyone else?"

"Yes. The other is this man who has arrived by boat. This man Matos."

Willie's eyes flared in interest. "How would Matos know anything about it?"

Clancy drew on his cigar and exhaled. "Because thirty-six years ago, Miguel Angel Matos was part of Operation Espresso."

Willie frowned. "The guy is a gangster."

"In a manner of speaking, yes. But in Cuba, gangsters were sometimes a part of political life. Different factions cut deals with street toughs, used them as muscle or as guns, and paid them for protection. It was part of the political tradition. Matos came from Old Havana, a tough neighborhood near the docks, and he had political connections in those rough quarters. He and his friends were also people used to their independence, so they didn't cotton to a communist revolution. When it came, some joined factions of the underground."

"And the underground cell he worked with was mixed up in Operation Espresso."

"Yes. In fact, it was Mr. Matos's job to hide whoever had to be hidden and help smuggle them out of the country through the port. He had contacts with foreign ship captains who he had bought contraband from and they were willing to help him."

"He never had a chance to do it."

"No, he didn't. The plan fell apart. In the end, he was the only person involved directly in Operation Espresso who was arrested."

"Charged with the killings of Carlos and Maria Player."

"Yes."

"Do you think he killed them?"

Clancy shook his head slowly. "I don't know. He had the same reasons other people did."

"Because he suspected that they had betrayed the plot and possibly because he wanted their money. After all he was a common criminal."

"That's true, although I believe he was truly committed to the underground. His arrest for the murder of Carlos and Maria was made public the very day the embassy was closed and we all left Cuba. We heard about it here in the States days later. Of course, a lot of people didn't believe Matos was guilty. They thought the government was just covering its tracks by blaming a thug. Those of us who were involved in Operation Espresso knew a connection really did exist between Matos and the Players. And when I found out later that certain people had doubts about the Players' patriotism, I knew that Matos had a motive to kill them."

"But so did other people."

"Yes."

"And if it was someone else who killed them, then Matos may well be here to find who really killed the Players and who sent him to jail for thirty years. Maybe he *is* doing exactly what he has told Bobby Player."

Clancy nodded. "And to make sure they pay. A man like Mr. Matos has a very long memory."

Willie thought back to his last meeting with Matos on that dark street in Little Havana. " 'This is personal business,' " he had said.

Willie studied Clancy. "It means he could come after you."

Clancy shrugged. "I'm not sure. We never met directly. He may or may not know who I am."

"Maybe you should take some precautions."

Clancy lifted the edge of his guayabera to reveal a 9mm Browning stuck in his belt. He wasn't happy about having to carry it. The glad-handing diplomat of their first meeting had disappeared. The pigeons—and ghosts—of his old CIA days were coming home to roost and it wasn't pretty. Just as he himself had said, conspiracies were treacherous even to those involved. Maybe one of his own would come after him, just as someone had turned on Carlos and Maria Player.

Clancy seemed to read Willie's mind. "You have to understand the tremendous pressures everyone was under at that moment," he said gazing into the past. "Hunted by security agents, fearing infiltration at every turn, feeling they had been betrayed. No contact with anyone who could help them. Trapped on an island. They were doomed."

The ensuing silence was broken by the sound of Willie's pager. He borrowed Clancy's phone and dialed the number. Ellie Hernandez was on the other end. She sounded frantic.

"Sam Suarez just found out where Bobby is hiding. Mike called to tell me. They're going with some security people. I'm afraid something will happen."

"Where is it?"

"An apartment right on the beach that the bank keeps for visitors." She gave the address. "Please try and get there. I'm afraid."

He told her he would go as quickly as he could and signed off. He stood up.

"They've found Matos and Roberto Player."

"Are they alive?"

"So far. I'm heading there."

Clancy escorted him outside where they shook hands. Clancy held on a moment.

"The times get more and more interesting, don't they? Be more and more careful, Mr. Cuesta."

Chapter 28

Willie did what he'd promised Ellie Hernandez, speeding on the Dolphin Expressway, cutting off a semi to catch the interstate north, crossing Biscayne Bay to the beach, running a red light, careening into valet parking outside a complex called Atlantic Palms on Collins. He crossed the lobby, jumped into an open elevator, and headed to apartment 309.

But he was still too late.

From the elevator he heard the first exchange of fire. Two shots, then several more. When the door slid open on the third floor he waited and then peeped out with one eye. In the hallway he saw Mike and Sam Suarez pressed against a wall. A man he didn't recognize lay in the hall holding his arm, a pistol near him on the floor.

Retreating down the hallway were Bobby Player and Aurora. Matos was shielding them, backing away, holding a gun in his left hand, covering their escape. With his other hand he held his own shoulder.

Willie stepped out of the elevator. When Matos saw Willie, the gun came up. Willie had no gun. He threw himself to the floor and saw Sam and Mike Suarez do the same. Matos didn't fire. Instead, he, Bobby, and Aurora ducked down a staircase and disappeared.

Willie got up and ran the length of the long hallway. The Suarezes were already seeing to the injured man. Willie passed them and headed for the staircase. He looked over the concrete stairwell and then started down slowly.

At the lobby level, he stuck his head out again momentarily, but saw no one. When he reached the parking garage, he heard car doors slamming. He stepped into the garage just in time to see Bobby Player's black Mercedes come tearing toward him, Bobby at the wheel. Bobby brought the car right at him, taking aim for the palm tree pattern on his shirt, and Willie had to duck behind a parked car.

He got up and watched Player drive right through and shatter a wooden cross bar and bounce over a speed bump. Then they were gone.

Willie climbed back up the service stairs. By the time he got there, building security guards were on the scene. Two of them were tending to the man on the ground, who Willie assumed was Sam Suarez's security agent.

He found Sam and Mike Suarez inside apartment 309. They were staring down at blood on the beige carpeting. It trailed out of the apartment down the hallway. Near the door stood the suitcases he had seen Matos and Aurora bring off the *Wayward Wind* three nights before. He turned to Mike Suarez.

"What happened?"

"My father found out they were staying here."

"How?"

"We had a client coming in who wanted to use the place and we called the maid service to make sure it was ready. But when the maid got here, she heard people inside. She called and my father figured it had to be Bobby. He had keys to the place."

"Then what?"

"The security man knocked on the door and we told them who we were. The next thing we knew they start shooting."

"They, or was it just Matos?"

"I don't know who it was. The door opened and then there were shots. Then you came."

Willie went and looked at a shattered sliding glass door overlooking the sea. It was close enough so they could hear the waves, mixed with the sound of sirens approaching in the distance. Bullet holes had also perforated the wall of the hallway. The firing had gone in both directions. The question was who had tried to gun down whom. Did

Sam Suarez prefer to have Matos and Roberto Player
dead? Willie went up to him.

"Why didn't you call the police when you found out
they were here?"

The elder Suarez said nothing. Mike Suarez answered
for him. "We wanted to try to talk to him, to get him away
from those people."

"Well, the police are going to be involved big time
now, *senores*. What are you going to tell them?"

Sam Suarez scowled. "I'm going to tell them he's helping an enemy of the Cuban people and they should hunt
him down."

He turned abruptly and went into the hall. His security
man was already being put on a stretcher by emergency
personnel.

Willie didn't have time to ask Sam Suarez more questions, although he had a few. The police were arriving and
again Willie didn't want to speak with them just yet. He
told Mike Suarez he would be in touch and then ducked
down the back stairs.

He got in his car, stopped down the street, and watched
as more patrol cars converged on the Atlantic Palms.
Willie decided to go see Olga Tuzzi. The address she had
given him was not far away.

Willie found the small building on the ocean side of
Collins about ten blocks north of the Atlantic Palms. It
was a narrow, two-story, pink place with exterior walk-
ways. Buildings like it had always been inhabited by old
people. That was before the beach had hit it big again and
the elderly drifted off to quieter, cheaper digs farther
north. That or they simply died off and went to that big
beach in the sky.

Willie parked on the side street where there were no
other cars. The only sound that reached him was the whisper of the surf. He took the stairs to the second floor, to
the end of the building closest to the sea, and found apartment 14. Willie pressed the bell and it sounded inside
emptily. He rang it again, but there was no reply. Maybe
Olga Tuzzi had gone to the beach.

Willie stepped to the head of the rear stairs that over-looked the ocean. Behind the building was a parking lot. A few cars sat there, including an older green Cadillac he had seen parked near the *Treasure Coast* the first time he had been there. Willie went down the stairs and found the car empty. He put his hand on the hood. It was cold.

He looked out over the sand. About halfway across the beach he saw several old wooden chaise lounges. All but one of them were empty. In that occupied chaise lounge sat Olga Tuzzi in her trademark toque—this one blue—and a white bathing suit. She was staring at the sea. You couldn't blame her for staring. The water was four or five different gorgeous shades of green and blue as it spread to the horizon.

Willie slogged through the sand and came up next to her. Even then she didn't glance away from the sea. Willie knew why. He knew the moment he looked down at her. Olga Tuzzi would never see anything more beautiful than what she was staring at right then. She was dead.

He looked up and down the beach and noticed a couple of old people strolling, but that was it. No one suspicious. He crouched next to Olga. The dead woman's cheeks were rouged as always, but underneath the skin was turning gray, bloodless. The eyes were open but no longer alive with seduction. He touched her and found she wasn't cold yet. She hadn't been dead long.

He tilted her chin to one side and her head fell lifelessly against the chaise. Right in the back of her skull was a bullet wound. The hair around it was scorched. She had been shot at point-blank range.

Willie quickly checked the pockets of the robe lying next to her but found nothing of importance. After that he didn't stay around. He gave her one last look. He hadn't known the old chorus girl well, but he had liked Olga Tuzzi. It made him feel bad that she was dead. Real bad. She sat staring vaguely in the direction of Cuba, scene of her early success. He hoped that when the bullet hit her she still had the sound of applause in her head from her latest success the night before.

He reached down and closed her eyes. Then he walked

back to his car, drove a few blocks, stopped at a pay
phone, and again dialed 911. He fed the female operator
the exact location of Olga Tuzzi's body, said she'd been
shot to death, not by him, and then hung up before she
could ask any questions.

Then he headed home as fast as the LeBaron could
carry him. Three people dead in two days, all of them
people he had talked to just hours before they died. It was
time to lay low before he talked to somebody else and got
them killed.

Chapter 29

Willie parked the car, took the stairs two at a time, opened the door to his apartment, and looked right into the barrel of Miguel Angel Matos's gun.

"Caramba!"

Matos was slumped on the couch. Next to him sat his daughter holding a bloody towel to his bare shoulder. Bobby Player was just coming out of the bathroom with another towel. They all stared at Willie. Matos wagged his gun and Bobby came over, closed the door, and frisked Willie. This time he had no gun to take.

"Well, it certainly didn't take you folks long to get here," Willie said.

He looked across to the back door and saw a pane of glass had been broken.

"You could have waited for me. I would have let you in."

"My father is hurt," Aurora said.

"Wait a moment and I'll get something."

He went into the bathroom with Bobby following him, gun in hand, and came back with first-aid supplies. He laid them on the coffee table next to the couch. He went to the kitchen, boiled water, and brought it back in a pan. He also brought back a bottle of rum and glasses and poured a healthy shot for the wounded man and for everyone else, especially himself. He turned on the ceiling fan and sat down across from them.

"That's a bad cut."

"It's just a scratch in the muscle of the shoulder," Matos said. "I've been scratched before."

For the next few minutes Willie watched Aurora tend to him.

"Maybe this would be a good time to tell me what is going on," he said finally. "Especially since the entire city is going to be looking for you now."

A siren sounded outside. All four of them froze until it faded into the distance. Matos looked back at Willie.

"We are here to take care of an old account," he said.

"You mean the killing of Roberto's parents."

"In part."

"And the fact that you went to jail for it."

Matos met his gaze. "The fact that I unjustly went to jail for it."

"You're saying you didn't kill them?"

"That is precisely what I'm saying."

Willie glanced at Bobby Player, who was sitting like a devoted student listening to a teacher. Here was a man who might answer the key question he'd had all his life—who had killed his parents. Matos was like a philosopher, a gangster philosopher, who had found the answer to the riddle of life and death, and he had Bobby Player's undivided attention. But there was still a question: Was the guru telling the truth?

"I know you've convinced Bobby of that," Willie said. "But why should I believe it?"

"Because it is true."

"Are you saying you didn't know them? That you weren't involved in the underground with them?"

Matos shook his head. "No, I'm not. We did work together."

"On Operation Espresso?"

Matos's gaze quickened. "You know about Operation Espresso?"

"A bit. I know it was a plot to poison revolutionary leaders. I know Carlos and Maria Player were key operatives. I know it fell apart at the last moment and I know that some of their fellow conspirators felt the Players had betrayed them. I figure maybe Cuban State Security killed them. Or maybe one or more of those fellow conspirators beat them to it."

"It was the second, not the first."

Willie watched the other man closely. "How do you know?"

"Because in jail in Cuba you meet many people, including former Cuban State Security operatives who have fallen out of favor. I talked to some and I found out things. And Victor Del Rey, the croupier, confirmed all that to me when I talked to him here. He had been told by State Security to watch the Players and anyone they were working with. But it had to do with smuggling money. It had nothing to do with Operation Espresso."

Willie frowned. "So you're saying the Cuban government didn't know about Operation Espresso at all?"

"Not until after Carlos and Maria Player were dead. They didn't know I had anything to do with them. They didn't know I had been to the Players' house that same afternoon."

Willie cocked his head to one side. "You were there that afternoon, the day they died?"

Matos nodded. "Yes."

"Why?"

"Because other people in our organization were being rounded up all over Havana. There had been some leak in the underground. It had always been my job to hide everyone once the operation was complete and I knew that Carlos and Maria Player would be in danger. So I took the chance and went to try to hide them. We made plans for me to return that night to pick them up, but by the time I got there, they were dead, shot to death. Killed before they could escape."

"So Carlos and Maria Player didn't betray anyone."

Matos shook his head. "No. They were the ones who were betrayed and so was I. I left their house, but the next day the Security trapped me and charged me with killing them and also charged me with being part of a plot to murder the leadership."

"Someone tipped them to you and to Operation Espresso."

"Yes. They had details of the plan. Details which could only have come from someone who knew of the plot. For that reason I was sentenced not just for murder but for crimes against the state. I spent thirty years in prison."

Willie watched him. Matos did have the hollow-cheeked, sunken-eyed stillness of someone who had spent a long time locked up.

"I dreamed of nothing but revenge," he said. "That and getting my daughter out of that country." He looked at Aurora, his normally expressionless eyes full of sadness. "Her mother had died of heartbreak and a hard life. Aurora would die of it too if I didn't get her out of there. I don't know if you can imagine what it is to grow up in a place like Cuba when your father has been accused of the ultimate crime against the state."

"It can't be easy."

"No. But then Roberto Player here showed up." Matos looked across the room at Player, who wore that same rapt, boylike expression. "He came to see us in the dirty corner of Old Havana where we were forced to live. And I told him the same story I've told you. I told him his parents were patriots. Brave, good people. I told him of those last hours and how his parents were betrayed by one or more of their former friends."

Another siren passed just then and again they went silent. They tracked it until it was far enough away. Willie turned back to Matos.

"Do you know everyone who was involved in the plot and who might have betrayed them?"

"I think I do."

"Did you pay a little visit to Armando Capitán? Did you firebomb his headquarters?"

Matos shook his head. "I know he learned of the operation in those last days. I also know it was he who used the escape route we had planned."

"On the Panamanian ship?"

"Yes. I learned later that he made it aboard that freighter and got out just a day or two after Carlos and Maria Player died."

"He would have had to pay the captain, I assume."

"Oh, yes. In advance. But my question is how he knew

about that ship and the escape plan when he wasn't part of Operation Espresso."

"Tuzzi could have told him."

"Tuzzi knew there was an escape plan, but he didn't know exactly what it was. No, the only people Armando Capitán might have talked with in those last days who knew the plan were Carlos and Maria Player. They knew because I told them."

Willie studied him. "So you may well have reason to kill Capitán."

"Yes, but I wouldn't have been so stupid as to throw a firebomb at him. We haven't seen him at all."

"But you did see Del Rey."

"Yes, but we left him alive. I knew Del Rey from the old neighborhood. He grew up near the Havana docks too. Later he went to work as a croupier at the casino. We had no cause to kill him. He wasn't involved and he posed no danger to us. In fact, he was sympathetic. He cared for Carlos and Maria Player as well. He too wanted to see their killers pay the price."

"How about Olga Tuzzi?"

"We haven't been able to find her yet."

"You won't find her ever."

Matos frowned. "What do you mean?"

"I just found her dead."

Willie watched Matos's face and that of Aurora next to him. It appeared that they hadn't known.

"How did it happen?" Matos asked.

"She was hiding at an apartment in Miami Beach. Somebody traced her there and shot her to death. Why was it you wanted to talk to her?"

"Because she worked in the show at Hotel Cuba. She knew both Del Rey and Tuzzi, people who were on opposite sides in those days. She also knew Carlos and Maria Player. After speaking to Del Rey we decided we had to find her."

"And her husband?"

"Of course we hoped finding her would lead us to him."

"You'll find him in the same place. The morgue."

Willie told them of the mobster's death. Matos looked at Willie suspiciously. "Are you telling us everyone is dead so we won't go after them ourselves?"

"Call the police. They'll tell you about all three—Del Rey and the Tuzzis." Matos was stunned into silence.

"Who else do you need to talk to?"

"Sam Suarez."

That surprised Willie. "Why Suarez?"

"Because we know he was involved. He was at the casino many times in those last days. And he visited the house of Carlos and Maria Player as well. He knew of the plot. Carlos told him. And he had contacts with the American embassy and the person there who ran the entire operation."

"James Clancy?"

The name had slipped out before Willie could close his mouth.

Matos frowned. "You know him? I never actually met him. Is he here? Do you know where to find him?"

Willie hesitated. He could deny knowing Clancy's whereabouts, but it seemed too late for that now, given the way Matos was looking at him. If he stonewalled, Matos might shoot him. Or at best, the three fugitives might disappear back into the city. He would have to wait and listen to the radio until Bobby Player showed up dead. He could do that, or he could find a way to save them—and himself.

"Yes, I know him."

"Where is he?"

"I can't tell you right this moment."

The gun came up and pointed right at Willie's chest. "Don't play with me. I have very little to lose at this point."

Willie couldn't argue with that. "You're being hunted and I'm not. I can help you resolve all this within a short time, but you have to give me an opportunity."

"I don't have to give you anything."

"If you kill me you'll have no chance of accomplishing your mission and you'll probably end up dead." He looked at Aurora a moment and back at Matos. "All of you. And believe me I don't want Roberto or your daughter dead. Or you for that matter, if what you tell me is true."

For a half minute the gun stayed pointed at him. Willie sipped his rum, figuring if he was going to get shot, a last drink was in order. Matos didn't take his eyes from him, but Willie could see his argument working on the man.

"What is it you are planning to do?" Matos asked finally.

"I can get the information that will tell us who killed the Players. On that you just have to trust me."

"How long will it take?"

"Hopefully, just a day."

"And in the meantime?"

"In the meantime you should be somewhere else, before some goon shows up here looking for me and finds you instead. As soon as it gets dark, you get out of here. The question is where can you go?"

Bobby spoke up.

"There's a fishing camp on the edge of the Everglades that I used to go to. No one will find us there."

He explained to Willie where it was, about fifteen minutes outside the city, a ways past the New Casino Cuba and the Delta-5 training grounds.

They waited two hours for darkness, mostly watching the television reports of the shootout at the Atlantic Palms, including descriptions of Matos, Aurora, and Bobby. Willie called out to a Cuban Chinese place, paid the delivery girl at the door and they ate. He put an old collection of boleros on the CD player softly in the background. At one point Willie sat down next to Bobby, who hadn't shaved in a couple of days and looked like he hadn't slept either.

"You holding up all right?" Willie asked him.

"I'm fine."

Despite his shaggy looks, Willie realized Roberto Player suddenly sounded calmer, more together.

"You're sure now that your parents' killers are here, aren't you?"

"Yes. Aren't you?"

Willie considered the question and nodded slowly. "Yes, I am."

"I used to go to psychiatrists and they told me I'd never be happy until I put the deaths of my parents behind me. Week after week, year after year, that was the message. Except they never told me how to do that. I had people preach to me that I wasn't a kid anymore and I should forget it all. I had women tell me I thought about it too much. That I was disturbed. I'm forty-two years old and I've heard that all my life. As if there's a moment in life when you should just forget that your parents were murdered. 'Today I'll forget it.' " He snapped his fingers. "Does that make any sense? All your life you're hurt by it, but now you just forget."

"No, I guess that never happens."

"No, it doesn't. The last two weeks have been the only time in my life that I've been able to see the possibility of peace. Nothing haunting me." He fixed more intently on Willie. "You know it isn't that I've never grown up, but I've grown up with a responsibility to the only family I ever had. Other people have responsibilities to their families, don't they?"

"Yes."

"Well, I have mine. It's just a lot different from other people's responsibility. It's finding who killed them. I tried to explain that to Ellie."

For the first time Willie saw Roberto Player as something besides a large boy. Maybe he was right. Maybe the only way for him to leave the ghosts behind was to nail his parents' killers. Maybe then Ellie Hernandez would have him to herself.

When it was dark, Matos announced it was time to go. He stood up and so did Bobby and Aurora. Matos turned to his daughter.

"I want you to stay here." She started to protest, but he shook his head. "It's too dangerous. Cuesta can find a place where no one will look for you. And I'll be in touch as soon as possible."

She started to complain again, but he embraced her

with his one good arm. The other was in a sling they had made from a torn bedsheet.

"Don't make me worry about you now."

He kissed her on the cheek and then he and Bobby Player went out the back way. Aurora looked as if she would follow, but Willie held her. She didn't struggle. Instead, tears came into her eyes. Willie put his arms around her and held her until she stopped crying. Her sobs emanated from nerves and fatigue and fear. When she looked up at him, he kissed her lightly on the lips. But it wasn't enough for her and she brought his face to her and kissed him harder.

When she pulled back she had a look of anguish. The look of someone alone and afraid. There were women who felt that and crawled into themselves. And there were some who, at times such as these, desperately needed someone, anyone. In her case, perhaps because she had lived in such isolation in the midst of other people all her life, a political outcast, it was the latter.

They stood there a while, Willie feeling her heart beat against his chest.

"We have to go," he said finally.

"Where?"

"Like your father said, someplace where you'll be safe."

They went down the front stairs, checked the street both ways, and hurried to the car. They made the five-minute drive to his mother's store. They entered past St. Lazarus and Francisca and found her behind the counter, stringing her sacred bead necklaces, watching her Spanish-language soaps.

"I have a friend here who needs a place to stay, Mama."

His mother peered at Aurora in the same appraising way she looked at any woman Willie had at his side, as a potential daughter-in-law, a potential bearer of grandchildren. Her eyes tended to stray to the hips. She looked at Willie, but sensed it was better not to ask why the young woman was being left on her doorstep.

"Do you want coffee?" she asked. "I'm about to make some." Aurora nodded.

Willie left as his mother was preparing *café con leche* for Aurora. Willie could have used one himself, but before he did anything else he needed to speak one more time with Clarence Ross.

Chapter 30

Willie headed once again to Miami Shores. From the highway he could see across the bay toward Miami Beach. It was Saturday night and the nightclubs had their searchlights scanning the skies. They were searching for clientele. He was glad they weren't hunting for Roberto Player and Matos, although lots of other people were.

He parked behind the old Volkswagen again and heard the muted sound of a band saw. He entered the garage through the side door and saw Ross, wearing goggles, bent over his task. It was past ten p.m. Either he really wanted those ham hocks or the widow in question had charms he hadn't mentioned. The old man turned off the saw when he spotted Willie.

"What brings you out here on a Saturday night, *compadre*?"

"I have a few questions for you."

"About what?"

"About your old Mafia buddies and their plans for killing Castro."

Ross brightened. "Ya don't say."

Ross stripped off the goggles and Willie followed him into the house. The grits were still on the stove, a slightly deeper shade of yellow. In the air hung the aroma of homemade barbecue sauce, which Ross served with ribs. He had cooked them for Willie lots of times.

The two of them sat where they had the day before, in the Florida room, and the old man cracked a beer for each of them. Willie filled Ross in on everything that had happened in the last day. Ross kneaded his chin and listened until Willie finished.

"So what is it ya need to know?"

"You ever hear of a plan called Operation Espresso?"

Ross swigged from his bottle and thought. He shook his head. "No. But if it had to do with tryin' to kill Castro then it was part of a bigger FBI and CIA program. They called it Operation Mongoose." Ross chuckled. "A mongoose is a critter that eats snakes and Castro was considered the worst kinda snake."

"And it involved the Mafia?"

"That's right. The Cosa Nostra and U.S. intelligence agencies were tighter than bed bugs back then. After all, when Castro took over, they were the big losers—the gangsters and Washington."

"And who went to whom?"

"The way I've heard it, the Feds went to the mob. They got in touch with a hood out in Vegas named Johnny Roselli. Roselli was a bad boy who had been a numbers runner and a thug in Chicago, but in Vegas and on the West Coast he made the acquaintance of a lot of legitimate businessmen. The CIA used one of those business types to make the contact."

"And they asked him if the Mafia would be willing to help kill Castro? Just like that?"

"Just like that, *amigo.* There wasn't nothin' fancy about it."

"And Roselli said yes."

"Sure thing. If somebody is screwin' with your operation, the way Castro was screwin' with the mob, and the U.S. government asks you to do it a favor and kill 'im, you don't got much to lose, brother. They ain't gonna come after you for it. And the Mafia boys were ready to go. In fact, they thought the CIA was draggin' its feet gettin' rid of the guy."

"Is that right?"

"Hell, yes. The first thing Castro did when he took power was close casinos. But the people who worked in them protested because it would put them out of work. The gaming tables also provided money for the government. So Castro let some of them stay open for the next couple of years. But the mob boys knew eventually it

would all come down. They figured out Castro right
away, but the CIA didn't."

"Why?"

Ross sipped and shrugged. "Maybe the Company thought
Castro went after the casinos only because they were run
by bad guys. But the mob knew that wasn't it because in
Cuba they weren't bad guys. Gambling was legal. And
they also knew eventually Castro was going to go after
the other legitimate businessmen."

"And the CIA didn't get that?"

"Not fast enough, not for the Mafia. Lots of the people
in Washington figured there was no way he would dare be
a red. These little Latin guys, we'd always had them in
our pockets. All we had to do was buy them off with some
money and some guns so they could keep their people under control. No Latin guy was gonna screw with us. They
didn't have the balls. If this guy did, then we'd find somebody close to him we could buy and have him killed."

"It didn't work that way."

"No, not by a far sight. Old Castro, he had bigger fish
to fry. The boys in Washington figured that out finally
and they went scrambling for help from the mobsters.
And one of the reasons they went to the Italians was they
didn't really think much of the underground."

"Why not?"

"For the same reason they didn't think much of Castro at
first. Those Latin boys couldn't cut it, not by themselves."

"So they got the mob to try and kill Castro."

"That's right. It went on for a few years."

"This Operation Espresso, it involved poison."

Ross nodded. "Probably botulin poison. Kills you before you blink twice. That was a favorite back then. They
also tried to shoot him, blow him up. They even had one
scheme to make him smoke a cigar that would make his
beard fall out. They figured without the hair on his face
nobody would recognize him." Ross shook his head. "They
were crazy as loons, some of those CIA boys."

"Would Roselli have known Cozy Costanza?"

"I'm sure."

"So he could have arranged for Cozy to collaborate with the Cuban underground against Castro."

"Can't see why not. In fact I knew when they all ended up back here, they were real close. I would be keepin' an eye on the mob boys and see them meetin' with exiled leaders and vice versa. I remember mentioning it to an old CIA boy and him tellin' me not to worry about it."

"You never got any sense that there was a falling out between them?"

"None."

Willie sipped his beer. "Do you think Castro would ever be willing to do business with the Mafia?"

"I wouldn't think so." Ross shrugged. "On the other hand, the mob and Castro, they both do exactly what suits them at the moment. So you never know. But if I was Castro I'd look at my rice and beans real careful every time I sat down to eat if I ever let the mob boys back in."

Willie sipped his beer and looked at the old man. "You've heard it all. Who do you think might have killed Carlos and Maria Player?"

Ross stared off into his hibiscus garden and shook his head slowly. "I don't know, but I'll tell you this. What some people were doin' back then, they said they were doin' for political reasons. Idealism. But you learn somethin' real quick in this world. The moment the political plan falls apart, then it's everybody for himself. People were counting on the Americans going in there and turning it all back to the way it was before. When it became clear that wasn't going to happen, some people started looking out for themselves. That's the way it was. It's the way it's always been in situations like that. In the end you need to know why people are involved in politics in the first place. There's always something they want for themselves— maybe money, maybe power, fame, occasionally the public good—and it always comes back to that reason in the end."

Ross fell into silence again, sipping his beer. Willie took a swig of his and thought. "I need to know exactly who did what after they all left Cuba back in nineteen sixty and sixty-one. People like Mando Capitán, Cozy

Costanza, Sam Suarez, James Clancy. I need dates and numbers. And I need to know more about Miguel Angel Matos."

Ross nodded. "Well, we have friends we can call both here and in Washington, but we can't call them at this hour, brother."

"In the morning."

"I'll give you a bunk here for the night. Our former colleagues on the Miami police force may be waiting for you at your place."

Willie agreed. He and Ross opened more beers and talked into the night. Willie finally lay down in the spare bedroom and thought some more until he finally fell asleep, the sound of a siren fading into the distance.

He woke once in the middle of the night with the fragment of a dream right behind his eyes. He was on a gambling boat, like the *Treasure Coast*, but much bigger and more opulent. It was crowded with beautiful people drinking and gambling, and Willie was searching among them for one person in particular. He started on the top deck and worked his way down from one gambling salon to another, seeing no one he recognized. Finally, on the bottom deck, he found a small room that he knew was reserved for private games played for the highest stakes. Standing behind a roulette wheel was the dead croupier Victor Del Rey, dressed in a white dinner jacket and black bow tie. They were alone. Willie stepped to the wheel and Del Rey spoke, maybe trying to tell him what number to play, but Willie couldn't understand him. Then Del Rey dropped the black ball in the spinning wheel. He fixed Willie with a knowing look as the ball clattered. Willie waited, but the ball wouldn't stop clattering, as if the wheel would never stop spinning and he would be stuck there forever staring into the dead man's gray eyes. It clattered and clattered.

Willie woke with a start. It had started to rain and water was running off Ross's roof and spattering his boat trailer outside. He listened to it for a while and finally fell asleep again.

Chapter 31

First thing in the morning, Willie got on the phone. During his time in Police Intelligence he had established contacts with banks and accounting firms around the city, people who helped him on money laundering investigations. Of particular assistance was an old bank auditor named Dennis Green, whom Ross had introduced him to. Dennis knew every other bank auditor and most of the bankers in town and could get information fast. He had a long history of working with police.

"I need some history that goes back to nineteen sixty-one," Willie told him. "I don't need exact figures, just someone with a good memory."

"The people I know can remember deposits to the penny if they were large enough," said Green. "You know that. But you're not a cop anymore, Willie. This is a little tricky."

"If you don't mention you're doing it for me, I won't mention I got the information from you. It'll be for old times sake."

"Gotcha."

Willie gave him names to check. "I need it kind of quickly, Dennis."

"How quickly?"

"This morning."

Green whistled. "Well, I'll do what I can."

Willie hung up and then dialed a call to Washington. He phoned a woman diplomat who had served on the Cuba Desk in the State Department, another contact from his days in Intelligence. Together they had kept an eye on Cuban exile organizations. Her name was Iris Clark, a

lady originally from North Dakota, who studied some
Spanish in school and lived most of her life amid the palm
trees of Latin America before taking a desk job in DC.

"Long time no hear, Willie. How are the Miami
commandos?"

"Restless."

"Are they making reservations for the Dominican?"

"Not this time."

Years ago, Iris had discovered that the members of a
minor commando organization had all suddenly booked
plane passage to the Dominican Republic, a popular spot
from which to launch attacks against Cuba. Coinciden-
tally, Ross and Willie had found a freighter full of weap-
onry on the Miami River headed in that same direction.
Together, with the help of the FBI, they had convinced
the would-be invaders to cancel their travel plans.

Willie said hello for Ross and filled Iris in on the current doings involving Delta-5.

"Well, as long as they aren't headed for Cuba I guess
we'll leave this matter in your capable hands," Iris said.

"I do have a question or two about the past," Willie
said. "Those last days in Cuba."

They spoke for a half hour, moving right from one of
Willie's questions to another. Those inquiries involved all
the individuals Willie had encountered in the case and
everyone he had discussed with Ross. He ended up with
several pages of notes with lines connecting one name to
another and all of them tying into Carlos and Maria Player.
The diagram included more than one question mark.

"Confusing, isn't it?" Iris said.

"Just a bit."

"Matters down in Cuba back then grew complex, more
complex than our people realized."

"Obviously."

"Good-bye and good luck."

Willie thanked her and hung up. Ross had prepared
breakfast. Eggs, sausage, a new batch of grits, coffee as
thick as molasses. Willie reviewed his conversation with
Iris. Then they waited for Dennis Green to call back. An

hour passed and then another and the phone didn't ring. Willie tried Dennis's number and got voice mail. He drank more of Ross's coffee and watched the old man tie fishing leaders and listened to some very tall stories about fish he had caught.

Finally, the phone rang. It was Dennis.

"Sorry it took so long, Willie. One of the guys was working out of town, but I got it all."

Willie debriefed him. In just a few minutes, Willie had the information he needed. He and Ross chewed it all over some more. Then Willie called Miami Police Homicide, asked for Compton, and gave his name. Moments later the detective picked up. He didn't beat around the bush.

"Where are you right now, Willie?"

"At the house of a friend."

"Which friend? What's the address?"

"You sound in hurry to see me."

"A man was found shot to death less than a block from your brother's nightclub last night, Willie. A thug named Rico Tuzzi. Have you ever met him?"

Willie thought it over a half second. "Yes, I've met him."

"Recently?"

"I spoke to him two days ago."

"It's a good thing you told me that. We found your business card in his pocket. It was crumpled up in a ball like he was planning to throw it away. But he didn't get a chance. Somebody shot him."

"It wasn't me."

"Is that right?"

"Yes."

"Well, I want to talk to you about it right now."

"I can discuss it with you a little later in the day."

"This isn't the time to play with me, Willie. The city is blowing up and it has to do with you and some people you know. Specifically, a Mr. Roberto Player." Compton had obviously been speaking to Sam Suarez. "Tell me where he is, Willie."

"I need a little time. If you can just back off for a couple of hours. Don't look for them. It will be dangerous. If you wait, I can tell you what you need to know."

"I'm not waiting for anything, Willie. As of right now, you're wanted for questioning about the events of the last two days. Be a fugitive if you want, but don't end up in the middle. You'll get hurt."

Compton hung up then. He sounded a lot like Armando Capitán had sounded two days before.

Ross was watching Willie. "Sounds like old Compton is reluctant to cooperate."

"Yes. But at least I know where he is," Willie said. "I better be going before he moves."

Ross patted the police scanner that he kept next to his BarcaLounger. "I'll keep an ear out for you," he said. "Don't do anything I would do."

Willie cranked up the LeBaron and headed again for the Everglades. He got off the Palmetto Espressway and headed west out the Tamiami. He passed the entrance to the New Casino Cuba, which was quiet now. He turned south and drove by the entrance to Mando Capitán's boot camp, which wasn't quiet at all. He saw even more activity out there than he had the day before, more cars, more new camouflage uniforms milling around.

He didn't stop. He was about a mile farther south when he saw the old, rusted BAIT sign Roberto Player had described to him. Fifty yards past it, he turned onto a dirt track crowded on both sides by thick vegetation—ferns, sawgrass, air plants, and trees, some of them burned and dead, apparently struck by lightning. In those trees sat dozens of black buzzards that looked down at him with professional interest. He remembered a song about a jungle path that led to love. He wondered if this one led to death.

He endured the buzzards' scrutiny about a half mile, then turned back east into an overgrown culvert. There, partially covered by brush, he saw Bobby Player's black Mercedes. He parked next to it.

He walked up the narrow trail and came into a clearing. In it sat a small, delapidated tin-roofed shack that looked decades old, Next to it was built a fishing hut, or chickee hut, as they called them in the Glades, a kind of tall lean-to with a thatched palm roof where you could gut and clean your fish and stay out of the sun. Old fish scales littered the dirt like dusty sequins. Just beyond those structures the Everglades had encroached, and a rusty old aluminum canoe was beached in shallow water.

Bobby Player sat on a rusted chair just outside the shack. He held a pistol in his lap, the one Matos had confiscated from Willie two nights before. When he saw Willie, Player suddenly grabbed the gun. Willie held up his hands.

"Slow down. It's me."

Bobby called out and Matos came out from the shack with his left arm still in the sling. Matos also carried a pistol in his free hand. He had a day's growth of silver beard.

"What are you doing here so soon? Are you sure nobody followed you?"

"Nobody followed me."

"What is happening?"

"Well, they're looking for you and they're looking for me, too, now."

"So you risk coming here and bringing them to us."

"I need to talk to you. I found out a few things this morning, but there's still something I need to clear up."

"Like what?"

"Like your part in Operation Espresso. It was smuggling out the other people who participated?"

"That's right."

"How exactly were you going to do that?"

"Through a ship captain, a Panamanian, who I had known for years. Smuggling people out was very hard right at that time."

"Why?"

"Because once travel restrictions were declared, people started to sneak out and State Security became angry. If you were planning to leave by sea you had to be picked up by a boat from outside the island. You couldn't find a Cuban boat. People were either with the government, like many of the fishermen, or they were scared. They would turn you in if you solicited them. The boats that came from the outside ran the risk of being shot at by the government patrol boats. The reason I was needed was that I had those contacts on the foreign freighters that came into the port. I had done contraband business with them for years, since I was a boy, and could get them to take stowaways if I paid them enough. Right then it was even difficult for me. But I found this one man, the Panamanian, who was willing."

"So Mando Capitán, for example, would have had a hard time smuggling himself or anyone else, or money, off that island if he planned to do it by sea. Without you, that is."

"Absolutely."

"How about by air?"

"That was even less likely. There were very few small craft and the government controlled all of them. Anyone boarding a commercial aircraft was identified and their belongings and bodies thoroughly searched. You didn't sneak out and you didn't smuggle money out."

"And what about the bankers, like Sam Suarez, and their access to wire transfers?"

"That I know nothing about."

Willie was about to ask him something else when suddenly they heard a vehicle come up the road and a car door slam. Both Matos and Bobby lifted their handguns as someone came through the bushes and finally into the clearing. It was Mike Suarez.

He stopped the moment he saw them and raised his hands to show they were empty. He looked at Player standing near the shack. "Bobby, it's me."

It was Matos who answered. "What are you doing here?"

"I came to talk to Bobby."

"And who did you bring with you?"

"No one. Bobby and I have come here for years. I figured this might be where he would hide."

Bobby Player lowered his gun. "You shouldn't have come here."

"You have to turn yourself in to the police, Bobby.

They're looking everywhere for you. They came to the bank. They went to your condo, Ellie's place, everywhere."

"I'm not going to do that."

"Give it up, Bobby. You're going to end up dead yourself. Come with me now. Ellie needs you. We need you."

Matos, still standing near the door to the shack had his gun fixed on Mike Suarez. From the look on his face, Willie knew he would never let Bobby Player or Mike Suarez leave there.

"And maybe you'll die before you go anywhere," Matos said to Suarez.

Then suddenly they heard the sound of more vehicles turning up the road. Through the vegetation, Willie caught glimpses of them as they roared by—the green Cherokee Mando Capitán drove, two more Cherokees, a couple of pickups filled with men in camouflage uniforms. They missed the turn off, but it wouldn't take long for them to find it.

Matos aimed right at Mike Suarez's chest. "You brought them here."

"I didn't. I swear."

"If you shoot him it will only attract the others," Willie said.

Matos didn't move. Willie was sure Matos was about to kill Mike Suarez right where he stood. The shot would bring Mando running and they would all go down in a hail of Delta-5 bullets.

Suarez's hands were still up. Then his right hand went slowly into his shirt pocket and came out again. Between his thumb and his index finger he held something red. Willie looked closely and saw the jagged half of a poker chip.

Willie went to Suarez and took the piece from his hand. He reached into his own pocket and brought out the other half. They fit together perfectly.

Bobby Player came toward them too and stared at the whole chip lying in Willie's hand.

"How long have you had that?"

"For a lot of years," Mike said.

"Why didn't you tell me?"

"I couldn't. But after what's happened in the last days I knew I couldn't keep quiet any longer. Maybe now I can help you find who killed your folks."

Chapter 32

What came next came quickly.

The Cherokees and trucks that had passed moments before came roaring back and screeched to a stop just down the dirt track. Doors slammed and they heard a voice shouting orders. Willie recognized it right away. It was Mando Capitán.

Matos came toward them waving his gun.

"We're getting out of here now."

He prodded Willie and Suarez around the side of the shack to the canoe.

"Put it in the water and get in."

Bobby Player jumped in followed by Suarez and Willie. Matos got in last and sat facing them, gun drawn. Willie, Player, and Suarez grabbed oars covered with moss, pushed off, and began to row as fast as they could in the only direction they could.

They paddled through a shallow rivulet that smelled of dead vegetation. Close on either side of them stood sawgrass, but it wasn't thick enough to hide them. They would be spotted in short order if they didn't find cover.

Mosquitoes swarmed all around. The sky was gray and swollen with rain. The trees overhead, like the ones lining the road, were dead, and more buzzards, dozens of them, peered down at them.

But before they worried about the buzzards, they would have to concern themselves with Mando Capitán and his men. As Willie dipped his oar, he turned and saw them coming through the underbrush in their camouflage uniforms. They had automatic weapons in their hands that would blast that canoe and its occupants to shreds. With the water less than two feet deep, the Delta-5 men could even stalk the canoe across the open Glades.

The rivulet widened suddenly into something approaching a canal. A large blue heron, startled by their appearance, rose off the surface of the water, wheeled in the air, and disappeared into the trees. It took off just in time.

A shot rang out, maybe fired into the sky, maybe not. Buzzards and small birds bolted out of the grass on either side and another heron, this one pure white, broke from cover and streaked across their path.

"Move!" whispered Matos.

Willie, Player, and Suarez paddled and suddenly they were clear of the canal. The Glades opened up before them in a moment, a savannah of shallow water stretching as far as the eye could see. It all hugged the earth with immense amounts of sky above them and almost no cover anywhere.

A hundred yards away sat three small islands where stunted bushes grew. They were narrow and no more than twenty feet long. But they would provide cover if the canoe could reach them before Mando's men broke into the clear. If not, they would be caught like ducks on a pond, dead ducks.

No one had to give the order. The three men paddled, right at those islands. Willie glanced back toward the underbrush where the shouts were coming closer.

He dipped his oar and hit the bottom. The water was less than two feet deep and grass floated on the surface. They could dip the oars only halfway so that they had to paddle very hard and fast in order to move at all. In front of Willie, Player and Suarez flailed at the water.

As they approached the islands, the water got shallower and made it impossible to use the oars. Willie jumped out of the canoe and immediately the mud was almost to his knees. He pushed the canoe the last few feet, shoving it behind the tip of the island, just as he saw the first camouflage uniforms come through the underbrush into the clear.

Willie threw himself down into the water at the edge of the island and hoped they hadn't seen him. His eyes, right

at water level, fixed on the first troops that came into
sight. They held their weapons across their chests. With
the mud as deep as it was, it would take them a good ten
minutes to walk through it to that first island. Willie saw
that he and the others might be able to move from behind
this island to the next and then maybe paddle like hell for
another thick stand of sawgrass about three hundred
yards farther away.

With the stench of the bottom mud in his nose, Willie
watched the camouflaged pursuers stop and stare across
the savannah toward them. It was dead quiet. He held his
breath. He stayed perfectly still watching them and then
he realized he was also being watched. He had felt eyes
on him from somewhere and now he turned and saw,
about twenty-five feet away, an alligator. Its craggy back,
maybe seven feet long, had a greenish tinge the color of
moss, and it almost disappeared into the Glades. But there
it was, lying in the reeds, half submerged in the water, its
arched eye sockets barely emerging above the surface,
black snout pointed right at Willie. It had probably been
sleeping, but it was awake now. Its viscous eyes were directed at him.

Willie froze. The only alligators Willie had ever been
close to he had seen at a fair when he was a kid. Some Indians had wrestled with them. Even put their heads in the
gators' mouths, which were frothy and white like cotton.
Willie cringed whenever he remembered those mouths
opening and seeing for the first time those terrible white
tongues. It wasn't the teeth that scared him but the thought
of disappearing into that horrible slather and whiteness.
He had been terrified. But those gators had been on
drugs. Morphine, heroin, whatever. His father had told
him. They had been addled. This particular alligator, on
the other hand, was almost certainly drug free. No dope-
head gator here, not in the Glades. It didn't move, but its
interest level was evident. With two strokes of its tail it
would be on top of him.

Fifteen feet from the canoe, the bushes blocking him
from the view of his human pursuers, Willie edged slowly
backward. The mud sucked at his feet as if someone be-

neath the surface were gripping him by his sandals. He didn't speak and he tried not to splash, which would only attract his admirer. He moved like a crab and didn't take his eyes from the gator.

A commotion broke out in the canoe as the others saw what Willie saw, but he held up his hand and they fell silent again. They began to come back for him.

Willie hauled his foot from the mud in slow motion now, a form of aquatic tai chi, and got one step closer to them. The gator watched Willie's stylized movement, seemingly bored. But when the canoe was still six feet away, the animal's curiosity, or boredom, got the better of him. Flexing his tail with one languid stroke, he came right at Willie. The detective was his drug of choice.

Willie turned and lunged for the canoe, the mud sucking at his feet like glue. He threw his hand out and Suarez reached and caught him by the wrist. Willie yanked one foot out of the muck and Suarez tried to haul him in. Player, on his knees, swung the other oar at the gator as Willie threw the top of his body into the boat and pulled in one leg. His trailing sandal dangled in the water as the snout came at him and suddenly opened. For one moment, Willie saw his ankle between the open jaws of that awful, frothing white mouth lined with triangular greenish teeth. He yanked with all his might, as the teeth hit the side of the canoe with the sound of enamel meeting metal. Willie shouted with fear and Matos fired at the gator. Willie tumbled backward into the canoe, the gator hitting the side and glancing off, almost capsizing them.

The animal disappeared quickly into the reeds. Willie lay gasping in the bottom of the canoe, covered in mud, as shots sounded, breaking through the underbrush and whizzing overhead. Delta-5 had heard the scream, the shot.

"Quickly," Matos said.

Willie and the other two men paddled, using the cover of the island. It had started to rain now, big drops pelting the water around them. When they got to the tip of the last island, Willie stepped out onto the spit of land and squinted through the brush. The men in camouflage trudged through the mud, the water halfway up their thighs.

Behind him Willie saw open water and then the thick sawgrass. If they could keep the island between them and their pursuers, they might make it.

"We're going back that way," Willie said.

He jumped back in and they paddled hard. Behind them they heard more shouting, but no shots. In five minutes they had reached the sawgrass. They paddled right into it until the canoe was totally covered and then they stopped.

They looked back toward the island and seconds later the first Delta-5 troops came slogging around it. Willie recognized the man who had been posted in the guard tower at Mando's camp. Again he was carrying an Ak-47 across his chest. So were the others. They prodded the bushes on the island with the barrels of the guns and then turned and looked toward the sawgrass.

"They don't see us," whispered Suarez.

"Not yet," said Matos.

Suddenly, the platoon leader lifted his weapon and opened fire. The four of them flattened themselves as far as possible in the canoe as bullets ripped through the grass to one side of them. Right away another commando opened up and then another. Bullets sang just overhead, clipping reeds so that the chaff fell on them.

Then it went quiet, or almost quiet. The troops had stopped firing and were not moving, just staring at the flat Glades. But a sound was approaching quickly from a distance. It was a motor, the roar growing louder so that it seemed to be coming through the grass right at them. Finally, it was right in their ears. A moment later it passed twenty feet from them and exploded out into the open.

It was an airboat. Sitting high up in a chair, just in front of the big propulsion fan, was a pilot in a red-billed cap. Perched in the bow, Ak-47s in hand, were Mando Capitán and two other commandos. Matos swore under his breath. He lifted his pistol and pointed it in Mando's direction. But Willie held his arm.

"Wait."

The other soldiers pointed into the sawgrass and yelled to Mando. The airboat turned, sliding sideways on the water, and came back at full throttle. It rushed right toward them, its motor screaming, and passed this time just yards to the other side of them.

Water sprayed them and the canoe rocked wildly in the wake. The sawgrass bent under and sprang back up, but only partway. Their cover was methodically being cut down.

The airboat reached about a hundred feet beyond them and then they heard it slow and swivel around again.

"We have to shoot that son of a bitch driving it," Matos said.

Willie shook his head. "No."

"He'll kill us or put us in the water for the alligators to eat."

Willie reached for the gun that lay at Bobby Player's feet. Player wasn't expecting it. He grabbed for Willie, but Matos held up a hand.

The airboat came screaming by them again, this time on the other side, even closer now, again covering them in spray and tossing the canoe. The smell of bottom mud, vegetation, and diesel fuel filled the air.

It turned now to come at them a third time, with no grass left but the stand in which they were hidden. It took a wide turn, and slid sideways as it started to gain speed. It straightened out, pointed right at them this time. It was sixty feet away, when Willie lifted the pistol and pulled off three quick shots.

The airboat was bouncing and the first two missed, but the third one found its target—the fuel tank just behind the pilot's chair and under the propulsion fan. Suddenly a small ball of fire appeared, followed quickly by a large explosion.

The airboat turned a complete circle on its own axis, the pilot went flying out of his chair and was flung into the water. One of the soldiers in the front of the boat also went overboard. Mando and the third soldier held on as the back of the boat erupted in flames, still spinning. Fire engulfed the pilot's chair, started to move forward, and they jumped off.

Another large explosion sounded, the boat went up

completely, and the shallow water was on fire. Mando
struggled through the mud, hauling one leg after the other
as quickly as he could. He was heading right for them,
trying to escape the burning water. Willie looked for the
gator, thinking he might deal with Mando for them, but
with the roar of the airboat and the explosion, any sane
gator would be long gone.

Willie handed Bobby Player the pistol back.

"Let's get out of here."

He and Mike Suarez picked up the paddles and flailed
at the water. The rain fell harder now. If they could disappear into another thick stand of sawgrass behind that curtain of rain, they would be almost impossible to find.

But all of a sudden they broke into the open again. The
sawgrass they had hidden in was no more than thirty feet
deep. What faced them was a wide open expanse. The
moment Mando and his men stepped into it they would
see the canoe and cut them down. Another stand of grass
stood two hundred yards away, their only possible refuge.
Beyond that Willie could see the roof of a building, which
he realized was the New Casino Cuba, but it was a half
mile away.

Matos swore under his breath and Suarez's paddle
froze in half stroke.

"Paddle!" Willie yelled. At least they could get far
enough to make the shot more difficult.

They paddled, but in the end they didn't get far at all.
They had gone maybe forty yards when Willie heard a
shout, turned, and saw Mando and some of his buddies
break into the open.

Mando's first burst of gunfire hit just to one side and
sent the four of them toppling into the water. From his
knees Matos fired two rounds in Mando's direction, but
with a handgun and at that range he missed badly. Mando
had to change clips and did so slowly, carefully, looking
at them as if he were deciding exactly how to shoot them.

Then a new sound was heard approaching from behind
Mando and his troops. At first Willie thought it was another
airboat rushing to back up Delta-5 and maybe Mando
thought the same. The *comandante* shoved the clip in, braced

his weapon, and was about to finish them off when a helicopter flying low, skimming the sawgrass, burst into the clearing and almost took his head off. Mando had to throw himself into the water and the men with him dove too.

The chopper passed Mando and flew over the canoe. On the underside was printed POLICE. It turned, hurried back, and hovered over the *comandante*. It was quickly joined by two other choppers, rifle barrels protruding from them, aimed at the water. A voice on a bullhorn told Mando and his men to throw their weapons down. One by one they did as they were told.

The chopper then flew over the canoe. The bullhorn gave them the same order.

Matos, after a moment's hesitation, threw his gun down. A person appeared in the door of the copter. It was Compton. Next to him appeared another face. It was James Clancy.

Willie turned to Mike Suarez, who was kneeling in the mud, rain dripping down his cheeks, his hands up.

"You better tell me how you got that chip and tell me quick."

Chapter 33

It didn't take long for them to be rescued. The four of them were plucked from the mud into the copter, like a scene from Vietnam. Mando was harvested by another copter. His men, on the other hand, were ordered to wade toward shore under the keen eye of SWAT team members hovering above. It would take a half hour to herd them back to land.

Willie, Mike Suarez, Bobby Player, and Matos were dropped onshore near the New Casino Cuba. The rain fell hard and Compton got permission to march them all into the club. Disarmed, they were placed in the ornate but now-empty dining room, with another mural of the conquistadors floating above them.

Compton came in escorting Mando, who was placed at an adjacent table, a separate reservation so to speak. Clancy, dressed in camouflage pants, a cold warrior back in his element, joined him. Willie turned to a club security chief and asked if he might order a Cuban sandwich, but the man informed him the kitchen was not yet open.

An official vehicle with its siren sounding pulled up in front of the club and moments later a police chauffeur strode into the dining room. He was followed by Sam Suarez and, just a few steps behind the banker, Cozy Costanza, again with a pink ball clutched in his fist. Willie, standing near the door, looked from one to the other.

"I didn't know you gentlemen traveled together."

Suarez glowered at him. "Mr. Costanza was in the bank when I received word. He wanted to make sure my son was all right." Costanza didn't argue with that. In fact, the mobster didn't say a word. He took a seat at the nearest empty table.

Sam Suarez inspected his son and Bobby Player from a distance, but fixed on Matos. Then he turned to Willie. He sounded as if he were rehearsing for television cameras.

"Good work. You've captured this terrorist before he could blow up my bank and my club, the way he did Delta-5, and before he killed any more people, the way he did Carlos and Maria Player. You'll get a check."

Willie's eyebrows danced with amusement.

"Well, thank you. But I didn't capture him and he didn't kill the Players, or blow up Delta-5."

Compton glared at Willie. "So who did?"

Suarez pointed at Matos. "He's a gangster. He's also in the country illegally, an agent of the Cuban government, and an assassin."

Willie shrugged. "Well, part of that is true. Matos and his daughter were smuggled into this country. But he isn't, nor has he ever been, an agent for the Cuban government. In fact, he spent almost all of the past thirty-five years in jail in Cuba, convicted of being an enemy of the government. I checked that this morning with an old acquaintance of mine at the State Department in Washington."

Compton stood right over Matos, but spoke to Willie. "So what's he doing here?"

"What exactly he might be doing here in the long run I can't say. Maybe running away from Cuba, looking for a new life, like a lot of other people. But these last three days he has been working with Roberto Player, trying to find the killers of Roberto's parents."

"And why should he do that?"

"Because the same person or persons who killed Player's parents also double-crossed Matos when he was with the Cuban underground. That resulted in Matos's spending almost all his adult life behind bars."

That bit of information made everybody, including Mando, Clancy, Suarez, and Costanza, look at Matos. He stared back at them, unblinking.

Sam Suarez revived first. "That's what he says, but what he is really here for is to carry out acts of sabotage.

He killed a man at a hotel downtown, I'm told, and a woman, Olga Tuzzi."

Willie shook his head. "I don't think it occurred that way. In fact, I know he didn't kill one of them."

"How do you know that?"

"Because when Olga Tuzzi was killed, Matos and Player were at the Atlantic Palms. In fact they were in the act of shooting their way out of the Atlantic Palms in your presence. I was the one who found Olga's body a while later and it was still warm, too warm for any of them to have killed her. And if they didn't kill Olga, then maybe they didn't kill Del Rey either."

Bobby Player spoke up. "So who did kill them and why?"

"Del Rey was killed because of something he knew about the deaths of your parents. And I figured Olga died because Del Rey, somewhere along the line, might have told her."

Suarez was livid again. "What could he tell her? Everybody knew Carlos and Maria had been in the underground."

"That's true. And everyone knew about the money Carlos Player had put away too. You did, Mr. Suarez, because you were the Players' banker. Mr. Costanza here and Rico Tuzzi knew because they were partners in the casino. Armando Capitán became aware of it because Tuzzi told him after they both developed suspicions about the Players' patriotism."

Mando scowled at Willie from across his table.

"You don't deny that, do you Mando? You were convinced the Players were communist agents and you also knew about their stash."

"What about it? That doesn't mean I killed them."

"No, not necessarily. James Clancy here knew about the money too. Carlos Player told him before the heat came down on everyone and they fell out of contact."

It was Mike Suarez who spoke up now. "So they all knew about this stash. That doesn't mean they killed Bobby's parents and stole the money. Government agents might have done that."

"That's true," Willie said. "And most of the people in

this room didn't have a chance to do it anyway. When the plan to poison the government leaders started to fall apart, they all had to make certain moves." Willie pointed at Mando. "The *comandante* here suspected that Carlos and Maria Player had betrayed the underground. He had observed them in the company of government officials. He didn't know the details of Operation Espresso or that the Players were setting up those officials. He went to Rico Tuzzi and asked Tuzzi. Player had never liked Tuzzi and vice versa. Tuzzi was ready to accuse Player of betrayal because he just didn't like him. Rico wasn't too smart."

Bobby Player came up out of his seat. "So the two of them killed my parents?"

Mando came up out of his chair as well. "I said I didn't."

The SWAT guys pushed both of them back down.

Willie had picked up a white napkin from the table and was dabbing at his wet face.

"Mando might have gone after Carlos and Maria Player if he'd had the chance, but he couldn't. He was being hunted himself and he went even farther underground until he finally managed to smuggle himself onto a Panamanian ship and escape Cuba. He doesn't know it, but he has Mr. Matos here to thank for that connection. Matos probably saved Mando Capitán's life."

Mando looked quizzically across the room at Matos, whom he had been trying to kill just a half hour before.

"And how about the Italians?" asked Compton.

Willie glanced at Costanza and then shook his head. "Neither Cozy Costanza nor Rico Tuzzi went to the Players' house either. They knew things were hot and they didn't want to get near anybody involved in the plot. Costanza had Tuzzi busy getting ready to escape the island. And since they left on a commercial flight and their belongings were thoroughly searched, I can be pretty sure they left without the half million dollars belonging to Carlos and Maria Player."

Willie glanced at Bobby Player. He was listening and watching intently. This was what he had been waiting to know for thirty-five years. Everyone of the people seated

at those tables had known his parents. Someone there
knew exactly how they had died. Bobby met Willie's
gaze. "So it wasn't either of them. Who else?"

Willie pointed at Clancy. "James Clancy here was also
forced to take one of those flights out two days later when
the U.S. embassy closed down. Every intelligence agent in
the embassy had been assigned Cuban government operatives who were following them everywhere day and night.
James Clancy was no different. I also checked that this
morning with my contacts in Washington. It seems impossible he could have killed anybody."

Willie got up, reached into his pocket, and brought out
the two halves of the red poker chip.

"The person who did go to their house that night before
your parents died was Sam Suarez. That was when Carlos
Player gave him his half of this poker chip. The other half
was with you, Bobby, here in the States. Your father was
afraid he wouldn't make it out of Cuba alive and he
trusted Sam Suarez to take care of you if Suarez escaped
eventually. Mike found the chip one day years later and
knew it meant that his father had accepted the responsibility of raising Bobby. Isn't that right, Sam?"

Suarez watched Willie as if he were watching a stock
ticker bringing news of a market crash.

"What about it?"

"At first you weren't eager to do that," Willie said, approaching the banker. "That's because you were convinced that Carlos and Maria Player were traitors, that
they had been working for the Castro government. Someone persuaded even you, an old friend of theirs, that Carlos and Maria had sold out the underground, just as
Mando Capitán and Rico Tuzzi had been persuaded."

Suarez was staring along his nose at Willie in that
way he had. "What about it? That doesn't mean I killed
anyone."

"No it doesn't. When you went to see Carlos Player
that last day at Casino Cuba, he told you he was expecting
someone who could smuggle money out of the country
without any problem. He asked if you wanted to sneak
yours out too. Yesterday you told me you didn't do it be-

cause of the risk. But that's not the truth. You didn't give your money to Player because you were no longer sure of him. You'd been warned by an acquaintance of yours to stay away from him and his wife. You thought that Player planned to take the money and turn you in to the government agents he conferred with secretly.

"The next morning you heard that Carlos Player and his wife were dead. You thought you knew exactly what had happened. That the underground had executed them and taken the money because the Players were traitors. It was all true what you had been told about them. You believed it because of who was telling you all this—the CIA."

Willie turned to Clancy.

"It was James Clancy who relayed to you this information. But it wasn't true. It was all part of his plan, a plan that included shooting the Players to death and then smuggling their money out of the country in his diplomatic pouch, the same kind of diplomatic pouch other diplomats used to help smuggle the visa waivers for Peter Pan kids."

Clancy, sitting just feet away, grimaced.

"What are you talking about? You yourself said just moments ago that I couldn't have killed anyone. I was being tailed constantly by Cuban State Security and couldn't leave the embassy."

Willie shook his head. "I said everyone was assigned a Cuban agent to follow them. But you knew the person assigned to shadow you in those last days, at least part of the time, was Victor Del Rey. One day when he was tailing you, Del Rey tapped you on the shoulder and told you he wanted to change sides. He told me himself that he had decided he was no revolutionary. He wanted out. He figured you were the perfect person to help him. You told him to bide his time, stay in place, report back to you. It was Del Rey who told you the Players were suspected by the Cuban government of hiding a large amount of money. You didn't know about the money until then. You also told him to stop following you and just fake his reports to his superiors, which he did. This left you free to move about Havana at certain times in those last days, unlike the other agents in your embassy. Del Rey, of course, later realized that, and he apparently told Olga Tuzzi. That's why both of them are dead."

Compton stared wide-eyed at Willie. "You're saying he not only killed those people in Cuba, but the ones who were murdered here?"

Willie nodded but stayed fixed on Clancy. "You heard that Matos was here. Matos was another person who knew of your connection to the events and he was looking for revenge. If he had enough time and freedom to move around he would find out the truth. So you decided to divert attention away from yourself and Operation Espresso and possibly bring heat on Matos and Roberto Player. You attacked the *Treasure Coast*. I think when the police question that gardener of yours who wears camouflage, they'll probably find the guy who helped you shoot up the gambling boat. After that, you had Tuzzi on your side. He didn't know it was you who had shot up the *Treasure Coast*. He was convinced the Cubans were after the Italians because of the rumors of the Mafia going back into Cuba. That was all right by you. It was another way to divert attention away from you. He helped you on the Delta-5 job, I'd guess. And he definitely helped you the night you came after me. When that attack backfired, you put a hole in poor Rico's head and left him behind."

All eyes were on Clancy now. Mando, sitting just two feet away, stared at him in shock. Clancy's face seemed to have turned even more red than usual. "You're crazy, *amigo*. The sun has gotten to you. There was absolutely no reason for me to hurt Carlos and Maria Player in the first place."

Willie shook his head. "Oh, yes there was. It all started because you knew that your foreign service career was ruined. You had made serious mistakes. To begin, you were one of the agents who underestimated Castro. You told your superiors that there was nothing to worry about in Cuba. There was nothing that these young Cubans could do that you couldn't handle. Your whole organization was known for these sweeping misjudgments back

then and in Cuba they came back to haunt you. You figured these Latin boys would come around. You knew
them from the clubs and casinos. They were good-time
people. No way they were real communists. You confused yourself with them. You were the good-time boy.
You drank too much, spent too much time with call girls,
at cock fights, and in casinos. When you did try to organize an operation, such as helping set up underground
cells or Operation Espresso, you were sloppy and left
your agents exposed. Many of them ended up dead."

Clancy made a noise in his throat. "You don't know
what you're talking about. My record back then was
excellent."

"Your record, which I was given an informal reading
of today by friends in Washington, says you were a disas-
ter. It said your gambling debts were so high, your drinking so bad that you were going to be yanked out of Cuba
any day and drummed out of government service. You
were told that by your superiors. It said you were vulnera-
ble to being co-opted by the enemy because of those
weaknesses. In fact, maybe you *were* co-opted. A traitor
couldn't have done more damage.

"And that's exactly what you were. You betrayed Carlos and Maria Player. You went to their house that night
to get the money to put in your diplomatic pouch, money
you knew you were never going to give back. You knew
you had to kill them. I can't say why you tortured Maria
Player. Maybe because they knew Operation Espresso
was falling apart and at the last moment they came to
suspect you and wouldn't tell you how to get the money
out of the safe. But the next day you anonymously contacted Cuban State Security and implicated Mr. Matos
here. You came back to the States, left the foreign service
before they fired you, and immediately started to use the
money, something we know you did because of bank
records.

"You had convinced Mando Capitán you were his
friend because you gave him the name of the Panamanian
sea captain who could smuggle him out. You convinced
Sam Suarez that you were his friend because you gave

him a little bit of money to help out when he first got here. You convinced them both that the Players had been traitors. But everyone agreed it was better that the communists be blamed for their deaths. Carlos and Maria Player were seen as martyrs and it was best that it remain that way. That's why no one would ever talk about what they thought had really happened with them. It was an oath everyone had taken."

Willie turned to Sam Suarez. "Sam here believed you about Carlos and Maria, but he took care of Bobby anyway and never told him his parents were suspected traitors."

For moments, there was total silence. Clancy had gotten to his feet, fuming but silent. Bobby Player was staring at him in shock. He finally had the answer he had always wanted and now he couldn't speak. He wasn't given time.

Matos stood up. From inside the sling he wore on his bad arm he produced another handgun, the one Bobby Player had left lying in the canoe. The police had taken one gun from Matos, but hadn't found this one. He pointed it at Clancy and pulled off two quick shots. They bent the tall man in the middle, like a stick breaking, and he fell.

Matos turned to Willie as if he wanted to say something to him, but he didn't let the gun drop. Several police opened fire on him. He took the slugs, fell back over his chair, moved as if trying to get up one last time, and then he too lay still.

Chapter 34

It was almost ten hours later that the police finally let them go. They had been transported to headquarters and questioned endlessly. Willie finally walked out with Bobby at his side. Waiting in the parking lot of headquarters were Sam and Mike Suarez. Bobby stopped in front of them. Sam Suarez had lost his bravado.

"I'm sorry, Bobby. At the time I believed what I was told."

"You took care of me anyway, Sam. That's all that matters."

"So you'll come back. You'll take a few days but you'll come back to the bank."

"Yeah, I'll be there in a few days." He embraced Mike and then he and Willie headed for the car.

Ellie was waiting for them at Bobby's condo. That embrace lasted much longer. Ellie heard the whole story of what had happened more than thirty-five years ago and over the past few days. She shook her head.

"Poor Olga Tuzzi. She always loved you, Bobby."

She looked from Willie to Bobby and back again. "And the girl? What happened to her?"

"She's in a safe place," Willie said, "and I better go see her now."

Ellie reached for her purse. "I have to pay you."

"That can wait until tomorrow." He figured if he got the check from Sam Suarez, he could let Ellie slide. He shook hands with Player and gave Ellie a kiss on the cheek. He hoped that what Player had said the day before was true and that he was ready to be happy.

He left them and headed for his mother's place. During the entire interrogation he had been asked only once by Compton about the girl who had been with Matos and Player. Willie had said he didn't know where she was. Bobby had told them the same. Willie had managed to make a call to his mother and told her the rudiments of what had happened.

Willie found Aurora and his mother together in the consultation room, the incense burning, the life-size statue of Santa Barbara looking on. His mother had spread the cards and shells on the table. She had probably spent all the ensuing hours helping the young woman cope with the news of her father's death.

Willie's mother scowled at him. "You lied to me about the danger you were in, but we will talk about that another time. It's too late."

She gave him a kiss on the cheek and exchanged an embrace with Aurora. "There's a bed made for you upstairs," she said to the woman. "You can stay as long as necessary." Then she headed up to her room.

Willie sat next to Aurora. It took her a few moments to speak.

"Did he die right away?"

"Yes. He didn't suffer."

"And he killed the man who betrayed him?"

"Yes."

She thought about that for a moment. "He knew that he would never survive this. There was no way he would get through it alive."

They sat in silence for a minute.

"What are you going to do now?" Willie asked finally.

She shook her head. "I don't know."

"As the daughter of a long-time political prisoner, you can apply for asylum. You shouldn't have too much trouble getting permission to stay here."

She closed her eyes. "Right now I'm just very tired."

He put his arms around her and held her for some time. She wept and after a while she stopped. Then he took her to the stairs and she went up to bed.

Willie turned off the lights and went out, the bell jangling over the door. The statues standing guard at the entrance, St. Lazarus and Francisca, watched him disappear into the night.

PENGUIN PUTNAM INC.
Online

Your Internet gateway to a virtual environment with
hundreds of entertaining and enlightening books from
Penguin Putnam Inc.

*While you're there, get the latest buzz on
the best authors and books around—*

Tom Clancy, Patricia Cornwell, W.E.B. Griffin,
Nora Roberts, William Gibson, Robin Cook,
Brian Jacques, Catherine Coulter, Stephen King,
Jacquelyn Mitchard, and many more!

Penguin Putnam Online is located at
http://www.penguinputnam.com

PENGUIN PUTNAM NEWS

Every month you'll get an inside look at our upcoming
books and new features on our site. This is an ongoing
effort to provide you with the most up-to-date
information about our books and authors.

Subscribe to Penguin Putnam News at
http://www.penguinputnam.com/ClubPPI